AWAKENED BY FLAMES

A Hot Paranormal Dragon Shifter Romance

VELLA DAY

Erotic Reads Publishing

AWAKENED BY FLAMES

Hidden Realms of Silver Lake

Book 1
Vella Day
Copyright © 2018 Vella Day

www.velladay.com

velladayauthor@gmail.com

Cover Art by Jaycee DeLorenzo

Edited by Rebecca Cartee and Carol Adcock-Bezzo

Published in the United States of America

❉ Created with Vellum

BLURB

The only thing between this werewolf and his destined mate is a portal to a different world.

It's crazy. Finn McKinnon knows dreams can't be real. So why does his wolf shifter side have the overwhelming urge to step through a portal into a mysterious new realm? Is Kaleena Sinclair his mate or just a figment of his overactive imagination?

For years, Kaleena has known that Fate has designated the deliciously hot man from Earth as hers, but she can't reveal she's a dragon shifter—at least not yet. Dreamwalking has been her only connection to him, but damn, Finn still thinks she doesn't exist. So what's a girl to do -- especially when Finn is her sole chance at survival?

Before he knows it, Finn is thrust into a dangerous journey—a journey so unique and sensual that the life he's known ceases to exist. The clock is ticking, and Finn must survive impossible odds if he is to save his future mate. But how in the world can they fulfill their destiny as fated mates if some ruthless force is hell-bent on keeping them apart?

around, a wave of nausea caused her to fall off the stool, but Christian caught her before she landed on the floor.

"I'm taking you to the Emergency Room," he said with fear tingeing his voice.

Kaleena was too disoriented to argue, but when he wrapped an arm around her waist to help her up, her mind snapped. Suddenly, she was convinced he was an evil dark lighter sent to harm her. Kaleena had been trained to fight, and she used what little strength she had left to swing a fist at his face, but it was as if the air was made of clay, and her delivery came out way too slow. No surprise, Christian was able to duck before she could connect.

Fight, dragon, fight, she pleaded.

"I'm trying to help you, Kaleena," Christian said.

Was he? So what if his support was all that was keeping her upright. "I'm okay."

"No, you aren't. You fell off the stool. Come on." Christian managed to weave them through the crowd toward the back entrance. As soon as she stepped outside, her vision turned black, and her knees buckled.

When Kaleena awoke, her head was pounding something fierce. She slowly eased her eyes open to find darkness. Where the hell was she? Only scant light filled the small, disgustingly smelly space. From the stench, this wasn't a hospital. The drugs were still in her system, and they were definitely messing with her ability to focus.

Pushing up on her elbows, she looked around, but she only remained in a semi-sitting position for a moment.

Weakness attacked her again, and she fell back onto what felt like canvas resting on a bed of rocks. Even though cold dampness seeped into her body, she didn't have the energy to rub her arms to warm herself.

Don't move, her dragon warned.

No problem. I couldn't if I wanted to.

To help ease the ache stabbing her eyes, she palmed her lids and pressed inward. The pain eased slightly. Not only was her head throbbing, her stomach was threatening to revolt. This had to have been a mistake. If she lived long enough to tell her family what had happened, they would make certain the perpetrator was punished for this.

Sounds slowly filtered into her drugged mind. Something clanked, feet shuffled, and moans sounded, but she couldn't quite figure out her location. Pleading with her body to get rid of this devil potion inside her, she rolled onto her side and held in a moan. Kaleena blinked and focused on the small dirty white sink jutting out from a wall made from stone. Next to it sat a metal toilet.

Cot, sink, toilet.

Was she in some kind of jail cell? Why? It wasn't as if she'd committed a crime. And where was Christian? He was supposed to have taken her to the Emergency Room. Or was he being held captive too? Goddess, this was such a nightmare.

When her vision finally cleared, her body turned even colder. Covering all three walls were knives that protruded at six-inch intervals. Their blades pointed outward. And not just a few knives, mind you—a ton of them.

With a gargantuan effort, Kaleena managed to sit up and ease her feet to the floor. An ache stronger than the ten dragon claws digging into her chest filled her, but she pushed aside the discomfort and glanced upward. Holy goddess. The eight-foot by eight-foot cell had daggers jutting down from the ceiling too. What kind of sick bastard had kidnapped her? At least the fourth wall was merely barred.

Why would anyone drug and imprison her? For money? Or did this person have a vendetta against her family? Perhaps her father or uncle had threatened to expose some deadly secret, and her kidnapper planned to use her as leverage to keep them quiet.

Think!

She was the head of public relations for SinCas Mining and Gems, but it wasn't as if she wielded a lot of power. Okay, that wasn't entirely true. Her extended family was one of the most powerful and wealthy in all of Tarradon since they owned the two largest mines in the realm and employed many of the local shifters and humans. And yes, she possessed a level of magic the Royals wished they had.

Not only were the workers at SinCas always treated well, the Sinclairs and the Caspians each gave to many charities. None of them would do this. She wracked her brain to think if she'd mentioned her last name to Christian. Even if she had, he didn't seem like the type to be after her for her money since he was a highly successful lawyer. Or had that been a lie?

Nothing made sense to her addled brain. At least if her captor demanded a ransom, her parents would find her. Whether she'd be alive or not was another matter.

Lay back down, her dragon said. *I need to heal you. Or at least try to.*

Kaleena did as her dragon asked, and she closed her eyes once more to help center herself. A combination of unwashed bodies, mold, and stale air, pushed past an acceptable level and caused bile to rush up her throat. She had to force herself to reach the sink that was a mere two feet away. Just in time, she bent over and vomited. To add to the humility, her knees weakened, and she dropped to the filthy floor. Jeez, she had to get out of there.

And she would too if only she could figure out how. Given all of the knives surrounding her, shifting was out of the question. Her nearly twenty-foot wings would be shredded in seconds.

As Kaleena inhaled deeply, her body became wracked with a coughing fit. After she forced herself to calm, she rose to her feet but instantly dropped back down as a wave of dizziness assaulted her again. Damn drugs. No one was going to stop her from doing what she needed to do however. She was a Guardian, for goddess sake—a dragon shifter imbued with magic and strength. She would escape.

With her lungs still on fire, Kaleena crawled back to the cot and dragged herself on top. One of her talents should enable her to escape. Only which one? She was strong and fast in the air, but shifting inside the cell wasn't possible. Cloaking only occurred in her shifted form too. Damn. If only she possessed the talent to teleport, she could get out of there right now.

Then an idea struck. There were hundreds of weapons surrounding her. All she had to do was extract one of the knives from the walls and wait for her captor to return. If he was a dragon—which she suspected he was—she would need to stab him in the top part of the heart where the one vulnerable spot on his body was located. With the element of surprise on her side, she might be able to kill him.

Renewed by her fresh idea, she tried to stand once more. This time she succeeded. Focusing on keeping her balance, she made it to the sink and held on. Not wanting to slice her hand when she tugged on the knife to remove it, she slipped off her lightweight jacket with the intention of wrapping it around the knife to pull it out.

Shit. The moment the fabric came in contact with the metal, it jutted out from the wall another ten inches. If she had brushed against the wall, the blade would have impaled her.

Strong footsteps sounded down the hallway. She quickly lowered her arm and slipped on her jacket but then had to grab the bars to steady herself.

"Who's there?" she called out.

A moment later, a man who was clearly a dragon shifter, wearing a khaki uniform appeared. Unfortunately, the small logo on the pocket wasn't something she recognized, and the letters were too small to read. He handed her a metal cup through the bars but said nothing.

Not wanting to piss him off, she took his offering. "Thank you. Can you tell me why I'm here?"

As he stepped closer, his sour breath made her lean back. The man opened his mouth wide and laughed. Oh, dear goddess, he had no tongue. What kind of monster would do that to another person—especially to a dragon? Acid burned in her stomach at the injustice.

She stood as straight as she could without wincing to show him she wasn't afraid—even though she was. "I'm Kaleena Sinclair. Please ask my captor to come here and face me." She hoped her name would mean something to him.

The guard slammed his hand against the bars and leaned forward as if to give her some kind of warning. He glared at her and then grinned before shuffling back down the hallway. Well, that didn't go as well as she'd hoped.

The energy drain to remain standing overwhelmed her, and she returned to the cot. Kaleena needed to go over what had happened with Christian in order to figure out how she'd ended up there. During the prelude to their two-minute dance, she tried to recall if he had hinted at anything to indicate he was involved in some scheme to retaliate against her family, but nothing came to mind. While she'd never met him before tonight, Christian seemed like a nice guy.

Gaining strength slowly, she stood and paced, assessing the situation. So far, only one guard had stopped by, but she wasn't so naïve to believe that there weren't others.

A whimper came from someone near, and Kaleena stilled.

"Hello?" Kaleena called out. "Who are you?"

Silence.

Perhaps the caged person thought this was a trap. "I'm Kaleena Sinclair. Maybe we can help each other."

"Sinclair?" The woman whispered the name with reverence.

Kaleena's pulse sped up. "Yes."

"My name's Danita. Why are *you* here?" she asked.

That was a good question. "I'm not sure, but someone drugged me."

"Me too." The desperation in the woman's voice tore at her.

"Are you a white lighter?" Kaleena lowered her voice when she said the last two words. It seemed like the only logical explanation for why they'd both been taken. Possessing magic was highly valued in Tarradon.

"Um...yes." It was as if she was afraid to admit it in case a guard could overhear.

"When did they take you?"

"I think a week ago."

Kaleena's shoulders slumped. This was worse than she thought. As much as she wanted to speak with this woman, there was no telling if anyone was monitoring the conversation. She looked around the hallway, checking the ceiling for any mounted cameras but found none. "How many other captives are there here?"

"I don't know for sure...three, maybe four?"

Kaleena returned to her pacing, careful not to walk too close to the walls. She stopped. "Are there knives sticking out of your walls?" she asked the other captive, trying to see if every cell was equipped with such torture.

"Knives? No."

A heavy door opened, wheels squeaked, and then what sounded like metal trays slid across the floor. One scraping noise. Then two. And three. Finally, the same guard who'd handed her a drink appeared in front of her cage. He bent down and delivered a tray under her cell bars.

Without making eye contact, he left the same way he came, implying there were four prisoners. Were they white lighters too? Or had some committed crimes for real? And were any of the prisoners at the other end dragons?

She glanced down at her food. The porridge looked bland, but the bowl of vegetables held some appeal. The problem was she didn't trust they wouldn't drug her again. For the time being, she'd go hungry.

Dropping onto her cot once more, she closed her eyes and allowed her mind to wander to Finn McKinnon—her safe haven each night. Even though she'd only connected with him in her dreams, he'd given her great solace. She'd been dream-walking with Finn, a werewolf from the Earth realm, for a while. He was her mate!

Finn was also her hero. Sure he was incredibly hand-some with his square jaw and kissable lips; and yes, his body seemed to have been sculpted by the gods, but it was his caring nature that excited her. When clients came to the bar he managed, he always listened to them—at least when she was given a vision of him in his life, that was what it seemed. But perhaps it was his sense of humor that really made her fall in love with him.

Over the last few weeks, their minds had merged into one, communicating and feeling with such intensity, she almost felt as if they were in the same room. When she dream-walked with him, they'd been intimate too. For her, love had bloomed, but she'd been careful not to scare him. Telling him they were mates—or that she was a dragon—might have caused him to shut her out, and she couldn't chance that.

As much as she wanted to stay awake to figure out some kind of escape plan, her best hope might be to have Finn—a man who didn't know Tarradon existed—help her. Hell, he'd asked many times whether she was real. Promising him that someday they'd meet didn't seem to be enough for him. Well, the time might be closer than he realized.

To contact him, however, she needed to dream, and that meant she had to fall asleep—something that would be difficult since she had no clue who had taken her or what they planned to do with her. Despite that and the lumpy cot, she had to try, as her only hope to contact someone in the outside world was to dream-walk with Finn.

CHAPTER TWO

Finn tossed and turned. Normally when Kaleena came to him in his dreams, her brightness soothed his soul and excited his wolf. Not tonight though. Everything was different—darker, somber, and even frightening. While her face was always a bit blurry and her long, red hair was swept behind her back, her body was in shadows this time.

"Finn?" Kaleena called as if she were very far away.

"What's wrong?" He'd become accustomed to her coy and flirtatious tone. While she shared some things about herself, he suspected she held back at the same time. Tonight was different. Something had changed.

"I need your help," she pleaded.

From the way her voice cracked, something was very wrong. In his dream world, Finn was invincible and capable of doing anything. *"What can I do?"*

"I'm being held prisoner. I need you to come to Tarradon."

He wondered why his imaginary woman had chosen this scenario to play out with him. *"Of course, I'll come. I'll ride in on a white steed and save you."* Not that he had any idea where this town of Tarradon was located.

"Finn, this is no joking matter. I'm real. You have to believe me. I need you."

Finn rolled over, his mind in a confused dream state. At times, he wanted to believe that the woman in his head was alive and that they'd even met at one time, but how could she be flesh and blood? Kaleena only appeared to him when he slept.

Because she sounded so desperate, he played along. *"Okay, I believe you. You said you live in Tarradon? Where is that exactly? And how can I reach you?"*

"Tarradon is a different realm from Earth—a parallel universe if you will. My best guess is that I'm still in Edendale, which is a town in the province of Avonbelle. Getting here will be tricky. You will have to find a portal in order to reach me."

"A different realm?" He had to be crazy to believe her. *"Listen, I don't even know how portals work."*

"Someone must know. Ask a white lighter."

"A white lighter?" He could guess what she meant by those words, but he wanted to be sure.

"You call them witches."

Since she used a name he wasn't familiar with, it gave credence to the fact she might be real. *"I'll try."*

"If you don't help me, I could die." Then the link broke.

"Kaleena?"

Nothing.

The idea that Kaleena was being held captive and in danger—while Finn was unsure if he could help her—was so horrendous that he bolted upright in bed. His forehead was drenched in perspiration, and his heart was beating way too fast. It took a moment for him to realize that he was in his bedroom and not locked in some cell. A prison cell? Where had that idea come from?

Usually, Finn's dreams took place at some glorious waterfall that spilled into a clear pool. It was so turquoise and clear he could see to the sandy bottom. Kaleena was always with him, smiling and beckoning him to join her in the refreshing water.

At night, they'd interact on many different levels, sometimes flirting and teasing. At others times, they'd delve into fascinating philosophical discussions. As crazy as it sounded, he was beginning to fall in love with her. Kaleena even promised that one day they'd meet. Hell, maybe that day had come.

Often, their dream session would end with them engaging in mind-blowing sex—well sort of engaging. She wasn't actually with him—just in his mind—but man did it feel real. His cock sure felt as if they'd had sex, and when he was kissing her, he could almost feel the pressure of her lips on his.

But he wasn't that delusional. Finn knew they hadn't actually touched despite reveling in her velvety mouth and enjoyed her warm, sensuous hands.

In this last dream, however, she'd been bathed in darkness, and he could feel her pain as it wrapped around his heart and squeezed.

It is a dream. It has to be.

No, his wolf responded. *Kaleena is real. And she needs you.*

Finn wanted to believe that was true, but sane men recognized dreams weren't real.

The light streaming in through his bedroom window

helped calm his clouded thoughts, but the sun didn't make things any clearer. Ever since this amazing woman had entered his thoughts a few weeks ago, he'd pondered whether he really had been talking to a woman he was slowly falling in love with, or if he had lost his mind. The only person who'd believed him was his twin, Chelsea, but could she help him now?

Finn snatched the phone from his side table and called her. Today was her day off from the vet clinic.

"Hey. You're up early. I thought you closed the bar last night," Chelsea said.

"I did. Listen. I need to pass something by you."

She didn't say anything for a moment. "You sound worried."

"I am." He told her about his dream and how scared Kaleena sounded.

"If she is in trouble, maybe Connor can help find her."

He wasn't sure how to explain it any better than he had. "She's in a different realm!"

Chelsea was silent for a moment. "A different realm? You mean Cargonia?"

Most shifters believed this other parallel realm existed, but that it was the only one. "No. This is a different realm, called Tarradon."

"Wow. Maybe you should be contacting Zane Barons. He claims to be from Cargonia. I know that's not this Tarradon place, but it is different realm. He might have heard of it."

Why hadn't he thought of that? "Thanks, Chels. I'll give him a try."

"Let me know."

"Sure."

Zane claimed he'd been cursed and sent to Earth, where he was asleep for one-hundred years until his mate found him. He now worked for the fire department as a janitor. Had Finn's older brother not vouched for him, Finn would have considered the man a bit loco. Why not call? He had nothing to lose.

Finn's mind reeled. "So it's possible the other realm exists?" he asked Zane.

"I believe so." Zane motioned Finn to take a seat on his living sofa. "But as I said, I've never been to Tarradon. I've heard that it is inhabited with many dragon shifters who rule their realm. As a werebear, I decided it was best to stay clear of the place."

"Have you met anyone who's been there?"

"No, I've just heard stories. Mind you, the last time I was in Cargonia was over a hundred years ago. A lot could have changed."

"I see. But if you know that other realm exists, it means Kaleena is telling the truth," he whispered. Finn leaned forward. "Can you tell me how telepathy works in your realm?" Finn never understood how he was able to communicate telepathically with Kaleena when they hadn't mated.

"What do you mean?" Zane asked.

"Kaleena and I have not mated—obviously—yet we can communicate when we sleep."

"You can dream-walk?" Zane asked, his mouth opening slightly.

"Yes. Why?"

"That only happens if both of you are witches." Zane waved a hand. "Of course, it might be different on her realm."

Finn dropped back his head and glanced to the ceiling. "Well, fuck—I'm no witch."

Zane shook his head. "How do you know?"

Maybe Zane didn't have his shit together after all. "I have no magical abilities."

"Maybe they are latent, and you just don't know about them. I've seen it happen before."

Talk about mind-blowing. "Then I guess I need to do a little investigating. Where I don't know."

"If this Kaleena is a witch who is able to initiate this dream link with you," Zane said, "then you'll need to find a powerful witch here to help you. She's far more qualified to know about these things than some lowly bear like myself."

Finn jumped up. "I'll speak with Ophelia—Silver Lake's most powerful witch." He faced Zane and held out his hand. "Thank you."

"I didn't do much."

"You helped more than you realize."

"Any time."

As soon as Finn left, he sat in his car and called Connor. True, his brother was skeptical about the existence of Kaleena until he told him what Zane said.

"It might be true about you having some special talents," Connor said.

Now it was Connor who was a bit crazy. "What do you mean?"

"Our great grandmother on Mom's side was said to have witch abilities."

Shock coursed through him. "So we're part Wendayan? That's nonsense." And he sure as hell never had blue sparks shoot off his body when he was sexually excited either—a sure indication he was part Wendayan.

"Don't be so hasty. You might have inherited some of her talents," Connor said. "You need to ask Mom about it."

"Oh, I will." Just as soon as he talked with Ophelia.

So, here he was, waiting in his car, ready to hear whether he was crazy or not. Finn had never spoken to the town's most powerful Wendayan because he'd never needed her guidance before. While she'd often been helpful to others —especially to his family members—she did have a tendency to talk in circles. Some claimed she'd been more frustrating than useful at the time they met her, but in the end she had always been right.

He shouldn't be nervous to meet her, but he was. *What if she tells me Tarradon doesn't exist? Then what would I do? Seek therapy because I believe my dreams are real?*

He didn't want to address that issue yet. He wasn't sure which would be worse though—learning that Tarradon didn't exist, or what he'd have to do if it did.

Aw hell, Ophelia was some ninety-year old lady who probably wasn't open to things such as realms. If she said other realms were a product of someone's imagination, he'd try another witch.

He looked around the wooded area, where Ophelia

was said to reside, but he didn't spot her. He wasn't sure where she wanted to have this conversation, but someone as frail as her wouldn't appreciate standing out in the cold. Finn debated searching for her, but he'd been told she could sense when anyone was near. Hopefully, she'd find him.

Sure enough, two minutes later a frail and withered looking woman, who couldn't weigh one hundred pounds soaking wet, emerged from the forest. Given her advanced age, he expected her to move slowly, but she seemed to glide rather than walk.

As if he'd lost track of time for a minute, she opened his car door. Christ, he hadn't even seen her cross in front of his vehicle. He must be losing it. Ophelia slipped in and reached out to take his hand. Even though she wasn't wearing a coat and the temperature was nearly freezing, her hands were warm to the touch. How was that even possible?

She studied him. "You're troubled."

Since this was the first time they'd met, Finn was more surprised by the blunt comment than at her observation. It was true the bags under his eyes were the worst they'd ever been because of his worry for Kaleena, but he didn't think he looked that haggard. "I am."

While he'd rehearsed what he was going to say, now that the petite woman was in front of him, it seemed his tongue couldn't work.

She squeezed his hand then let go. "No need to explain. Dream-walking can be very troublesome to your sleep patterns and quite confusing, if not downright disturbing."

Tension rippled through his muscles at her insight.

Never in a million years did he expect her to know anything about that. "What do you know about it?"

She smiled. "You'll find out soon enough. Right now, you need to worry about that mate of yours. We don't have much time—or rather Kaleena doesn't."

Finn's head nearly exploded. Ophelia knew her name? How? It was almost too hard to grasp. "So she exists?"

Mate, mate! his wolf chanted. *I told you so.*

Finn had hoped it was true, but he understood he had a better chance of winning the lottery than Kaleena being flesh and blood.

Ka-ching, ka-ching. His wolf cheered. *Better than the lottery.*

"Of course, she exists," Ophelia said, as if she couldn't believe he doubted it. "Her family is very important in Tarradon."

It didn't matter if her parents were important or not, Kaleena was his main focus. "What can you tell me about her?"

"She's a Guardian who's been kidnapped. Don't ask me how I know that, or why that is a big deal, just believe me. As much as I'd like to tell her parents that Kaleena's being held hostage, I don't want to interfere with Fate's plan for true mates. It's up to you to follow the path that Fate has set out for you."

She wasn't making a lot of sense. "So you won't help her at all?" He failed to keep the censure from his tone.

"I didn't say that. I will do what I can, but I suspect when Kaleena doesn't show up for work, they will begin searching for her."

Her information was becoming increasingly more frustrating. Finn didn't know whether to ask what a Guardian was or what he could do. "You said you could help. How? You're here and she's..." he nodded upward. "There."

"I can help by aiding *you* in reaching her."

Finn prided himself on his strength, but right now his bones were about to melt and his head explode. "Me? How?"

"I can show you the location of the portal."

Joy sprang up. "I can go to Tarradon and help Kaleena?"

"That's the plan." Her modern use of language threw him for a second.

Then reality struck. "Even if I reach Tarradon, what can I do? Suppose I manage to find her family. They might not believe that Kaleena called out to me." This was getting worse by the minute. It had all sounded so doable at the time. Only then did it occur to him that Ophelia might be pulling his leg. "How can you be so sure you can find a portal?" No one that he knew of had been successful —other than Zane who had come from another realm.

Ophelia sighed. "You young people and your need for proof." She pulled something out of her pocket and held open her palm. "This is a dragon scale imbued with magic. With it I can communicate with someone in the Guardian Circle—someone with the power to help you reach your destination."

A dragon scale? For real? It did look like it could belong to a dragon. The mostly black scale was about one-inch by one-inch and was iridescent in parts. Finn straightened his shoulders. "Where did you get that?"

"It was given to me many years ago."

"How does it work?"

She waved a hand at his incessant questions. "Suffice it to say, it's magic. Magic you don't need to understand. Just know that I can contact this person and ask him to open a portal where someone from Kaleena's family will meet you."

Finn had his doubts, but to voice them would piss off the old lady, and he needed her. Ophelia's lips had already thinned, and she seemed to be losing her patience with all of his questions.

Regardless of her changing attitude, he decided to call her bluff. "When can I go?"

The tension lines around her eyes seemed to soften. "The portals open everyday at noon and midnight. So you will go tomorrow at midnight."

"Why not tonight?" While it wouldn't give him much time to get ready, he didn't want Kaleena to suffer any more than necessary.

"I need to make sure I can contact the right person on Tarradon. I also figured you'd need time to get your affairs in order."

She was right. He had a job he needed to square away, and a lot of people to say goodbye to. His shifter family and friends were more accepting to strange occurrences, but he doubted everyone would be open-minded to his attempt at inter-realm travel.

Now that she was handing him this golden opportunity though, he wasn't sure he was ready, mentally or physically to leave this world. "What is it like?" he asked.

"What is what like?" Her brows knitted together.

"The portal. How long does it take to reach Tarradon? And will it be a difficult trip?" Even though he was willing to deal with any kind of hardship for Kaleena, he needed to be as prepared as possible.

She let out a breath. "One second you will be here and the next there. I doubt you will even realize you've moved."

That was too good to be true, but how did she know? Had she herself been through one? And was it to Tarradon? Portal rides might be different to different realms. Finn had to admit this sounded like something out of a science fiction movie, but if Zane was to be believed, he'd come through one, so it must be okay. "If traveling between the realms is so easy, why haven't we even heard Tarradon exists?"

"It's complicated. I'm sure Kaleena's family explain once you arrive."

Kaleena never mentioned that her realm was dangerous, but if she was imprisoned somewhere, it must be. More questions surfaced. Once Finn stepped into this portal, would he dematerialize or stay in his human form? Jeez. What difference did it make if it worked? Like toppled over building blocks, a ton of additional questions bombarded him, but he forced himself to hold them back.

Then his practical side surfaced. "What should I take?"

He had to assume the air was compatible to that on Earth. In Zane's realm of Cargonia, it seemed to be. As for how cold or hot it was there, Kaleena never complained of extreme temperatures, but even if Tarradon were blistering hot or icy cold, he'd deal. From what she'd said, Tarradon had the same modern conveniences as Earth, but given that royalty lived in castles, it implied a hint of the medieval mixed in.

"I suggest you limit it to one change of clothes. Anything else can be purchased there."

With what? Dollars? That would imply the two realms interacted often, and somehow he doubted that. Jeez, the number of unknowns was mounting.

Now that he'd been shown what was possible, could he leave his world, his life, his family?

"Now run along and do what you need to, but tell no one other than your family, and be sure to swear them to secrecy."

His heart dropped to his stomach at the thought of leaving. He loved all of his siblings, but it was his twin sister he'd miss the most. "What should my parents say as to why I'm not around?" This wasn't fair to them, or to his uncle who counted on him to manage McKinnon Pub and Pool.

"They are strong. They will figure something out."

Finn understood none of it, but Ophelia must have her reasons for wanting his journey to remain a secret.

"Thank you." Those words seemed so inadequate.

"I'll be in contact soon. Be prepared to leave tomorrow night at midnight."

"I will." Or so he hoped.

She opened his car door and floated back into the forest. Hopefully, she had a warm place to live. These mountain winters could be hard on the elderly.

Even though he had a lot of things to do to prepare for tomorrow night's adventure, Finn sat there, stunned and unable to move. His thoughts were swarming like a poked hive of bees. He inhaled and dropped his head back against the seat. Kaleena was real! He could hardly believe it.

But why had she contacted him of all people? He was just a bartender from a small Tennessee town. From the way Ophelia spoke, and from what he'd figured out, Kaleena was larger than life. That made him question once more why a woman from another realm would reach out to him. Was it because Fate had destined them to be mates as Ophelia implied?

Zane had told him dream-walking only happened if each person had some magical ability and not because they were destined for each other. It looked like it was time to have a talk with his mother.

CHAPTER THREE

Soaring then dipping along the warm currents, the delicious air kissed Kaleena's body as she flew over Tarradon. The landscape below, with its majestic mountains cradling large fertile valleys, was dotted with villages and sprinkled with the occasional stone castle. The sight made her grin and laugh.

Hundreds of years ago, when the Royals' rule was supreme, their *slaves,* also known as serfs back then, had huddled nearby their kingdom, but no longer. Cities had formed and people had begun to spread out. When the dragons began visiting Earth, progress changed Tarradon for the better.

Kaleena spotted a castle in ruin, and her heart ached for the foregone beauty, but she was thrilled that the serfs, who long ago had been forced into labor, were now free. It galled her that the Royals still managed to enslave a few, most of whom were humans.

Tarradon contained four provinces, the largest of which

was Avonbelle. Edendale, the largest city in her province, sat in the middle. Humans, shifters, and witches for the most part lived in harmony as they bustled around the city streets. Horns honked and store front lights flashed. Even though it was a lot smaller than Denver, Colorado, Edendale was of great importance in the realm.

Kaleena darted over the tallest of the buildings and then slowed as she reached her building—SinCas Mining and Gems. She sighed knowing that the work she and the other Guardians did helped keep their people free. While all dragons possessed some magical abilities, the non-Royals bred with whomever Fate designated them to be with—whether it be white lighters, humans, or other shifters—whereas the Royals either bred among themselves or with dark lighters, most of who were not their Fated true mates.

Over the years, problems had developed for the Royals. Weaknesses began to crop up from these non-sanctioned matings. It was why, Kaleena believed, the Royals were trying to bolster their declining magical powers through theft.

Out of nowhere came a hurricane-force wind that made Kaleena careen toward the ground.

"Wake up," came a demanding and loud voice.

Wake up? Who was talking to her? Kaleena flapped her wings once more to reach a different current. Before she could glide upward, she was met with blackness—and then reality.

You're dreaming, her dragon said, sounding quite disgusted. *Open your eyes.*

Damn it. Rousing from a deep sleep, she looked up to

find two men looming over her.

Fuck. She wasn't free and hadn't been flying high above. Far from it. She was still in this dingy cell. "What do you want?" she managed to say despite her dry mouth.

One of the men was the mute guard. The other was larger and seemed more menacing, probably because his face was scarred.

"Cuff her," the larger one said.

Cuff me?

Before Kaleena could put up much of a fuss, the larger man held her down while the mute slapped a thick metal cuff on one wrist and then did the same on the other. He then pressed the two cuffs together, locking them tight.

As hard as she tugged, Kaleena couldn't break them apart. What little strength she had seemed to be draining quickly from her body. "You don't need to do this. I won't escape." If they believed that, they were gullible, but right now she'd say anything for a chance at freedom.

The guards yanked her up to a standing position, and her knees buckled. Something was happening to her. She'd been stronger a moment ago.

Dragon, heal me.

I'm trying, but something is stopping me, her animal said.

"Get moving."

When the mute opened the cell door, adrenaline rushed through her system, and Kaleena could almost smell freedom. As much as she wanted to run, her legs wouldn't oblige, damn it. The best she could do was stutter-step out into the hallway. Just as she glanced around to get her bearings, the second guard blindfolded her. Asshole.

"Where are you taking me?" she asked in her haughtiest voice.

He shoved her, forcing her to her knees. Had she not had quick reflexes, she would have done a face plant. As much as she wanted to yell at them to leave her alone, she understood they didn't give a damn what she wanted. Someone was giving the orders, and they planned to obey.

One of the men jerked her to her feet again and then kept his hand on her upper arm as he led her down the hallway. They turned right, left, and then who knows where. Many minutes later, a sudden influx of fresh air implied they'd stepped outside, but her excitement was short-lived. They reentered the cold, dank interior not long after.

The outside smells however reminded her of the Plantera bush, which she'd only smelled twice in her life. The first time was when she was little and her parents had taken her to the coast in the province of Thedia. She remembered running through a field bordered by this sweet smelling bush. It thrived in the dampness and overcast skies. She'd been told it rarely grew in Avonbelle—a drier area of the realm. The only other time she'd smelled it, was on a rare visit to her cousin's castle. Was that where she was now? The hard, rather uneven floor convinced her it might be.

By the time one of the guards knocked on a door, Kaleena had no idea where she was.

A moment later a voice from inside called, "Come in."

Maybe now she might learn why she'd been taken.

As soon as she took a few steps forward, the blindfold

was removed. When she saw who was seated behind the large wooden desk, she went speechless.

"Sit down, Kaleena."

Finn wasn't looking forward to this conversation with his parents about his departure. His family was tight—probably tighter than any other he'd ever known, which made this so much harder. Informing them that their youngest son wanted to leave Earth because he believed a woman was in danger would be hard, if not impossible to explain. His one sliver of hope was that if it was so easy to get to Tarradon that returning should be just as quick.

His dad in particular wouldn't buy into the idea of his running off, but his mom would probably be more sympathetic to his cause. She'd break down for sure when she learned she might never see him again though, and Finn didn't know if he could stand hurting her like that. But he had no choice. Even if he assured him that the transportation part was easy, he really had little knowledge of what Tarradon was like—or how friendly they'd be to wolf shifters.

At least Chelsea would understand and even encourage him to follow his heart, but he sure would miss her.

The worst part might be that he was leaving before the Christmas holidays. That in and of itself would be akin to a sin in his household.

Finn would never have the conversation until he got his ass in gear. Starting the engine, he took off. Halfway to his parents' house, the right front wheel ran off the pavement and hit a patch of ice, jerking his attention back to the road. Damn. He'd been thinking about Kaleena and seeing her soon—not on driving.

Focus.

When he arrived at his parents' house, Finn blew out a breath and shut off the ignition. He eased out of the seat, braced against the chilly air, and forced his feet to reach the front door. He knocked lightly before heading in. "Hello? Anyone home?"

"Is that you, Finn?" his mom called from the kitchen.

"It's me." He was quite relieved his mom was home even though she'd be the first to cry.

Wearing the apron he'd given her for Christmas when he was twelve, she came out of the kitchen, wiping her hands on a towel. The apron was frayed and stained, but she wore it often because she loved the saying on the front that read: *My mom's the best cook.* His heart warmed at how happy she'd been at the gift. He still remembered the hug that followed.

Her smile lit up her face. "What a nice surprise. I'm finishing up the final touches for Connor and EmmaLee's mating party tomorrow night."

"Mating party? When did that happen?" He'd spoken to Connor briefly yesterday, and he said nothing about it. Or had Finn walked through some kind of time warp?

"Yesterday. We would have waited a few days before celebrating, but the white moon is tomorrow night and EmmaLee will be shifting for the first time."

This was almost too much to take in. "I see."

"Can you get off work?" she asked.

He forced a smile. "I wouldn't miss it for the world." But it would be the most difficult time of his life to sit through a party and have his brothers and sister know that he might not see them for a while—for a long while.

"Wonderful. How about coming back into the kitchen and tell me what's happening in your life? You don't look good, by the way."

His mom always worried about the family. "I'm okay."

"Come, come. I'll fix *you* a drink for a change."

That brought out a smile—one he sorely needed. "Where's Dad?"

"He's here somewhere." She stilled for a moment, as if she had just telepathed him that Finn had arrived. "He'll be right down."

Footsteps sounded and his dad appeared. "Hey, son. Nice of you to stop by."

It wasn't as if he was a stranger. He'd been there last week. Finn sat at the kitchen island while his mom made him a chocolate shake like the kind he used to crave as a kid. She didn't know she was making it more difficult for him to leave.

Finn cleared his throat. "I had a disturbing dream last night."

"Really? What was it about?" Concern colored her tone.

"Recently, this one woman has been occupying my mind. She's amazing, beautiful, and we've connect on an amazing level."

"I thought you said it was disturbing," his mom said.

"Last night's dream was. At first I thought I was crazy. I

mean, come on, a dream is a dream, but Kaleena, that's her name, feels real."

"But last night was different?"

"Yes. She said she was being held captive and asked if I could help her."

His mom sucked in a breath. "When she's talking to you, is it telepathically?"

Finn stilled. "Yes."

Her jaw slackened. "Then you were dream-walking," his mom announced, her voice sounding far away.

Stunned, Finn had to swallow to gain some control. "What do you know about that?" Her hands stilled, and she glanced to the ceiling. "Mom, what is it?"

She looked back at him. "I honestly haven't thought about my grandmother in a long time."

His mind spun. "What about my great grandmother? Connor mentioned something about her being a witch. Is that true?"

"Yes. She was a Wendayan, and not just an ordinary one either. She possessed a lot of power and magic."

His heart beat hard. He glanced at his father who didn't look surprised. "Why didn't I know about this before?"

Her eyes widened. "I saw no reason to bring it up. I didn't want any of you kids to get your hopes up."

"How so?"

"My mother, their only child, didn't exhibit any symptoms of magic, and when I didn't either, nor did any of you kids, I figured that gene had disappeared—until now."

Once more, he was stunned. "So you believe my dream-walking is real?"

"Powerful witches, like my grandmother, could dream-walk. You must have inherited her talent, and it never manifested itself before now."

This was almost too much to grasp. "Then Ophelia was right. Kaleena must be real."

Yay. His wolf cheered.

"You spoke with Ophelia?" his mother said.

Now came the hard part. "I had to see her about my dreams. She told me that Kaleena exists. And here's the incredible part. Ophelia can help me reach her."

"Why that's wonderful!" While her cheer seemed to reach her eyes, his dad seemed frozen to the spot.

Finn leaned forward, trying to decide how to break the news to them. "It is fantastic, except that Kaleena lives in a different realm."

"On Cargonia?" his father asked in his gruff and commanding voice.

Cargonia was the only realm anyone had heard of before. "No, on a parallel universe called Tarradon."

"Tarradon?" his father asked. He glanced over at Mom.

"Have you heard of it?" Finn asked.

His mother nodded. "Yesterday. Your brother and EmmaLee were picnicking near the caves—the same caves were Zane was found."

His palms sweated. "Where they looking for a portal or something?" EmmaLee believed in dragon shifters and wanted confirmation they existed.

"Yes. While they were there, her stalker showed up."

His fists tightened. "Slater Coghill found her?"

"Yes. Only this man said he was from Tarradon and that he couldn't have her reveal that dragons exist. It's why he wanted her dead. Before he could tell them more, he shifted into a dragon."

"Holy shit."

His dad moved closer to the counter. "Connor said that he shifted into his wolf and tried to fight him off, but he was no match for the beast."

Nothing made sense. "How is he still alive then?"

"Connor can give you more details, but right before his eyes, the dragon disappeared."

"Disappeared?"

"Yes. This is what makes me think Tarradon isn't a safe place," his father said.

Finn shook his head. "No, that proves I need to go. Kaleena really is in danger."

His mom grabbed his dad's hand, and the color drained from her face. "So you're really going after her? For how long?"

"I don't know, but I'm hoping I can return." He really had no idea how this portal system worked. Would he be saying goodbye forever?

Her lips pinched. "Is she a wolf shifter? Is that why she needs you to help? Or is she human?"

He'd asked Kaleena, but she'd always flirted with him instead of answering. "I don't know, and honestly I don't care. Mom, I know this sounds totally crazy, but she is my mate. Not only that, I have been falling in love with her since the first time I saw her in my dreams." Okay that sounded even crazier than he'd thought.

"I see." She looked over at Dad. Clearly, the two were talking. "What are you going to tell everyone?"

"I'm not. Ophelia said that only the family can be told

about my going to this other realm—no one else, at least for now." He added that last part. Finn believed no shifter or Wendayan would leak the information to the humans.

"What about your Uncle Garth?" Dad asked. "He needs to know why his manager has decided not to show up for work."

"Fine. Tell Uncle Garth, but that's all. I've been training my assistant in case I wanted to take some time off. I'm sure he will do a fine job."

His mom grabbed his hand. "Why can't Kaleena's family save her? Why does it have to be you?"

"Because they don't know she's in trouble yet. Besides, she's my fated mate, and I love her."

His mom sighed and nodded. "Then you must go and help. You are such a wonderful boy." She hugged him. "But how will you find her? You know nothing of this other universe—how advanced it is, what kind of shifters there are, or anything."

That was a big issue. "I know, but Ophelia thinks that if I go, I can help. Her family will meet me at the portal entrance."

"I see. Did she say if the travel is safe?" his father asked.

"Yes. One minute I'm here and the next I'm there."

"I'll be damned," his dad said. "If it's that easy, I wonder why we've never heard of this realm."

"I wish I knew the answer to that."

Finn slipped off his stool, walked around the counter, and hugged his dad first and then his mom. "I love you both."

Mom leaned back, her cheeks wet. "I love you too. Come back to us. Please."

"I will try."

After another fifteen minutes of goodbyes, he told them he would be at the party tomorrow night to celebrate, but that they had to pretend as if nothing was wrong.

"I'll try not to cry," his mom said.

"Thank you."

CHAPTER FOUR

"Well, well, if it isn't cousin Rathan," Kaleena said. She should have guessed. She never trusted the guy. "What the hell is going on?"

His brow furrowed. "Sit down, Kaleena."

"No."

He waved a hand. "Suit yourself."

She straightened, but it was becoming increasingly more difficult to focus as something was affecting her balance and vision. "Why am I being held captive?"

He might be Prince Rathan Abercrombie to the constituents in Avonbelle, but that didn't mean he necessarily held any power over her.

Rathan leaned back in his chair, looking way too confident. He wore an expensive blue suit and a white shirt opened at the throat. If he weren't such a despicable man, she'd say he was almost handsome with his thick black hair slicked back and his rugged features.

"I need your help," her cousin said.

That was a joke. A member of the Royal family never asked for help from a Guardian—not that he realized she was one. To him, she and her family were merely owners of a mine who possessed magical powers. It didn't seem to matter that their mothers were sisters and grew up in this castle.

A snarky comment shot to her lips, but the old adage of honey working better than vinegar came to mind. Besides, with her hands in cuffs, she didn't have much leverage.

For a moment she debated shifting and taking him on, until a flash of reason surfaced. That wasn't an option in this room either. While she was confident the change would annihilate the cuffs, his office was a mere four hundred square feet and the ceiling only twelve feet high— three feet shorter than her dragon height.

Not only that, she was not at full power and she needed to be if she expected to defeat Rathan. The Royals compensated for not having as much magic as others by training intensely—like the American Special Forces. When she'd visited Earth, she read about them in the news.

That made the Royals quite difficult to defeat, which meant fighting Rathan now would most likely result in her death. Even if she did manage to get close enough to attack, the two goons standing watch would charge in.

"What do you need from me?" She was pleased she managed to speak with a less acidic tone, though what she wanted to do was yell and spit in his face.

He nodded to the two men at the door. "Leave us, but don't go far."

"Yes, Prince."

As soon as the men stepped outside, Rathan sat up straighter. "I'll be honest. The dark lighters who have provided us with our magic are getting old. We need fresh blood."

Her pulse soared. This implied that the adrenaline rush the Royals received with each infusion of magic was decreasing. Good. "And that would involve me how? My magic abilities are only used for good."

He threaded his fingers together. "That can be changed quite easily."

Kaleena's legs weakened at what he implied. She took a step backward and bumped into the chair. A second later, her rear hit the seat. Kaleena had seen the spells put forth by the dark lighters, and they were incredibly powerful. She doubted they were growing weaker, only more taxed as more Royals were born. "Can you explain what you mean by that?"

"Oh, my dear cousin, you are so naïve. The dark lighters are trying to give us royal dragons what we need, but they are overwhelmed with work right now. Rest assured, we will soon be more powerful than any other dragon shifter— including you and your family."

An intense spike of fear coursed through her. The only way her family could boost their abilities was to use dark magic, and they would ever do that. Besides, the Guardians had no desire to conquer and were content with the magic Fate gave them. "You will never have more magic than us," she said, hoping that statement was true.

He shook his head and blew out a breath, acting as if he were talking to a child. "Surely, you've noticed the Royals are on the rise. It's only a matter of time before we take back what is rightfully ours—and that includes land and *resources*. With your help, we can do it sooner rather than later."

He must be referring to her family's mine, and that wasn't going to happen. "Take back what is rightfully yours? That's a joke." He'd never get his hands on SinCas Mining and Gems. "You will never get what you want. The Guardians will help protect what is rightfully ours."

"Guardians, ha. Let's not belittle my intelligence. I know more than you think about those so-called saviors. Soon, they will have many surprises coming their way. Let's just leave it at that, shall we?"

What an ass. He couldn't know that she was one. Her family kept it secret that they were the protectors. Rathan was just testing her, but she wouldn't fall for it. "Don't think your constituents will give you any money either. They already pay more taxes than is fair. Hell, you practically torture a good portion of the human population to do your bidding and then tax the crap out of them so they can't live any kind of life."

He lifted his chin. "They are compensated. We provide some of them with living quarters."

"That doesn't mean it's right. I can understand why you think it's okay to treat humans so poorly. Most of them don't fight back. Clearly, they've forgotten how the Royals of old kidnapped their ancestors from Earth and then turned them into slaves."

Rathan planted a hand on his chest. "You're so harsh in your assessment, my dear. In case you haven't noticed, the Royals do a lot of good here in Avonbelle. Who do you think takes care of the roads, keeps the water clean, and the countrymen educated and healthy? We do! And that takes money."

He was delusional, but she wouldn't get into a debate about how poorly managed everything was. If it weren't for her family's help and that of the Caspians, no progress would have been made in Tarradon. To argue with him would do no good, however. "And the other dragons? How did you lure them?"

He waved a hand and lifted his chin. "Lure is an ugly word. Those who joined us were the smart ones. Plain and simple. They saw the value in joining the winning side."

Hogwash. Dragons always had a weakness for treasure. She was sure Rathan promised them riches for their loyalty, but she questioned how often he actually delivered. As interesting as this line of questioning was, it wouldn't help her figure out how to gain her freedom.

"What did Aunt Teresa say when you told her you had kidnapped me?"

Rathan shifted in his seat. "She doesn't know, nor will she ever."

That didn't surprise her. "How are you going to keep that fact from her?" Once her family realized Kaleena was missing, her mom would call her sister and ask for her help. All staff gossiped.

Kaleena suddenly realized the answer—he planned to use her then kill her. He didn't care what his mother thought. Crap. She would have to escape sooner rather than later. Kaleena Sinclair wasn't part white lighter for nothing. "You won't get away with it, you know."

"Just leave that to me. Shall we get down to business?" He smiled as if this were a friendly conversation about the weather. "Here's what I need you to do for me. First, I will have my best witch teach you how to reach your dark side. She'll start simply by having you kill some small animals, and then we might move on to humans. After that..."

She couldn't listen to anymore. Rathan explained acts of evil so horrific that Kaleena managed to shut off her brain until he stopped listing the litany of terrible deeds he expected her to perform. By the time he finished speaking, her hands were trembling. "I won't do dark magic. It will kill me."

"Come, come. Surely you exaggerate. I only need your help for a month or so. Then I'll let you go."

His eyes almost morphed into slits. She knew the signs. Rathan was working hard to keep control from all the lies he was telling. Without a doubt, he would kill her once she was no longer of use. First and foremost, Kaleena had to find a way to get word to her family. Given how weak she was though, escaping on her own now seemed impossible, but she wouldn't stop trying.

He held up a finger. "I would consider letting you go sooner if you're willing to pass your magic onto me right now. Just place your fingers on my temple to donate your abilities and say that magic word only you know! Then I'll set you free."

If she did that, she'd lose all of her abilities. She hadn't realized Rathan was losing his grip on reality. The man needed to be shown just who he was dealing with. Partially shifting and then shooting fire at him might make him think twice about keeping her jailed, especially if she caught him off guard.

Kaleena jumped up with the intent to distract him.

"You're insane, Rathan. I will never give you my magic or help you in any way. Trust me when I say once your father learns what you've done, he'll take out his revenge on you."

She lifted her hands to partially shift and shoot fire, but nothing happened. What the hell?

Rathan's eyes widened, probably matching her own surprised expression. He then laughed. "What's wrong, cousin? Don't tell me you were trying to shift? Can't do it, can you? Not even partially. What a shame."

The extent of his demonic ways finally sunk in. "What did you do to me?"

"Not much. Those cuffs are sending a bit of poison through you, just enough to keep that damn dragon of yours busy. You can't shift, fully or partially, so don't even try."

Kaleena stumbled toward him and planted her palms on his desk. "You bastard."

He smiled. "It's for your own good. I don't want you hurting yourself. Oh, and by the way, your magic has been bound as well." He looked over at the door. "Guards, get in here," he demanded.

The door flew open and footsteps sounded behind her. "You won't get away with this," she said between gritted teeth.

"I already have. I'll be sending in one of our dark lighters to help you see a bit of reason. Please do as she asks. I'd hate to have to kill you."

"Fuck you."

"Tsk, tsk, such language." Rathan waved his hand, and one of the guards grabbed her arm while the other blind-folded her again. This couldn't be happening.

Help me, she begged her dragon.

I'm trying.

The two guards escorted her out through the door, each having a strong hold on her. Her energy waned with each step, yet somehow the trip back to her cell didn't seem as far as the walk there. Possibly they took a different route to further disorient her. The sounds and smells intensified, implying her dragon was helping somewhat to fight off the effects of the poison, but it wasn't nearly as fast as she'd like.

The cuffs were solid, about a half-inch thick, so how the hell were they poisoning her? She'd have to examine them once she reached her cell.

It's dark magic, her dragon announced, sounding quite certain.

Of course it was. Rathan was a bastard. At her first opportunity, she would kill him.

The guards stopped and then opened her cell door. One of them undid the blindfold and then shoved her inside. Her knees crashed into the cot and she tumbled forward. Kaleena could endure pain. What she wouldn't do was perform dark magic, partly because the more she performed it, the more her white light would disappear until eventually, complete blackness would kill her soul. She'd rather die than be evil.

Rathan would be sending a dark lighter to her soon, but whatever the woman demanded, Kaleena would resist, assuming she had the strength.

From the light coming in the windows in Rathan's office, it wasn't yet noon, but even if she could sleep and enter Finn's mind, he wouldn't be going to bed for many more hours. Damn.

Rest, her dragon said. *I need to work at keeping this poison at bay to the best of my abilities. Mind you, these cuffs are thwarting me at every turn.*

Only because she had nothing else to do did she lie down and close her eyes. Her mind instantly swam with unpleasant images. Rathan could have kidnapped other white lighters more powerful than herself, so why choose her?

The mole the Guardians had planted in the castle told of how Rathan's father, the King, watched his wife very carefully and restricted her contact with her two sisters, Kaleena's mom and Iona Caspian once they moved out of the castle. Maybe by harming Kaleena, Rathan was trying to get back at his two aunts for mating outside of the royal kingdom and leaving his mom alone.

But did her cousin's motive really matter? She was here, and Rathan seemed determined to make her pay for something. Could she augment the magical abilities of the Royals? Sure, but she wouldn't. Not ever.

Finn will save you, her dragon said.

As much as she wanted to believe her optimistic animal, she was a realist. The chances of him finding his way to Tarradon were slim. Even if he did, how could he find her? As a wolf shifter, it wasn't as if he could fight dragons.

Well, shit. She never should have asked him to come, because the man she was falling in love with just might try.

By the time Finn returned home from his brother's mating celebration, it was close to eleven thirty. Only thirty minutes to go before he would be landing on Tarradon. Unless that is, he'd been a naïve fool to believe the old witch. Could she really make the portal work? Ophelia said she would call him, but so far there had been no contact. If he had her number, he'd call her, but his brother's mate and her mom were the only ones able to contact her.

Hoping for the best, he busied himself by packing a change of clothes, praying the preparation wasn't for nothing.

But what if I imagined it all? he asked his wolf.

Stop doing this to yourself, his wolf said. *Kaleena is your mate. You heard Connor. He and EmmaLee met a dragon from Tarradon. Kaleena is real.*

You're right. Sorry.

When eleven fifty came and went, and Ophelia had not contacted him as promised, a wave of depression set in. She'd always been so helpful to his family, so why did she have to pick now to lead a McKinnon astray?

Even if she arrived in the next few minutes, by the time they drove to this portal, it would be past midnight. He could only assume something had gone wrong. Finn picked up the bag he'd set by the front door and returned it to his room. He stared at the bed. Maybe he should try to get some sleep, in the hope that Kaleena would dream-walk with him again. He might even ask her to show him their waterfall haven so they could make love once more.

Someone knocked on his door, jarring him out of his daydream, jacking up his heart rate. He didn't sense a shifter signature so it couldn't be one of his relatives stopping by to check up on him. Finn rushed to the door and threw it open. It was Ophelia! Blood thrummed through his body, adding pressure to the growing headache.

"Better get out here, boy. We only have a few minutes left." Ophelia turned and headed toward his front lawn, wearing only a thin gray dress.

Oh, crap. Maybe she didn't have enough money to buy a coat.

Move, his wolf warned.

"Let me get my case," he called after her.

He ran back to his bedroom and grabbed his bag and jacket. Once outside Finn shivered as he rushed up to Ophelia. "So now what?"

"We wait here for the portal to open."

That didn't sound all that promising. He slipped on his jacket. "Are you saying it will open in my front yard?"

No one had accused her of being batty, but maybe old age had finally caught up with her.

Ophelia placed a hand on his arm. "I told you this is a special portal—one that will deliver you someplace safe. So, yes, it will be near. Now look for some air disturbances, and be quick. We only have another minute or two."

Air disturbances?

Whatever. He'd humor her and look. With his overnight bag slung over his shoulder, Finn stepped back to the street in order to have the best view. His wolf growled and urged him to head toward the spare bedroom window. Finn wasn't sure why, but he went with his animal's instinct. When he drew near, a slight whirring sound made him stop. Did portals make noise? "Ophelia?" he called.

When she didn't answer, he turned, only to find she was

nowhere in sight. What the fuck? Had she walked around to the back of the house to look for it?

"Ophelia? Where are you? Did you find the portal?" he shouted.

No answer. A strong wind whipped around the house and caused chills to race up his body, but he wasn't sure if it was the cold or from nerves. No car sat in his drive, which meant someone must have dropped her off. If that person had picked her up just now, he should have heard the engine.

Finn rushed to the back and called out once more, but she wasn't there. *Fuck me.* He'd been fooled by a diminutive Wendayan. Just as he was about to head back inside and figure out how to admit to his folks that he'd been duped, another whirring sound reached him, only this time it was stronger. Once more, it came from near the bedroom window.

Check it out, his wolf urged.

He agreed only because he wanted to make sure this wasn't another trick by Ophelia. *I'll look one more time, and then I'm heading inside where I plan to get stinking drunk.* Heaven only knows he'd never fall asleep now.

As Finn moved over by the bedroom window to investigate, his vision blurred and his body seemed to stand still.

"You must be Finn," said a giant of a man, slipping out from behind a huge tree.

What the hell?

CHAPTER FIVE

The large stranger extended his hand, but Finn was leery of taking it. The moon backlit the giant, preventing Finn from seeing his features clearly. Bottom line, this guy was trespassing on his property.

Just as Finn was about to go on the defensive, he realized the air was balmy and smelled like pine and rich loom. What he could see of the dark landscape was lush, not stark like the trees in Tennessee. They were at the end of a field. No street. No streetlights. No other houses. His gut clenched at the differences.

Holy shit. The portal worked. Or was he just dreaming?

The man lifted Finn's hand and shook it. *Answer him,* his wolf urged. "Yes, I am Finn. Who are you?" He hadn't meant to sound harsh, but his senses had overloaded.

"I'm Jamison Sinclair, Kaleena's father."

Stunned, Finn struggled to say something coherent. "Her father?"

"Come. Ophelia wouldn't tell me what was going on,

only that you had some very important information for me regarding my daughter."

Finn dug his thumbnail into his index finger to make sure this wasn't a dream. Thankfully, it hurt. "I do. At least I think I do." Finn's eyes finally adjusted to his surroundings enough to look around. "Is this Tarradon?"

"It is. Now tell me," Jamison said. "Do you know where Kaleena is? She didn't show up for work today, and we're worried."

"She's been kidnapped."

The giant moved closer. "What? By whom?"

The man's intensity was palpable. "I don't know."

Jamison Sinclair looked around. From his stiff posture, his senses were on high alert. He glanced upward then back at Finn. "It might not be safe to talk here. We need to go back to our headquarters in town where I'll ask the others to assemble. The rest of my children are very anxious to hear about their sister."

What danger was Jamison speaking of? No one was anywhere near them. Even with his shifter sight, all he could see were mountains in the distance and some trees that surrounded the field. Only a few lights dotted the distant landscape.

Trust him, his wolf said. *He's Kaleena's father.*

So he says.

In truth, if Chelsea had been missing, Finn would be more than anxious—he'd be in full panic mode—so he understood the man's urgency. "How did you get here?" he asked.

"I flew."

Something was off. "Then where's your plane?"

The man had the nerve to laugh. "I'm sorry. I know this must be overwhelming, and I will answer your questions soon, but time is of the essence. Ophelia did share that you and Kaleena have been in contact through dream-walking. In any of those times did she ever tell you what kind of shifter she was?"

"No."

The large man blew out a breath. "This may be hard to believe, but she's a dragon shifter."

Finn's heart dropped to his stomach. "So it is true. My brother Connor ran into one yesterday, or at least he believes he did. The damn creature disappeared on him though."

"Ah, yes, that would be Slater Coghill. As I said, I'll answer your questions later. We need to go now."

A flock of large black birds flew overhead, and Jamison looked up. Or were those birds really dragons flying high in the sky? "Are you going to turn into a dragon and ask me to hop on?"

"I could, but it's a lot safer if I carry you."

The man had gone too far. "I'd rather walk."

"It will take days to reach the city on foot, and that's if you're lucky. Given you're only a wolf shifter, you might not make it. I'm sorry, but I have no choice."

Only a wolf shifter? What the hell? A second later, wind rushed by Finn as the man in front of him shape-shifted into a huge dragon. Holy crap! He had to be as tall as a two-story building. His long black snout was rather pointed and spikes protruded from his back, but it was the majesty of the wings that impressive Finn—long, curved, and sleek. Jamison Sinclair's eyes glowed teal, and some of his scales pulsed silver. The sight took Finn's breath away.

His fascination with the glorious creature won out over his desire to flee. If he hadn't mentioned he was Kaleena's father, Finn would have shifted and hightailed it out of there—assuming his muscles worked. Not that he'd like living as a wolf on a strange realm, but if he managed to escape, he could survive.

Jamison opened his wings that spanned a good forty feet. The webbing between the bony ridges of the wing was close to being translucent and appeared to be made out of some kind of rubbery substance. Fascinating.

With one flap of his wings, the dragon swooped toward him and grabbed him in his talons. Finn's first instinct was to fight, but when the grip remained gentle, he relaxed a bit. He had expected the claws to puncture him, but instead they merely cradled his body.

Most of the bar patrons considered Finn unflappable, but right now, all he could do was yell out as they soared higher and higher. He shut his eyes, not wanting to see anything—including the belly of the large beast. He didn't mind flying in an airplane, but being exposed like this was unpredictable and downright scary.

After a minute or so, the even flapping of wings helped to slow his heart enough for him to brave looking over his shoulder at the world below.

The moon bathed the land in soft light, and the vastness of the plains and mountains was stunning. The beauty of the landscape actually helped to calm him somewhat.

Not wanting to take any chances though, Finn grasped the talons tight, but even if he let go, he doubted Kaleena's father would drop him—not when his daughter's life was at stake.

After a few minutes, Finn accepted the fact he'd be safe and almost enjoyed the ride—almost being the operative word. The wind was cooler this high up, but it wasn't uncomfortably cold. In fact, it was refreshing.

Just as he was used to this mode of transportation, the dragon slipped over a mountain crest and dipped toward a rather large city below. Streetlights and building lights helped illuminated the movement of cars. It looked an awful lot like the States.

Like an expert hang glider, they landed on the roof of a building, and Jamison set him down softly before shifting back into his human form. Finn expected him to be naked like he always was after a shift, but Jamison was dressed in the same clothes as before. How was that even possible? Now wasn't the time however to discuss the differences between shifter types.

"Follow me," Jamison said. He pulled open a large metal door that led to a flight of stairs.

Now that the shock of his arrival in Tarradon was wearing off, Finn's curiosity was building. "Where are we again?"

"This is where SinCas is located—where Kaleena works. It's a metal and gem mining company short for Sinclair and Caspian. My wife is Moira, and her sister, Iona, is married to Laird Caspian. I'm sure you'll be meeting them soon."

The information overload kept coming. They only went down one flight before exiting the stairwell. Jamison then led Finn down a well-lit corridor, enabling him to take a good look at the man. Once more, Finn had to question what was real and what might be his imagination. This dragon didn't look older than forty, which would make Kaleena at most twenty, yet she claimed to be much older.

"Have a seat in this room while I round up a few people," Jamison said.

This place looked to be straight out of a New York City executive's office, complete with a view of the city. A large mahogany conference table that sat twelve took up most of the room. High tech equipment, including a projector and screen, covered one wall, while the remaining space on one end was filled with two brown leather sofas and large comfortable chairs. Nothing seemed alien to him, so was he really in Tarradon?

"This is incredible," Finn said in awe. "If you told me I was in a major US city, I'd believe you."

Jamison smiled. "We do love Earth. Much of what you see has been *borrowed* from your United States."

"How?" Other than Slater Coghill, he wondered how many others had visited?

"Your questions will be answered in due time. Perhaps you could use a drink." He nodded to the credenza on the far wall. "Help yourself. I'll be right back."

As soon as Jamison left, Finn became light-headed. All of this was so new, overwhelming, and a bit frightening. If Kaleena's father hadn't transformed into a dragon in front of him and taken him on the flight of his life, Finn might not have believed any of it.

Curious to learn what the Tarradons drank, Finn eased over to the credenza. Normally, he wasn't one to drink when he needed to stay sharp, but he'd make an exception today. Drinking glasses and bottles of liquor covered the table. On it was something so familiar that he began to doubt once more if this was a different realm. He picked up a bottle of Captain Morgan Rum and studied the label that said it was made in the Virgin Islands. Was this some kind of joke then? He had to be on Earth. Telling him he was in a different realm had to have been some ploy to convince him to help Kaleena. Regardless of his location, he believed her future was in trouble, and that she really did need his help.

Finn poured himself a glass and tossed it back, the wonderful smooth flavor helping to relax him. But he stopped at one. His senses were already over stimulated. Finn walked over to the large picture window to study the view of the bustling metropolis. It looked like every other large city he'd been to—tall buildings, buses and cars in the streets, and even flashing neon lights that signaled all-night bars.

Suddenly out of nowhere, two dark shadows cut through the light cast by the buildings. Finn blinked. What was that? A thump sounded on the roof above him, and then footsteps trod on the stairs. A second later, the door to the conference room burst open, and two huge men appeared.

"Where's Dad?" the larger of the two asked.

"You mean Jamison?"

"Yes."

They both acted like they knew who Finn was. "He went somewhere to round up a few people. I'm assuming you're who he was looking for?"

Both closed the gap. The larger one held out his hand. "Yes. I'm Declan, Kaleena's older brother."

They shook hands. "Finn McKinnon. I'm not sure what I am, except that your sister and I have been dream-walking for a while." He hoped like hell that wasn't some secret.

Declan smiled. "Nice to meet you."

"I'm Thane," the other man said. "Stone, Tory, and possibly Ramsey will be here soon."

"Kaleena mentioned she had a large family, but I had no idea how large."

Thane nodded. "The family also includes our cousins, the Caspians. One or two of them might show up too. We're all worried about Kaleena."

"Is Tarradon that dangerous?"

"For us Guardians it is."

"Guardians?" Finn asked. That was the same group Ophelia had told him. Once more his brain was having a hard time putting all of the pieces together. Maybe the travel through the portal had affected him more than he'd realized.

"It's a long story. While we wait for the others," Declan said, "I might as well explain a few things so you know what you're dealing with."

"I'd appreciate it."

The three of them sat at the large conference table. "All dragons are born with some abilities, or rather magic," Declan said. "The Royals—those who rule us—have always refused to pollute their gene pool and marry outside of the highborn class—unless it's with a dark lighter."

"That's an evil witch, right?"

"Yes. The rest of our forefathers—the non-Royals—mostly mingled with humans, white lighters, and other shifters. Over the centuries, the bloodlines of the Sinclairs and Caspians grew stronger and stronger because of it."

Thane cleared his throat. "Don't forget that Fate had a hand in making us special."

Declan held up a palm. "Very true. Our mates are always chosen with care and for a reason. Anyway, as a result of Fate's guidance, we became powerful. We believe it is our duty to protect those who are weaker against all tyrants."

Finn saw some similarities between his Clan and the Guardians. "On Earth, we breed with our fated mate too, but she doesn't have to be a shifter. We often mix with witches and even humans. Kind of like the Guardians, my family has stayed strong throughout the centuries too. My father was our Clan leader, and my oldest brother is now the Alpha."

"Clan, you say?" Thane asked. Finn nodded. "We don't have Clans per se, just families."

More footsteps sounded on the roof, and a short while later three more people rushed in. One of the men and the lone woman had similar traits. Both were tall with sun-kissed skin and straight black hair. The third man, while large, had lighter skin and brown hair.

The woman rushed up to him. "Are you really Finn?" Excitement laced her tone.

He didn't know how she knew of him. "Yes."

"I'm Nessa Caspian. Kaleena has told me all about you, but I never thought you were..." her voice trailed off.

"Real?"

"Yes."

He saw no point in saying he questioned whether any of them was real too.

Jamison burst in. "Oh, good. Most of you are here. I just received a call from Anderson at the precinct. Kaleena's car was spotted at the bar she usually visits on Friday night, which doesn't bode well for her. I asked him to question the bartender to see if he remembers seeing her." He stabbed a hand through his hair. "Everyone take a seat and we'll find out what Finn knows."

CHAPTER SIX

After hours of trying to sleep, Kaleena finally dozed off, but she failed to contact Finn. Damn. Either he wasn't asleep or that witch's curse had affected her dream-walking abilities. More and more, Kaleena wanted to kill her cousin, but first, she needed to find a way out of this cell.

Something tinny sounding rattled against her cage and roused her. Was it morning already? She couldn't have slept a full day.

Just a few hours, her dragon said. *I needed you to rest so I could keep fighting this poison.*

I hope you succeeded.

Not as much as I'd like. It's a constant battle, but you should be stronger for a while.

Kaleena opened her eyes and sat up. As if a strong force willed her, she stood.

"Good, you're awake," said a tall willowy woman with long brown hair. She looked to be about forty, but Kaleena was never good at telling the age of a human. Dressed in a long black sheath type dress, Kaleena figured she was Rathan's dark lighter, mostly because her cousin told her he was sending someone to *train* her.

Good luck with that. Kaleena would never use her magic to enhance the Royals.

"Who are you?" She didn't want this new person to think she was some pushover who would do what she asked.

The woman opened the cell door without touching it and handed Kaleena a cup that seemed to be filled with water. What Kaleena wouldn't give to be able to open locks with her mind.

"Have a drink then come with me," she said without answering her question.

"Where are we going?"

"Outside."

A split second of excitement ran through her at the possibility of escaping. Kaleena took the proffered cup, pretended to take a sip, and then set it in the sink. No matter how parched she was, Kaleena wasn't going to drink anything someone evil had given her.

As they stepped down the hallway, the two familiar guards filed in closely behind them. Just what she didn't need. If Kaleena couldn't shift or do magic, she was doomed to being held captive for a long time. "What are we going to do?" she asked.

"You'll find out soon enough."

Friendly sort. Not. Actually, Kaleena was surprised the witch was allowing her to see. If she ever managed to take down a guard, she'd know which way to the exit.

As Kaleena walked by the other cells, she glanced

inside. Most of the occupants were on their cots, asleep. None were Christian.

If it was nighttime, why not wait until morning? Or didn't the dark lighter want anyone watching what she was about to do? She remembered a few of Rathan's comments about killing animals and maybe even people, and a cold shiver tripped up her spine.

Without warning, a wave of nausea attacked her, and her vision clouded. Kaleena halted, and just as she grabbed her stomach, the guard behind her ran into her, knocking her to the ground

"Watch where you're going," he commanded.

Kaleena's heart pounded, and she palmed the cold stones in front of her. Oh, no. "I can't see."

The dark lighter cackled. "Did you think I'd let you? I can't have you know your way out."

Bitch. "A blindfold would have sufficed," Kaleena managed to say.

"True, but this is more fun."

Maybe for someone completely evil it was.

Kaleena rose to her feet and expected the men to guide her, but they didn't. That was okay. From the woman's spicy scent, Kaleena was able to follow her. Even the dark lighter's footsteps were enough to indicate when Kaleena needed to step up and then down again. Perhaps it was her imagination, but the trek outside seemed longer than when she'd gone to Rathan's office. Finally, a door creaked and fresh air greeted her. Kaleena inhaled and almost smiled at the sweet scent.

A smaller, cold hand grabbed her arm and led her farther outside. A finger snapped, and when Kaleena's vision cleared, relief rushed through her, but so did her apprehension. That was some magic trick. Rathan really had sent his most powerful dark lighter.

Right now, she didn't care what this person could do. Kaleena was just thankful she had her sight back. Being blind would have hindered her ability to do her job and fight the Royals. While she refused to praise this one for her significant talents, Kaleena was impressed. What a shame this woman decided to use her skills for evil purposes—assuming she had a choice. Tales had been bandied about when Kaleena was growing up about curses that changed a white lighter into an evil, dark lighter. Kaleena could only hope that it had been a made up story to scare little kids, though right now she doubted that.

Heart pumping, Kaleena looked around. Because it was dark, she couldn't see a lot other than that they were behind the mammoth castle on the expansive lawn that was bordered by a forest. No guards were in plain sight, but she had no doubt they were around.

The woman stopped and addressed the two guards who'd been following them. "You may go back inside. I'm sure I won't have any trouble with Kaleena."

Like hell she wouldn't. Kaleena was fast—at least she was when her magic was intact. All she had to do was make it to the forest and she could hide.

"What are you going to do?" she asked her captor.

"So many questions. I'm going to help you do what the Prince wants. And if you give him your magic, he'll let you go."

That was a lie, and no doubt this woman knew it too. Because this dark lighter was not being cooperative,

Kaleena let her lead her closer to the forest line—closer to where she planned to escape.

"We'll stop here. The art of dark witchcraft is all about learning to focus your powers. Do you see that rock over there?" The woman pointed to a stone approximately fifteen feet away from them that was about one foot in length and maybe six inches tall.

"Yes."

"Watch."

The woman leaned slightly forward as if she wanted to direct some kind of mental laser beam on the stone, not paying Kaleena any heed. Even though she still wore her cuffs, if she shifted, she could escape easily enough. Kaleena didn't care that her cousin claimed she was no longer able to perform any kind of magic.

Stepping back, out of the witch's sightline, she closed her eyes and imagined her wings flapping, like she did when she shifted—only this time nothing happened. After a second attempt, she admitted defeat and worked hard to tamp down the fear. Damn Rathan.

Her hatred for the man surged, and her stomach churned at the injustice. This time the ache wasn't from the slow poisonous drip into her body. This dark lighter, or someone like her, really had managed to cut off all of her abilities.

Even though Kaleena had never been helpless before, she wasn't going to give up. If she couldn't fly, she could certainly run. First, she needed to judge how long it would take her to reach the forest. Before making her next move, her gaze drifted back to the witch, and true to her word, the rock the witch was so focused on began to lift and then swirl in the air. Two seconds later it shot forward twenty feet, as fast as any bullet from a gun.

Now or never, she barked at herself.

Running as fast as she could without the use of her arms to pump was difficult and made her gait rather awkward, but she was making progress. She was halfway to the forest when a solid cement wall suddenly formed in front of her. Had she not had shifter sight, she would have run right into it. A second later, the sound of laughter reached her.

"Did you really expect to escape?" the dark lighter called.

Yes. Kaleena touched the wall to make sure it was solid. It was. Where had that come from? She could have sworn it wasn't there a minute ago.

Out of nowhere, the woman appeared beside Kaleena. Either the witch had the ability to teleport, or Kaleena had blacked out for a moment.

"You can't get away," the dark lighter cackled. She gripped Kaleena's arm again in a furious squeeze. "Let's go, now!" Her tone sharpened at the last word.

Before Kaleena could decide whether to obey or not, her legs suddenly gave out and she crashed to the ground. She looked up at the evil woman. "What did you do to me?"

"I'm just making sure you know I control you right now, so you might as well give up fighting me. Now, get up!"

Kaleena hated to give in, but without her ability to shift, use her own magic, or run, she had little choice.

Perhaps if the witch taught her how to move objects with her mind like that, she could use it to help her escape.

"I won't fight you, I promise, but if I'm going to obey you, can you at least tell me your name?"

"Sanditra."

"Sanditra." The name tasted like acid.

"Now let's begin."

Really? "Just out of curiosity, how can I do magic if my abilities have been disabled?"

"The dark magic inside of you is still available," she said matter-of-factly.

What was she talking about? She sounded like Rathan. "I don't have any dark magic."

"Rathan told me you were quite naïve. He was right. We all have good and bad inside of us, some more than others. Your magic is strong. I can feel it, but believe me when I say it comes from a strong dark side."

Kaleena never had the urge to use her magic to destroy things, but arguing with her would only prolong her *education*. "If you say so."

The dark lighter smiled, and Kaleena's heart squeezed. The battle of the wills was about to begin, and she had a sick feeling she wasn't going to win.

Kaleena had never felt so ill in her life. She was nauseated, her head kept pounding, and the sharp stabbing behind her eyes was becoming unbearable. She'd tried to act like the eager student when Sanditra showed her a few more tricks, but it was nearly impossible to do. While Kaleena had learned to move objects with her mind when she was a child, she'd never been able to make them fly so fast they could break windows and fell trees—like Sanditra could. With practice, Kaleena believed she could improve.

Unfortunately, that was the only *trick* Sanditra showed her that was moderately harmless.

After that, her new teacher taught Kaleena how to locate and kill small animals. Naturally, Kaleena refused to give it a whirl. Defiance however was not rewarded. Every time the evil woman thought Kaleena wasn't putting forth her best effort or downright refused to participate, Sanditra would weaken her by waving a hand or chant an incantation. First, Kaleena would feel a sharp stab to the ocular nerve, followed by rolling spasms of bile that cascaded from her stomach to her throat, which made her double over a few times. After a few of those spells, it didn't take much to bring Kaleena to her knees. She was positive that if it hadn't been for the poison dispensed from the bracelet cuff, she could have held out longer.

The worst part was that Sanditra told her they would continue these exercises tomorrow, and the next day, and the next, until Kaleena was willing to embrace the dark side.

When the guards finally escorted her back to the cell after spending an agonizing session with the witch, the sun was beginning to peek over the horizon. On her return trip, they blindfolded her, but from the smells and sounds she encountered, she suspected they had walked in circles a bit before returning her.

"Breakfast will be delivered shortly," the tall guard grunted.

As much as Kaleena didn't want to eat their slop, she needed her strength. They were already poisoning her, so how much more harm could they do?

Hoping her dragon could heal her further, she rested on the cot until the familiar sounds of plates scraping roused her. This time, she took the bowl of porridge and managed to down some of it. Too bad she felt worse afterward.

I'm not sure how much more I can take, her dragon said. *Just as I start the healing process, more poison enters your body. This might kill me before you.*

She didn't have the strength to say that only a jab to her upper heart could kill her. Kaleena returned to her cot, fully aware of what her dragon was going through. *Do you have any suggestions on how I can fight her?* she asked her inner animal.

Her damn dragon was always making comments at the most inappropriate times. The least she could do was offer a good idea now.

No.

Just as she suspected. Kaleena had to believe her family was looking for her. The problem was even if they were aware she was in the castle, they'd never gain access to this dungeon. Rathan would see to that.

She looked up at the one slim ray of light that sliced into the cell and a teardrop rolled down her cheek.

"Are you sure Kaleena didn't say where she was?" Jamison asked.

Kaleena's father, his three children, two nephews, and

one niece were seated around the table, all focused on Finn.

"No. I swear I've been over this many times. She just said she was being held captive, and that I had to find my way to Tarradon."

"How did she sound?" Nessa asked. "Kaleena is normally so strong."

Finn repeated the conversation in his head. "Scared, I guess, but hopeful. When I woke up, I thought I was in a cell. I'm thinking maybe it was because Kaleena was in one."

Jamison slapped his hand on the table. "She has to be in the castle then. Nothing else makes sense."

"Castle?" Finn asked.

"It's a long story and quite complex, but the short of it is that we and the Royals don't see eye-to-eye. In no small part, it's because the queen's two sisters married me and my cousin. They were then banned. Now the king won't allow them to interact. I think he believes his wife will want to leave the castle and its rigid rules. As you can imagine, we butt heads at every turn. I'm thinking this kidnapping might be his way of retaliating."

Declan, Kaleena's brother, sat up straighter. "I've been hearing rumors that the Royals are kidnapping white lighters and using them to infuse powers into themselves."

Finn had no idea that was even possible. "Kaleena would never do that."

His father nodded. "We know, but dark lighters are powerful. They have their ways of turning the best. As much as I want to storm the castle tonight, I think we'd have a better chance tomorrow morning."

"Why? We would have the cover of darkness, and our eyesight is better than any Royal dragon," Declan said.

Kaleena's dad's eyes darkened. "I'm not ready. We need to contact your aunt Teresa to see what information she might have about Kaleena."

"I bet Aunt Iona wouldn't mind being awakened when it's this important. If you were holed up in the castle, under who knows what conditions, wouldn't you want us to come after you as quickly as possible?"

"I would hope I could save myself, but if Kaleena is under some spell, she might be helpless. Your Aunt Iona might not mind being awakened, but your Aunt Teresa would. Remember we have one chance to get this right."

Declan dragged a hand down his chin and blew out a breath. "You're right, but there has to be something we can do now."

"As much as I want to go to the castle, wherever it is," Finn said, "if I'm stopped, I can't think of any reason why I'd be snooping around at one in the morning. I'd need a cover story." He hoped the family could provide him with one.

"Finn's right," Jamison said. "If we tip them off, they could hide Kaleena away for life or worse."

What seemed like a blast of cold air crawled up his body and clawed at his heart.

"I agree with Uncle J," Logan said. "Sometime tomorrow we should fly overhead and deal with those guards who patrol the airspace. Some of the other Guardians could disable the ground guards and go inside," Logan offered.

"You forget they are excellent fighters. We need to

really think this through. We'll come up with a good plan," Jamison said, and Logan nodded.

"As hard as it will be," Finn said, "I'm going to try to sleep tonight. I'm hopeful Kaleena will try to dream-walk with me again, and when she does, I'll ask her for all the pertinent details. She might have learned where she is being held."

Every face at the table brightened. "Sounds good. Let me show you where you can stay," Jamison said. "We'll reconvene at ten tomorrow morning. Iona should be able to contact Teresa by then, and hopefully the queen will have something to tell us."

Finn hoped like hell he never ended up in a relationship as messed up as that one. Right now though wasn't the time to delve into the dynamics of the Royal family. He desperately needed to talk with Kaleena—if only to reassure her that help was on the way.

CHAPTER SEVEN

"I did fall asleep," Finn said, answering Thane's question the next morning, "but as hard as I tried, I couldn't connect with Kaleena."

Jamison's hands clenched. "That proves she has to be under some kind of spell. Damn."

Nessa's cell rang. The design of the model looked suspiciously like the one Chelsea owned, but Finn didn't know how that was possible.

"It's Mom," she said to the group before answering. She pressed the phone to her ear. "Did you get a hold of Aunt Teresa?" she asked. "And what did she say?" Nessa listened for a moment. "Are you sure she's telling the truth? Okay, thanks. We'll be in touch when we know anything." Nessa disconnected, slipped her phone back in her pocket, and glanced from one person to another as if she needed some time to break the news. "I'm not sure it was a good idea for Mom to call because while Aunt Teresa was upset that Kaleena was missing, she was downright livid that Mom would suggest someone at the castle had her."

Declan scrubbed a hand down his jaw. "Aunt Teresa is loyal to the king for some unknown reason, so I'm not surprised she is offended. Your mom would have known if she was telling the truth though. The problem is that if the king ordered Kaleena's capture, he wouldn't have confided in his wife. I was hoping she'd heard news some other way."

Everyone around the table grumbled.

The door burst open and a woman with blonde hair Finn hadn't seen before rushed in. "Sorry I'm late, but man, I've been sicker than a green dragon." She grabbed a chair next to Jamison and dropped down.

Her father clasped her arm. "Are you okay, sweetheart?"

"Not really. I'm convinced I'm feeling Kaleena's pain." She looked over at Finn. "I'm Tory, by the way, Kaleena's twin. To answer your next question, we aren't identical. Even though my sister has dark auburn hair instead of blonde, we look enough alike to confuse people."

She seemed more outwardly emotional than Kaleena too, but that might not be accurate since he'd never met his mate in person. "I'm Finn McKinnon...from Earth." He wasn't sure how else to introduce himself.

She smiled briefly. "I've heard. Kaleena speaks about you often."

Her dad clasped her hand, squeezed, and then let go. "Tell me what you're feeling."

"Nausea, exhaustion, and fear...then add in dejection and that about sums it up."

Finn was confused. "Are you saying you're feeling what

Kaleena is feeling because you are twins?" She nodded. "How is that possible? I'm a twin also, but I don't think either of us or our wolves have been physically affected if one or the other was ever injured."

"It's different with dragons, I guess," she said.

Jamison leaned closer. "Did you learn where she was?"

"No, but once I realized the connection was that strong, I contacted Delisa Contreau. She'll be here shortly." She looked over at Finn once more. "Delisa is a powerful white lighter who can help enhance the twin link."

Tarradon and Earth were more different than he thought possible. "I've never heard of that. How does it work?"

"She'll use me to reach Kaleena and possibly be able to see where she is. At the very least, she'll be able to detect sounds and smells that might help lead us to my sister."

Jamison grunted. "I should have thought of that."

"Dad, you went into attack mode the moment you learned that Kaleena was missing. It's how you always operate."

A few of the others seemed to be fighting a smile.

Someone knocked and peeked her head in. "A Delisa Contreau is here."

Tory pushed back her chair. "Send her in."

Finn was totally fascinated. While he'd heard of people who could channel the dead, he hadn't been aware someone specialized in living twins.

Tory held out her hand to the newcomer. "Thank you for coming so fast, Delisa."

The tiny woman had long curly white blonde hair and blue eyes, but it was her alabaster skin that gave her the look of purity. She appeared to be in her mid thirties, but he had no idea if humans on Tarradon aged as slowly as dragons did. He didn't sense she was a shifter, but being surrounded by so many of them could have thrown off his abilities to detect one.

"Hi, everyone." She gave them a weak smile. Delisa nodded to the two chairs near the window. "I know you are anxious for me to reach your sister. Shall we begin?"

"Yes."

"Sit in the chair, and I'll stand behind you. You know the routine. I'll place my hands on your temples and try to connect with Kaleena."

Tory did as she asked, and Delisa moved behind her. With her fingertips in place, she closed her eyes. "Focus only on Kaleena and the last time the two of you were together."

"Okay." Tory inhaled, clasped her hands on her lap, and closed her eyes.

After fifteen seconds of remaining motionless, Delisa began to hum and sway. "I hear shouts." She then winced as if she were feeling pain. "I'm seeing a lot of stone and metal, along with a small cot." Delisa wrinkled her nose. "It's someplace unclean. Wait a minute...she's calling out someone's name...a Frin...or maybe she's saying friend. I can't tell."

"Finn?" he said, his heartbeat elevating.

"That could be it. Finn. Something about a warning not to come."

That made no sense. She'd begged him to help her. He was just about to say something when Declan squeezed his shoulder and shook his head.

"I'm hearing footsteps. Several sets of them," Delisa said. "Kaleena is very anxious. Wait...someone is saying that the prince will not be happy with her." Delisa's body shook, her shoulders slumped, and then her body sagged. She then lowered her arms and opened her eyes. "The link's gone. I'm sorry. I'm not sure if I helped." Her gaze traveled around the table.

The tension rippling across Jamison's face was palpable. "You helped a lot, Delisa. I think I know where she is."

"I hope so. Will there be anything else?"

"No. Go home and rest. It looks like you could use some. And thank you."

With rather stooped shoulders, Delisa slipped out the door, but Tory remained in the chair. Gripping the arms, she pushed herself up. "That was not fun."

"I imagine not, but it was necessary," Jamison said. "While we can't be certain, given the noise and activity level, I'd say Kaleena's not being held in one of the castle rooms, but rather in an area where many are being held. The mention of the prince implies any one of those good-for-nothing nephews of mine are up to something evil."

"Who?" Declan asked.

"Omar is too greedy to bother with Kaleena, but Tarik might need more power for his dragon soldiers. Then there's Rathan. He's just mean enough to do something like this. Shit. It could be any one of them."

"Bottom line, Dad, is that we believe she's in the castle," Declan said. "I think I have a plan. Want to hear it?"

After two hours of back and forth debate as to the best way to help Kaleena, they came to a consensus—more or less.

Only Finn disagreed with the decision. "I still think I should be the one to go in. They won't suspect a wolf shifter. You even said my scent is different from those shifters on Tarradon. Besides, I know I'll be able to sense where she is, assuming I can get close."

Jamison's cheek twitched. He looked around the room as if he was waiting for confirmation before swinging his gaze back to Finn. "Are you saying you and Kaleena are mates?"

Finn sat up straighter. "Yes, sir. I'm sure of it. At least my wolf is."

His features relaxed. "I'm happy for you two, but if you're caught, you'll be no match against a dragon."

"I'm aware of that, but I came here to find Kaleena, and I aim to do just that."

All eyes were on Jamison. "I appreciate that more than you can know. We'll first survey the area to see how many guards King Edwardo has this week before we make our final decision. Last time I checked, he was running a little thin. If some opportunity opens up, we can always change our minds and let you go in and find her."

The group stood, acting as if Jamison's word was final. Finn would do whatever they asked, but it didn't mean he had to like it—unless he was allowed to find her.

Because the castle was situated several miles outside of town, most in the group said they would fly there and then wait for Finn and Jamison on the edge of the property. Probably because Finn had been a bit squeamish on his first dragon ride that Jamison suggested the two of them drive. Most likely he was just being nice. He told Finn he'd take the car because it never hurt to have a vehicle nearby in case someone became severely injured.

The ride through the bustling city into the countryside was pretty, but it was hard to focus knowing his mate was in so much pain. Twenty minutes later, Jamison parked along the roadside near where the others were huddled together. Once Jamison went over his ideas once more, they split up. Declan and Griffin went with Finn, while the others planned to circle above at a distance, ready to help if need be. They would keep hidden by the dense forest until they were alongside of the massive castle, and then move in after cloaking themselves. Jamison explained that their ability to become invisible required a lot of energy and often failed at the most inopportune moment, which was why they would wait until the last possible minute to cloak. Stress, he said, was often the culprit that broke the ability to keep the shield.

Finn watched while the men shifted and then lifted gracefully into the air. A few seconds later, they were nowhere to be seen.

"Come on," Declan said, nudging his arm. "Remember, it's up to us to scope out any escape routes. And don't forget this is a reconnaissance mission only."

"Got it." Finn was on unfamiliar territory and had to defer to them.

They made their way near the castle entrance, ducking behind bushes, while they waited until the guards disappeared around a corner. When the three of them had gone about as far as they could, Declan leaned close. "Griffin and I will shift and put up our shield of invisibility but rest assured we are nearby."

"Okay."

Finn was about to head in on foot and pretend to be a sightseeing when Declan grabbed Finn's arm. He motioned to a guard, smoking a cigarette, whose back was to them. "I just thought of something," he whispered. "Finn, can you incapacitate him? The guard won't be expecting a wolf shifter. Given your scent is different, it gives you a better chance at avoiding notice."

"Piece of cake," Finn responded. When Declan's mouth twisted in confusion, Finn realized he must not know that idiom. "Sure, no problem."

"Good luck." With that both he and Griffin shifted then disappeared.

This was it. Show time! As quietly as any animal could move, Finn snuck up behind the guard and cut off his air until he dropped, nearly taking Finn down with him.

"Let us move him," came a voice out of thin air.

Not having any idea where they were, Finn stood still as the guard's body seemed to move on its own into the bushes. Finn followed.

In a flash, both men reappeared. They were out of sight from the entrance, and no other guards seem to be about, so Declan and Griffin must have deemed it safe.

"Help me undress him," Declan said.

"Why?" Finn asked.

"New plan. Put on his uniform. It's the perfect disguise. I want you to go in and look for Kaleena."

Adrenaline shot through every vein. "What about what your father said?"

"He said we could improvise. Listen, all we need is a location. With that knowledge, we can hopefully free her. No heroics, do you understand?"

This was what he'd wanted in the first place. A short while ago they'd said it was too dangerous for a wolf to be inside the dragon's lair, but that was before he had a legitimate uniform. "Yes."

He donned the rather over-sized clothes and hoped no one noticed they didn't fit. At six-two, Finn felt short among these giants. From the looks of satisfaction on Declan's and Griffin's faces, however, he might pass for a guard, though the khaki outfit didn't exactly scream castle guard to him. Back home, many mechanics wore clothes like this—only with more grease stains. If he'd had a baseball cap to shield his face, he'd have felt better.

"If anyone stops you," Declan said, "tell him this is your first day on the job and that you're filling in for someone. Act as if you're totally taken by the grandeur of the place."

"Not a problem." He wouldn't have to do much acting. Finn was already in total awe of it all. It was almost as if he was in the Scottish highlands.

"We'll give you fifteen minutes tops," Declan said. "If you're not out here by then, we're coming in. But if we do, it will get ugly."

He understood the warning. "I'll locate Kaleena and nothing more. Can you give me twenty minutes? This is a big place."

Declan flashed him a brief smile. "Go with speed."

Kaleena's heart rate spiked, and something akin to lust shot throughout her. The strange sensation was so out of place in this hellhole that she sat up and tried to figure out what was happening to her. Was this another cruel joke by that bitch dark lighter, Sanditra? Did she think if she turned Kaleena on that she'd cooperate?

Your tormentor isn't that creative, her dragon said.

You better be right.

When no one appeared in the corridor, Kaleena chalked it up to her over-active imagination. Enclosed spaces filled with knife blades had a tendency to make her thoughts go wild. Add in her growing weakness from not eating enough, and she was probably hallucinating.

Just as Kaleena was about to continue her much-needed rest, her whole body shot to high alert again. What the hell was happening to her?

She used the rest of her energy to stand, needing to cling to the iron bars for support. Listening intently, she heard slow moving footsteps off in the distance. They were too light to belong to the mute or to the scar-faced guard. While she assumed the castle had several shifts assigned to watch the prisoners, she had yet to meet any other than those two.

From the left, heavy footsteps sounded and she tensed. When the mute's face came into view, she moved back. While he'd not done much to harm or assault her, she didn't want to piss him off, so she sat down on her cot and looked off to the side. Thankfully, he passed by without a second glance.

No sooner had she let out a long-held breath than the hair prickled on her arms and her pulse sped up again—

almost as if the poison had miraculously disappeared. As much as she wanted it to be one of the Guardians come to save her, she didn't sense any new dragon signature close by.

A shadow formed on the far hallway wall opposite a corridor. A second later, a guard she'd never seen before appeared. Crap. She'd been hoping for a miracle.

Dejected, Kaleena leaned back on her elbows. The man stopped and looked her way, but instead of fear or disgust blasting her, a warm wave of desire and comfort washed over her, almost like a lustful protective hug. Confused, she stared back at him. When he lifted his head, the dim over-head lamps illuminated part of his face, and she sucked in a breath. It was Finn!

Sure, she'd never met him face-to-face, but she'd know him anywhere. While he was not much above six feet, Finn was muscular without being bulky, and his gaze was bouncing around in a tentative manner.

Mate, mate, her dragon said with wonder and awe in her voice.

Before he reached her, the guard with the scarred face entered from the left. He looked at Finn then stalked toward him. Kaleena held her breath and prayed.

"Who are you?" Scarface demanded.

Oh, shit, oh, shit.

She stood and gripped the bar hard, awaiting Finn's reaction. Kaleena debated causing a distraction, but for some reason, she believed Scarface would ignore her.

"One of the guards took sick, so they pulled me off the landscaping crew and told me to report to duty," Finn said.

Just hearing his deep, rich voice in person made her body tingle.

"That so? Did they tell you what your duties were?"

Please Finn don't mess this up. If only both of them had been asleep, she could have coaxed him.

"Just to make sure no one escapes. Seemed simple enough to me."

Scarface huffed. "Then get to work."

Finn saluted and moved toward the cells. She had to admit he thought rather well on his feet. He glanced at her and nodded but said nothing. He then moved out of sight. *Come back, Finn!*

Finn said something to the occupant in the cell next to hers before stepping in front of her.

"Kaleena, is that really you?" he whispered. His eyes went wide with surprise.

"Yes, it's me." Her dragon became wild with excitement, and joy raced through her at a speed faster than that dark lighter could throw a stone. Kaleena reached out to touch him just as Scarface returned.

"No patronizing with the prisoners, garden boy. Get moving."

"I was just telling her to keep away from the bars. Insolent prisoner." Such convincing vitriol. Oh, my. Kaleena had to fight a smile.

The regular guard nodded, and then headed back the way he came.

Finn returned his gaze to her and pumped his fists. "Don't worry, I'll be back," he whispered before turning around and rushing back the way he came.

As much as she wanted to yell after him and tell him that finding his way there meant the world to her, she didn't since it would arouse too much suspicion. It was possible Finn was working alone, but she doubted it. The Guardians had to be behind this. It screamed of a Declan plan.

She sat on the cot with her hair covering her face to hide her excited smile. Finn was here! His presence gave her a strong sense of comfort, as if a positive light of hope had been lit inside her body and overpowered the poison for a bit.

She opened herself to her dragon and shared these feelings, hoping it would give her some peace as well. Then she leaned back on the cot and closed her eyes.

Together, Finn and her family would save her.

CHAPTER EIGHT

"I found her," Finn said once he reunited with Declan and Griffin, who thankfully had disengaged their invisibility shield. His heart was still galloping from the ordeal after finally meeting the literal woman of his dreams.

What's wrong with you? his wolf whined. *We were so close. Not even a kiss! Not even a touch!*

You don't think I wanted to? I didn't want to get caught!

Declan motioned they move out of sight of the entrance. Once on the side, he faced Finn. "Where is she?"

Only now did the conditions under which Kaleena was being held hit him. Finn had mostly been oblivious to the surroundings, because he had been too focused on looking at her. If any of his brothers had been in this situation, they wouldn't have become sidetracked. Finn's only excuse was that he wasn't trained for this kind of stealth mission.

She's our mate. You were overwhelmed by her, his wolf shot back. *No one can blame you.*

He did blame himself, but in his defense, it had taken

all of his energy just to keep his wolf in check. His animal had been so desperate to be with her that Finn's teeth had sharpened to a point, and his beard had thickened. He was actually surprised Kaleena recognized him.

Answer his question, his wolf growled.

"Kaleena's in a cell down one flight of stairs through a long ass maze." He detailed the circuitous path he had to take to reach her. "In all honesty, if I hadn't felt Kaleena's pull, I'm not sure I could have found her. It must take weeks for the guards to learn where every corridor leads."

"How the hell did you find her then?" Griffin asked with a hint of awe.

"Like I said, Kaleena is my mate." Finn lifted his head and dared either one to deny it. They didn't. "The moment I reached the bottom of the steps, it was as if she'd attached a string to..." He'd been about to say his cock, but he refrained. "...to my body and reeled me in."

Declan patted him on the back. "I'm glad that Kaleena will finally mate, but there can't be any celebration until we free her. Understand?"

"Absolutely." He hadn't realized until Declan's comment just how excited he must have sounded about having finally connected with her in person. "I don't think I can pull it off again though." He then explained how one of the guards had already questioned him about why he was there.

"We'll figure something out, and I'd like to do it with as little bloodshed as possible."

Jamison stepped out from a wooded area and moved toward them. Two dragons flew overhead, dipping their head before moving on. Finn suspected they might be Kaleena's family.

"Did you find her?" Jamison asked in a voice raspy from the strain.

"I did."

"I saw you disable the guard, but I don't know what happened after you entered the castle Tell me what you saw, and how hard is it going to be to free my daughter?"

Finn gave him as much detail as possible, including the location of a box he'd spied on the wall. "Someone must have been careless when closing the door, because I could see a row of keys inside. Possibly, they open the prison cell doors."

"Excellent. That actually gives me an idea." He turned to Declan and Griffin. "Meet me at the Four Sisters Pottery Shop."

Ten minutes later, he and Jamison drove through a small town that couldn't have contained more than five streets. He parked in front of a pottery store and cut the engine.

"Let's go inside and I'll explain everything."

It was about time, but once they entered, Finn was more confused than ever. Why were they in a pottery shop? Sure, the handmade pitchers, plates, bowls, and cups were exquisite, but how was this visit going to help free Kaleena?

A tall woman with light brown hair braided in back, wearing a tie-dyed T-shirt and white jeans streaked with clay came out from the back.

She beamed then hugged Jamison. "My, my, but this is a pleasant surprise."

Jamison introduced them. "This is Acacia, a wonder with clay."

"Jamison, you flatterer."

"I need your help."

She smiled sweetly, acting as if this were an everyday occurrence. "What can I do for you?"

Jamison introduced Finn to her, and then explained about Kaleena's capture.

"That's horrible! Do you know where she is?"

"In the castle cellar," Jamison said. "A few of us went there to scope it out, when Finn here knocked out a guard and was able to sneak in. He found Kaleena. We'd like to go in again, but we fear he'll be recognized. I was hoping you could do one of your *face swaps* for us, so he can return without arousing suspicion."

Face swap? Finn must have heard him wrong. "Excuse me?"

Jamison's grim expression brightened for a moment. "It's an illusion, that's all. Anyone looking at you will see the other man's face. It's magic if you will."

"I can help," Acacia said, "but the spell will only last a few hours. Are you sure this man is still unconscious?" She waved a hand. "I only ask because we don't need two men who look alike to be in the same place at the same time." She giggled. "I bet that would give somebody a scare."

It would creep him out that was for sure.

Jamison looked over at Finn. "Do you think he's still unconscious?"

Finn shrugged. "I've never strangled a dragon shifter before. I don't know how long he'll stay out, but he did drop like a stone."

"Then I'll go now and make certain he doesn't move," Acacia said. "I'll return shortly. Where exactly is he?"

Finn explained the best he could where the man was located. She assured him everything would be okay and then disappeared right before his eyes. Holy hell! He glanced over at the door, but it didn't swing open like it would have if the person had merely become invisible. What was going on?

"Can all white lighters here to do that?" Finn asked.

Jamison chuckled. "Hardly. These sisters are...unique."

Five minutes later Acacia reappeared, right where she'd been standing before.

"The guard will not give anyone any trouble for the next few hours," she stated sweetly.

"Thank you, Acacia," Jamison said.

Before she could perform this very strange face swap thing, the rest of the crew arrived, and Jamison outlined his plan.

"Dad, don't you think one of us should have the face swap?" Thane said. "I mean Finn will be impersonating a dragon, but he won't have a dragon shifter signature. Someone is sure to notice."

"From the way Finn described the passages, I'm not sure any of us can find Kaleena."

During their discussion, another woman, taller with darker hair, had come out of the back and had been arranging some pots on the shelves. She stopped doing her chores and came over. "I overheard your concern. I might be able to help."

"How?" Thane asked, acting as if he were suddenly in charge.

"I can give Finn a shifter signature, but like my sister's facial magic, it will only last a few hours."

Who were these women? It was almost creepy that he was about to be transformed—albeit temporarily—into another man, but to be given a shifter signature different from his own? He doubted even Ophelia had that kind of power.

Thane smiled. "That would be fantastic!"

Both of the women surrounded Finn. "Shall we begin?"

Finn admitted he was nervous—if not downright scared shitless—about being solely responsible for rescuing Kaleena. Sure, when he looked into the mirror and saw someone else's face, he had kind of freaked. The texture was different than his usual skin, and he could almost feel his wolf fighting to exercise its dominance over this fake dragon shifter inside him. He hoped he'd still be drawn to Kaleena, and that the dragon spell didn't block his mate's allure. If it did, he might never find his way out of the dark maze.

"Ready?" Jamison asked.

"As I'll ever be."

He clipped a cell phone onto Finn's hip. "As soon as you go in, turn on the camera. One of Kaleena's cousin is back at the office, and she'll be monitoring and recording every-thing. In case something goes wrong, she can contact us."

Let's hope she isn't needed, though having some kind of backup made him feel better. "Thanks."

"Ready for your ride?"

"It's not dark yet," he said.

Jamison smiled. "Don't worry. No one will see us. When

I cloak, whatever I'm touching becomes invisible too. Now let's go. The others have their assignments."

Finn could hardly say no. "Okay."

They stepped outside to find the sun had almost set. A second later, Jamison burst into his dragon splendor, and Finn couldn't help but admire his shiny black scales, dotted with iridescent silver ones. This time when the large claws came at him, Finn was ready—or so he thought. Despite knowing what to expect, the speed with which they rose still took his breath away. Finn might have enjoyed the scenery more had Kaleena not been on his mind—or so he told himself.

Finn was terrified. If he messed this up, the woman he loved might be lost to him forever.

You can do this, his wolf said. *I won't let you fail.*

You better not.

Once Finn entered the castle and headed down the stairs, he focused on Kaleena's sensual draw to guide him. It didn't take long before his wolf found her again.

Is she in the same place as before? he asked his wolf.

Mate, mate, his animal panted.

Focus. That's not what I asked. We need to find her and save her. Is she in her same cell? Finn asked again, wanting to strangle his wolf. He wouldn't of course because he needed him too much.

Yes, he growled out. *She's still caged. I can feel her pain and frustration.*

Stop it.

Thinking about Kaleena's dire situation tormented him enough. If he expected to save her, he needed to be able to think clearly. The moldy corridor was making him cough and that wasn't helping him remain unnoticed. After five minutes of turning right then left so many times he was confident he was lost, he spotted the box that contained the keys.

Heart pounding, he glanced around, but saw no one. He eased open the metal door, and the resulting squeak was enough to wake the dead. *Shh*, he called out. At least someone hadn't locked it in the last hour.

Hanging on hooks were six keys—marked only with a number. Fuck. Which one opened Kaleena's cell? He didn't remember seeing any numbers on the cells. Dare he take all of them? Even if he did, wouldn't it draw too much attention when he had to try one, then the next, and then the next? And if he did walk out of the castle with them all, how could the prisoners ever be released? On the other hand, these keys might come in handy if the Guardians wanted to free some of the others.

Rather proud of himself for thinking ahead, Finn grabbed them all and stuffed them into several pockets to make the theft less obvious.

That's the right move, his wolf snapped.

Thank you. Not that he had to answer to his animal, but it was his ability to sense Kaleena that would make this a successful trip.

He closed the key door, and the clasp snapped shut. Good. It might take a while for a guard to notice anything was amiss.

Knowing that Kaleena's family was waiting, he

continued on his way. Needing to remain calm, he inhaled and let the scent of his mate draw him to her. Thankfully, his wolf did not disappoint. When he rounded the last corner and saw her in the cell, he almost shouted.

Be cool, his wolf said. *This is the hardest part.*

Like I don't know that? Sheesh—I've got this. You need to keep from messing things up now.

She's so beautiful. His wolf sighed. *I want her now. Hurry.*

This was what Finn feared—his animal going crazy after all these weeks of wanting her. *Keep my claws and sharpened teeth in check. We don't want to give anything away.*

His wolf just grunted.

Fearing it might cause one of the guards to check on her, Kaleena forced herself not to pace in her small cell. Having seen Finn in person was a bigger high than she'd thought possible. The problem now was that her damned dragon had become even more anxious for release.

Her animal whined once more.

Stop complaining. You can't shift even if I let you, Kaleena told her.

If Finn comes around, I might be stronger than any curse.

If only that were true. *Just hold on for a little longer.*

I can if Sanditra doesn't show up today and try to force me to perform unspeakable acts, Kaleena told her dragon

That was one of Kaleena's biggest fears. What if the witch took her someplace when her brothers or Finn showed up? Then what?

Now that her location had been discovered, she hoped

Rathan didn't learn of the breach and move her. Needing to wash up before she was rescued, Kaleena stood and moved over to the sink. Having Finn see her in this filthy place upset her, but from the way his eyes had changed colors when he was close, he hadn't really noticed the dirt or her stench.

Footsteps echoed from down the long hallway—the same one Finn had come from—and her pulse soared. When she glanced up, the air left her lungs. It wasn't Finn, but another guard she hadn't seen before. *Please walk on by*.

That not only didn't happen, he made a beeline toward her. Oh, no. Had Rathan found out about what had happened? She edged toward the back of the cell, and then stopped. Her body tingled, and waves of euphoria washed over her. Okay, she must be hallucinating, or else that dark lighter had put yet another spell on her. She shouldn't be reacting to this creep.

When he reached her cell and made eye contact, she could have sworn his eyes turned amber—not the usual dragon turquoise. From his pocket he pulled out six keys. The guard stuck one in the lock and twisted it, but it didn't open the door. He mumbled something under his breath. Was the guard going to transport her someplace else?

It's Finn, her dragon said.

It can't be. He didn't look anything like Finn, so why was she reacting to him in a lustful way?

The man tried another key. It too didn't work. She was about to make some snarky comment when the third key opened the door. Without a word, he motioned for her to exit.

Mate, mate, her dragon chanted, sounding way too cheerful.

It's not Finn, she tossed back.

Yes it is!

"Where are we going?" she asked in the most confident tone she could muster.

"The prince wants to see you," he said loud enough for the whole castle to hear.

Kaleena stilled. That voice. Even though it came out quite deep, it sounded like Finn. "Is that you?" she whispered. If the man were a real guard, he'd think she was just crazy.

Finn nodded and then checked the hall running parallel to the cells. "Yes. Come on. It's time to get you out of here. My disguise won't last forever."

Disguise? It didn't matter. This was Finn. Her mate! Kaleena wanted to hug and kiss him so badly, but then they'd never leave. "Wait. You'll have to blindfold me. I'm never allowed out of here without one."

"Fuck." While he sounded like Finn, he didn't look anything like him. That sure was some disguise. Finn glanced around then nodded to her jacket on the bed. "How about using that?"

"Good thinking." Now full of energy, she rushed back to the bed and lifted her jacket. "My hands are linked together. Can you help?"

Finn rolled up the thin jacket, placed it over her eyes, and then tied the sleeves behind her head. When he was finished, Kaleena lifted the covering a little to leave a bit of viewing area out the bottom.

"Ready?" he asked.

"Yes, but if any guard comes along, you have to grab my arm or shove me hard. You must act like you're superior, and I'm just a lowly prisoner."

"I can't do that."

Kaleena almost smiled at the horror in his voice. "To make it look legitimate, you'll have to."

"Let's hope it doesn't come to that. Now, do you know the way out?" he asked.

"No. Why can't we go out the same way you came in?"

"If another guard shows up, I wouldn't be able to convince him I'm not trying to help you escape. The corridors I came through only lead to the front of the castle."

"Well, fuck."

CHAPTER NINE

Finn had to stave off his urges to touch Kaleena, urges that were stronger than anything he'd ever experienced. This was his mate, the woman he loved, but he needed to wait a bit longer.

Touch her now, his wolf begged.

What if we're caught, you horn dog?

Grr.

You don't think I don't want to wrap my arm around Kaleena's waist to make sure she doesn't trip? I do, but if anyone saw my act of kindness, they'd question me for sure. Besides, I don't trust you not to go further.

Kaleena moaned and slowed as if she were suffering. "Are you okay?" he whispered.

She nodded, and she pressed on her stomach. Her shoulders slumped. Kaleena was a brave woman. "We need to keep going," she groaned out.

"Keep moving, prisoner," Finn said with authority.

While he didn't see any other guards, his voice probably carried.

After what seemed like hours instead of probably minutes, they reached a set of stairs going up. "Be careful. There are four steps," he whispered.

Kaleena swayed and stumbled, but Finn caught her. She'd told him the cuffs contained poison, and it must have injected her with another dose.

"I'm okay. Now please, keep slightly behind me. Shove me if you have to. That's how the guards always do it."

If anyone overheard that conversation, they'd both be tossed in a cell. If only he could communicate with her telepathically, like when they were asleep, it would make traveling a lot easier. He didn't like having to act like an ass, but their freedom depended on it. "Got it."

You will be able to communicate whenever you want after you mate, his wolf reminded him with too much glee. *I bet she'll talk dirty to you all the time.*

Shut up. I can't think about that now. You don't think I'm this close to finding an alcove and making love to her? We just don't have time for that, Finn shot back, angry that his animal was so shortsighted.

Come on. Her scent is driving me crazy, his animal stated. *No one is near. At least rub your hands down the soft curve of her back for me. You want to. I can tell.*

No! We have to wait until we are clear of the castle.

This time his wolf didn't respond.

Frustration bit into him once more when another guard drew near. When they reached the top of the stairs, Finn had no choice but to grab a hold of Kaleena's arm and jerk her forward, which was a big mistake on a personal level.

That one touch caused a strong electric surge of lust to rip through his body at the intimate contact. He quickly let go.

Without intending to, he raked his gaze down her back and along the curve of her waist down to her strong, shapely legs. A sharp bolt of desire straight through him, enough to light him up.

Shift, his wolf urged.

Finn sobered. *We'd be caught for sure.* He didn't blame his wolf for wanting to touch her all over, but now wasn't the time. Why couldn't his animal understand that?

Even if his distracting mate hadn't been with him, he wasn't sure he'd be able to tell if he'd walked in circles or not. This maze of hallways was intricate. Finn had a camera attached to his hip, but if he stopped and replayed their path, there was no guarantee he'd learn where he'd made the wrong turn. At school, he'd been told that if he kept his right hand on the right side of a maze and continued around—like forever—eventually he'd reach the end. Time, however, didn't allow for that luxury.

"Hold up for a sec," Finn said. "We need to mark where we've been so we don't make the same mistake twice." Or three or four times.

Finn closed his eyes and focused on extending his claws. Only when he was going into a full shift did they remain in his wolf form, but if he concentrated hard enough he could control how long his claws remained. The bones in his hands morphed, and when he looked, his paws appeared. Without wasting time, he scraped a claw down the rock that thankfully left a mark.

"This will be enough to let me know we've been down

this path before. I'll do one scratch for right and two for left." Had there been loose stones around, he'd have used them.

She flashed him a smile, and he instantly remembered that look from the many times in his dreams when they'd been swimming under the waterfall and making love behind it.

"Good thinking."

"Do you know how long it should take us to reach the outside?" He kept looking for an exit sign at the end of a corridor but none existed.

"When the dark lighter led me outside, it only took about fifteen minutes to get there from my cell."

Shit. He hoped like hell they weren't lost. "Let's keep going then."

They were halfway down the next corridor when she planted a hand on his arm to stop him. "I hear voices," she whispered.

Her touch flared his desire. *Not now*, he told his wolf. It didn't matter the flood of hormones helped cancel some of the anxiety rushing through him.

Sorry, his animal said, though he seemed more over-joyed at her touch than contrite.

Finn inhaled to push aside the lust and was able to make out some female as well as male tones. "I'm not sure we should head that way. I don't want someone to ask where we're going and then escort us to the prince."

"That would be deadly," she said.

After another ten minutes, Finn stopped at an intersec-tion. "Crap. Here's my claw scrape. We've been here before. The two slashes imply we went left before, so we need to go right this time."

"Don't worry. We'll get out of here."

He loved her optimism. If he'd spent days in a cell, he wasn't sure he'd be so calm. Kaleena led again, but this time it was as if she was drawing on some internal sensors to guide her.

She took another step and her knees buckled, landing on all fours before he could catch her. Panic tripped through him. Not sensing anyone near, he lifted her up, trying not to think what her touch was doing to him. "Are you all right?" he whispered.

"Kind of, it's just these stupid cuffs. They sent another dose of poison into me. The waves seem to be coming at shorter and shorter intervals."

"Your dragon can't heal you?" His wolf would be fighting hard.

"Yes, but even she is growing weary. Plus, I haven't eaten much."

Shit. "We'll rest then."

"No. We can't afford to."

"We'll go slow then." Her determination made him love her more. He led her down the corridor. After a hundred more feet, he stopped. "Do you smell that?" he asked.

"What?"

"The air is fresher."

She inhaled. "Yes. I think we're close. Okay, when we get to the door, you must grab my arm and pretend that you're forcing me outside."

He didn't like it, but he understood that he had to make it look good. No telling what was on the other side.

Totally focused on his sense of smell, he found a large wooden door, bordered by wrought iron and dotted with steel. It looked very much like what he'd expected to see in the Dark Ages. Holding his breath, he pushed it open and was met by a warm breeze. *Hello, outside world!*

He clasped her arm, and soon as he made contact, his wolf howled and the bristles on his face began to sprout. Finn silently grunted.

After several steps, Kaleena whipped off her blindfold and grinned. As much as he wanted to hug and kiss her at their success, they weren't safe by any means.

Do it, his wolf begged. *I'm not sure I can hold out much longer.*

Damn it, you have to.

His wolf growled back at him.

The sun had set but a faint pink glow resided in the upper clouds. His shifter sight allowed him to see well enough to make their way to the forest's edge. It also allowed others to see them cross the expansive field.

"I know you can shift, but can you do that wearing those cuffs?" Finn had no idea if the force of the shift would be strong enough to break them. He'd never tried to change into his wolf form while being handcuffed. Come to think of it, he'd never been handcuffed, even by a woman.

Her eyes widened for a moment as if she hadn't been sure he knew what kind of shifter she was. Kaleena held up her wrists. "Even if my animal could break through these, a dark witch put a spell on me. I have no magic and can't access any of my powers."

He held in his disappointment. "There goes plan A." He could shift and race to find the others—wherever that was—but he'd never leave her. "We have to make it to the forest then."

"We can't run or we'll attract attention."

"Then we'll walk. If someone stops us, I'll say we're out here because the prince ordered you to be punished, but he didn't want anyone to witness it."

A sparkle came into her eyes. "It's really hard to flirt with you when you look like someone else, so I'll give you some suggestions later on how to proceed with that kind of punishment."

He groaned at the image. Jeez, he was falling more in love with her each minute. Kaleena was amazing. Her life was at stake, and her powers were gone, yet she could joke at a time like this. "I can't wait."

Loud roars and whooshes of air, along with sounds of explosions of fire, jerked his attention to the sky. Finn grabbed Kaleena's arm to keep her safe. He had to blink a few times to make sure what he was seeing. Against the darkened clouds, dragons were fighting other dragons, but their images kept disappearing then reappearing.

Kaleena followed his gaze. "That one with the hint of red is Declan and the one with the golden sheen is Thane —two of my brothers."

"I thought they could stay invisible?" In those few seconds, everyone became visible.

"When a dragon goes into battle, it takes too much energy to hold the shield. To be honest, once you're spotted, there's really no use." Instead of fleeing, Kaleena continued to watch as the solid black dragon flew underneath Thane and gave him what looked like a kick in the chest with its large clawed foot.

She winced and turned her head. "We need to go while there's a distraction. We certainly don't need others rushing outside to watch. The Royals love nothing more than a good fight—especially since their guards often win."

Even though he'd only known her brothers for a short time, the ache would crush him.

Just as they took off, another high-pitched shriek came from their left. When Finn turned, he saw nothing, but a second later he was airborne with Kaleena in his arms. He might have screamed from the sudden upward movement had he not felt the security of the dragon's front claw around his back and Kaleena pressed against him.

He held onto her with all his strength. "I hope like hell this is a Guardian and not one of the Royal Guards." With the fast rushing air, Finn had to shout. From the way Kaleena hadn't tensed, he figured it was the former.

As if to show off its body, the high flying dragon appeared for a few seconds then disappeared.

Kaleena smiled. "It's my cousin Nessa."

He'd met her. "Are you sure?"

"Her beautiful purple scales interwoven among the black ones are distinctive to her alone."

"Thank you, Nessa," he called out, even though he felt a little silly doing so.

The dragon dipped her head as she flew over the dark forest below.

"Where do you think we're going?" Finn asked, finally willing to admit that they might now be free.

She leaned closer, and his wolf howled. "Some place safe."

Kaleena wanted to pinch herself. Being carried in the air wasn't her preferred mode of travel, but holding onto Finn was a dream come true. She leaned even closer, wanting to say so much to him but not sure where to begin. "I can't believe you came."

"How could I not have come? Your life was in danger," Finn said.

As if they'd timed their escape perfectly, Finn's face suddenly transformed from the pitted face of the guard to his handsome self. Wow.

He ran his hands down his face and then grinned. "I'm back. That was cutting it close."

"I'll say." Oh how she wanted to run her fingers down his strong jaw that was dotted with stubble. His once-almond colored eyes were pulsing amber—her favorite color.

With their faces only inches apart, he leaned forward and gently pressed his lips to hers. Her dragon roared. Maybe a kiss from her prince could bring back her inner beast.

"How did you find your way here?" Goddess, she had so many questions. She'd have to spend weeks, if not a life-time, having him answer them all.

"This powerful white witch, Ophelia, helped me. She seemed to know all about portals and even claimed to have a direct line of communication with your dad. I guess she did."

"Ophelia? Well I'll be damned."

"So you know her. How?" Finn looked down for a

moment and then returned his gaze to her face as if it was safer that way.

As she was about to elaborate, Nessa swooped over the SinCas mines and Kaleena reached out and grabbed Finn's hand just as her cousin landed. "Lift your legs," Kaleena called a second before they reached the ground.

Once Nessa released them, her cousin shifted and rushed into Kaleena's arms. "I can't believe you're safe," her cousin said. She turned to Finn, stepped over to him, and kissed him on the cheek. "Thank you for saving her."

"You know as well as anyone that it was a massive team effort." Finn wrapped an arm around Kaleena's waist and squeezed. Heat rippled up her body at his touch. As much as she wanted to drag him into the bed and ravish him, she wanted to have both of her hands free to touch him fully.

Without warning, her knees weakened, but Finn caught her. "Are you okay?" he asked.

No. "I just need something to eat. I also need to get these cuffs off me. I'm not sure how much more my dragon can handle."

"How can we remove them?" Finn asked.

"I don't know. They contain a dark lighter's curse."

"Well, that sucks," Nessa said. "I can't help you then, but I'm pretty sure one of the Four Sisters can."

A burst of energy shot through her. Their magical abilities were like nothing she'd ever seen. "I hope so too."

Nessa pulled out her phone, looked up a number, and then pressed a button. She turned her back when someone answered. She explained Kaleena's situation. "Are all four of you away then? Oh, I see. Later tonight maybe? That would be great. Thank you so much." She disconnected and faced them. "The sisters are in Hearndon province and won't be back until later. I hope you can hold out a little longer."

Finn stepped forward. "That's bullshit. I saw Acacia teleport. She could be here in seconds."

Kaleena touched his arm. "While I appreciate you valor, Finn, there are limits to what the sisters are willing to do."

He studied her for a moment. "Are you saying they will grant your family only so many favors?"

"No one has put it that way, but that's what we think."

"Then there has to be another way to get them off," he said.

I think the poison has stopped, her dragon said.

Kaleena planted a hand on her stomach. "Actually, I'm feeling better, and my heart isn't racing as fast."

His eyes widened. "Do you think being away from the castle helped?"

"I have no idea if the curse has any kind of range. It could just be that the poison ran out. I did get quite a few doses during the escape." Thinking her powers might have returned, she stepped back and tried to shift but she failed. "Damn. My magic is still gone though."

"I'm sorry."

I can heal you now, her dragon said.

That would be wonderful.

"While my dragon is healing my body, I'd like to clean up, eat, and maybe rest until it's time to go visit the sisters," Kaleena said.

Nessa rubbed her shoulder. "Sounds good."

Kaleena faced Finn. "What about you? Do you need to clean up?"

"Even if I didn't, I don't think even those palace guards could separate us," he said just before he kissed her.

Her whole body melted against him. Her skin shimmered with excitement and her dragon roared. She was definitely feeling better. "Let's hope you never meet one again," Kaleena said once she broke the kiss. "They aren't a friendly bunch."

Nessa cleared her throat. "Ah, gang. Before the Royal scouts do find you, we need to get you inside."

"You're right," Kaleena said with a chuckle. "Being this close to Finn messes with my mind."

Once shielded from the outside world, Finn leaned over. "Is there really a shower in here? It's a mine!"

This whole complex must appear rather strange to him. "Believe or not there is. To the outside world, it looks like an ordinary mine—albeit the largest one in the realm. While it is highly productive, deep inside is a huge complex that has several bedroom suites as well as meeting rooms and offices. The inner workings of SinCas mostly takes place in the office buildings downtown, but in the bowels of the mine, the Guardians keep everything they prize safe—and that means us."

As they went in through the first entrance, a bank of lights automatically came on. "They could use some of these sensors at the castle," Finn said.

Kaleena chuckled. "I agree, but the Royals don't like progress very much."

"So I've seen. Why is that?"

"For a lot of reasons. For one, the smarter the locals

become, the less likely they are to put up with their shenanigans. I wouldn't be surprised if there isn't a revolt in a few years. Most of us want a democracy. Clearly, the Royals don't. The Royals were wealthy and respected back in the day, but now they struggle to keep control."

"That makes sense."

Nessa led them to the entry door. She pulled out her dragon scale key, swiped it over the rock, and waited for a portion of it to glow. When a spot lit up, she placed her scale on top and the door clicked open.

"That is really cool," Finn said. "How does it work exactly?"

Kaleena smiled, loving the wonder pouring from his eyes. "It's magic."

Nessa spun to face them as they stood in the doorway. "Why don't you two do your thing, and I'll pick up some food. I don't believe the cook is here now. Any preferences?" she asked.

Kaleena glanced over at Finn. "How about a nice juicy steak for both of us? And some wine too."

"You are doing better." Nessa smiled. "Coming right up."

"Before you leave, do you know what happened to Declan and Thane?" Kaleena asked.

"No. When I saw you'd finally escaped, I came right over to escort you out. As I neared the castle, I caught a glimpse of your brothers battling. The Royal guards must have figured something was up when one minute you two were in the middle of the field and the next you'd disappeared. They took off toward the woods, but couldn't find us. I saw Declan and Thane charging them again. That's all I know."

"Thanks. I'm sure they'll be fine." Or so she hoped.

Nessa returned the way they came, probably heading to Antoine's for takeout.

"Ready to get wet with me?" Kaleena asked, as she stretched up and kissed him lightly on the lips.

"I've been ready for weeks."

CHAPTER TEN

Finn's head and body were spinning so fast from what had happened that it took all of his control to follow Kaleena down the white corridor lit by bright LED's. Cameras mounted from the ceiling lined the way.

"I hope the security is only in the common area," he said, a bit worried they were being watched.

She looked over at him and smiled. "There are cameras everywhere, but unless there is a widespread breach, they won't be on in the bedrooms. Trust me."

Did she say bedroom? his wolf asked, panting more than usual. *I can't wait to taste her.*

You better not show yourself you horny bugger, Finn said.

After passing several doors, Kaleena pressed down on the handle and opened the door. "This is where I stay when I come here. Tory and I share it since there aren't enough rooms for everyone to have their own."

It was a nice space with a king-sized bed against the far wall and a built-in wardrobe across from it. Next to the bed sat two matching side tables, and above the bed was a picture of three stallions racing across the plains. If he didn't know he was in a different realm, he'd swear he was out west somewhere. The third wall had a door that led to a bathroom, while curtains covered the fourth wall. "What's behind those?" he asked. It couldn't be covering a window. They were underground.

"Only a light bar that mimics the sunrise, so it will look like morning at the appropriate time. Being underground is depressing enough, and if we have to be down here, Dad wanted to give it an above ground feeling."

"That is really cool." For many reasons.

"Thanks. Dad and Uncle Laird—that's Nessa's dad— along with a few of their siblings designed and built this place."

"I'm impressed."

Kaleena stepped over to the closet door and then looked down at her outfit. "Well, damn."

"What is it?" Finn placed a hand on her shoulder.

She lifted her cuffed hands. "How can I take off my shirt and bra with these on?"

He had a solution, but he didn't know if she'd like it. "We'll have to cut off your clothes."

Kaleena almost cracked a smiled. "Since I have to shower, I see no way around it. It's probably for the best if I trash these since they'll remind me of my ordeal."

"I'm sorry," Finn said, sobering at the reality of what she'd been through. "Do you have anything else you can put on afterwards?"

"I have clothes, but how can I thread my arms through

the sleeves? I have a few halter tops back at my place, but not here."

While he should be sad at her ordeal, he couldn't help but grin. "You could go au natural."

She punched his chest lightly with double fists. "Not going to happen. A ton of people are down here all the time."

"Think of it as taking a vacation at a nudist colony." He dipped his head. "If it will make you feel any better, I can stay naked with you."

She laughed, draped her arms over his head, and rested her wrists on his shoulders. "You are good for me, Finn McKinnon. Now help me undress and then join me in the shower. I'm pretty useless without my hands."

"My pleasure." This was too good to be true. While their dream-walking had been exceptional, he'd always wondered if Kaleena had experienced the event exactly as he had—exciting, sensual, and loving. From the joy in her voice, he suspected she had. "Can I ask you something?"

"Anything."

"When we dream-walked, what was it like for you?" He drew her tight to his chest.

"The same as it was for you. We were together, remember?" She nipped his bottom lip with her teeth.

"Trust me, I remember every detail. Here's the thing, when we kissed, I could have sworn I could taste and feel your lips on mine. How was that possible?"

"It was magic!"

"All of Tarradon seems to be full of magic."

Kaleena chuckled. "It is."

"One thing has always confused me. Could you see me

clearly? Because you looked as if you were behind a gauze veil."

"I could see you quite well, but I remained indistinct because I feared that when I became excited—which happened often—you might have seen my rose colored scales glow under my skin, and then you'd have learned I was a dragon shifter."

"Why didn't you want me to know?" What else had she hid from him?

"Seriously? Your kind didn't know dragon shifters existed, and I couldn't chance you'd pull away."

Relief washed through him. "You didn't have to worry. I fell for you, not for who your shifter was, though to be honest I might have freaked out a little at first if I'd seen the scales."

"I'm sure you would have, but how about we put that in the past and start making new memories?" Kaleena winked, and his pulse skyrocketed. She unhooked her arms from around his neck.

"I'm with you all the way."

"Help me get out of these clothes."

He grinned, though his wolf howled. "Absolutely." He extended his claws. This was going to be fun, but if he looked into her eyes, he'd be lost. "Turn around."

Starting at the bottom of the hem, he sliced upward until the back opened. With care, he dragged her shirt down to her hands only to realize he'd have to cut open the sleeve in order to free it from her body. A minute later, her shirt lay in a mutilated heap on the floor.

Needing to drink her in, he rotated her back around and retracted his claws. As if on automatic pilot, his gaze dropped to her breasts—breasts he'd touched, sucked, and fondled in his dreams. "When we made love, did it feel as if our skin was really touching?"

Her brows furrowed. "It was touching."

Blood thrummed through his head. "How was that possible?"

"I teleported you to Tarradon by putting you into an altered state. It only felt like a dream at the waterfall, because I wanted you to believe it was. In truth, it was real."

Every muscle froze. "That's incredible," he whispered, his mind in chaos once more.

Her eyes widened, and then she grimaced. "No, I was only kidding about you being here, though I wish I could have transported you to Tarradon to be with me."

He opened his mouth, loving her wonderful imagination. "You had me fooled. It must have been wishful thinking on my part."

"I'm sorry. It was my most sincerest wish too." She tapped his chest. "Speaking of being Earthbound, did I ever mention that I went to the University of Colorado to study business?"

"What? You've been to Earth?" Or was that make believe too?

She nodded. "Many Tarradonians have gone there. It's how we learned about cars, electronics, and entrepreneurship. Several of my brothers went to the Colorado School of Mines."

So that was why their cellphones looked so familiar. They were probably copies of the ones made on Earth—or else they came directly from there. "No one has ever mentioned anything about dragons. I never had a clue they even existed—anywhere." Until his brother and his new mate, EmmaLee, told him about the one they'd seen.

Stop stalling, his wolf said. *I need her. Bad.*

"That's because we always cloaked ourselves when we shifted."

"I'll be damned." Once more, he wished he had that talent. Since Kaleena seemed to want to delay her shower, he'd play along. "Was it a difficult transition to live in the US?"

What are you doing talking about transitions? Drag her into the shower if you can. I'm about to shift, his wolf cried.

Finn swallowed and then repositioned his weight as his cock pressed harder against his zipper.

"Some things were more difficult than others, like learning your English idioms." Her eyes glowed a pretty violet right before she grabbed the waistband of his jeans. She tugged him closer, and his libido went crazy. "How about we table my Earth experience until after we shower?"

Here he thought she wanted to stall. "You won't get an argument from me. Let's get you out of that bra. As much as I hate to ruin it, you can't shower with it on."

"No, I can't. Be quick though. My dragon is heating up thinking about what I want to do to you."

After he unhooked the back, he once more extended his claws and cut through the straps. The bra found the floor.

Her dragon was heating up? Did that mean she was as anxious as he was to make love? Kaleena should be in his shoes. His wolf was howling up a storm, begging him to hurry.

"Are you sure you're up for this?" he asked turning her around, keeping his gaze on her face. "You could barely stand a few minutes ago." Finn didn't want to exhaust her. She and her dragon had been through so much already.

Don't be a fool. She can handle it. His wolf was close to being out of control.

"Like I said, the poison seems to have stopped, and my dragon is doing an excellent job of healing me. Or else being with you has thrown my body into overdrive."

He liked the sound of that. "Then I won't try to talk you out of anything."

Finn lowered his gaze and zeroed in on her perky tits again, and the urge to lick them nearly caused him to shift.

Kaleena held up a finger. "No touching yet. We need to shower first."

Finn inhaled and refocused. "Fine. If you kick off your shoes, I'll help you remove your jeans."

She wore easy-to-remove sandals and discarded them a second later. Kaleena even managed to unbutton and unzip her jeans before he helped her slip them off.

Confident that she might be ready for some real life loving, he dragged his hands up her bare legs. Whoa. Pink scales glowed under her skin. "Kaleena?"

"Yeah, that was what I was talking about. Maybe now you can see why I kept my image in the dream obscured."

He smiled. "I like them. They're pretty and rather exciting." So exciting that he almost threw her on the bed and impaled her. She might imply she desperately needed to clean up, but all he could smell was her heat—that unique essence that was overpowering him right now, calling for him to get his mouth on her. "I'm assuming you'll need help washing your hair and your back, right?" he asked, trying to focus on the mechanics of showering instead of on his increasing desires.

She grinned. "Yes, silly, but even if I didn't, I want you too much for us to take turns."

This was too good to be true. She was as desperate as he was. At that thought, several blue sparks shot off his arms, and he jumped back. "Whoa."

Even Kaleena looked surprised. "What was that?"

"Oh, crap. I recently learned that I am part Wendayan —a witch if you will—and when I'm turned on, I'm supposed to glow blue." At least that was he'd heard would occur. "Only this is the first time it has ever happened. Our dream-walking seems to have activated my Wendayan gene that my great grandmother passed down."

Kaleena ran her fingers over his arm, sending his body further into sexual turmoil.

"I've never seen anything like it before from a white lighter or any kind of shifter."

"Then I guess our witches on Earth aren't like yours."

"I guess not," she said, her lips quirking up into a smile. "I see I'll have to explore your Wendayan side later. It's time to shower. And if you plan on helping me, I suggest you get naked too, Sparky."

Finn kicked off his shoes and stripped off his pants. As soon as he removed his shirt, Kaleena turned around and sashayed into the bathroom, driving his wolf even crazier.

"You are a cheeky minx, aren't you? It's time to show you some more sparks!" Finn hoped his heart was strong enough for what was about to come.

Kaleena smiled as she stepped into the shower. Finn was everything she'd imagined him to be: kind, cute, funny, resourceful, and perfect for her.

To make room for the two of them, she moved the teak wood seat out of the way before turning on the water. A few seconds later, Finn's shadow graced the doorway, and she couldn't help but face him. Viewing his divine body up close and in person had her breath caught in her throat. When he smiled, the lust turned worse, and a wave of heat rushed through her veins so fast she almost staggered. Finn was magnificent, from his broad shoulders and flat stomach to his larger-than-life cock. This Finn McKinnon was even better than the one in her dreams.

"Come on in," she said.

Finn slipped in and locked his gaze on her face. "You are truly beautiful." Oh, how she loved the awe in his voice.

He dragged a knuckle down her cheek, and then when he swiped it across one nipple, swells of lust caught her off guard once more. Kaleena grabbed onto one of his arms to keep from dropping, and it wasn't from any poison this time.

She nodded to his cock. "You aren't half bad yourself, but before we get down to business, how about helping me wash my hair and then my body? I am at a disadvantage here." She lifted her hands to remind him.

He chuckled. "Don't mind if I do." Finn grabbed the shampoo off the shelf while she ducked her head under the water. Kaleena was unable to hold in a groan from the glorious heat and soothing flow.

"Feel good?" he asked.

"You have no idea what living in filth for a few days can do to a girl." As she stepped out from the divine spray, her legs weakened. Finn grabbed her and managed to stabilize her. "Easy now. I've got you."

"I'm okay." Kaleena had never needed any kind of help before.

"No, you aren't okay. I thought you said the poison was gone." He pulled over the one-foot square teak bench to the middle of the shower. "Sit down, and let me take care of you."

"It is. I swear. My dragon needs a little more time to complete the task. That's all."

He wagged a finger. "You better be telling the truth."

She laughed. "I am."

He put down the shampoo and picked up the bar of soap, lathered it in his hands, and then washed her face, her stomach, and then her legs. Those few rubs caused her pussy to rejoice.

That's because he's your mate, her very tired dragon reminded her.

She swallowed a smile. *How well I know.*

Before she made a fool of herself by melting right in front of him, she slipped the soap from his hands and washed between her legs.

A deep growl came out of Finn. "I was going to do that," he said painting on a fake frown.

She laughed, feeling a bit better now that she'd had a moment to rest. "I'm sure you were, but my dragon might have become a bit too feisty."

"I'm plenty feisty too, but I see your point." Finn

removed the handheld shower attachment from the wall and rinsed her, careful to avoid her eyes.

Following the scrub and long rinse, Kaleena almost felt normal.

"Hair cleaning time," Finn announced. He squirted some shampoo on her head then massaged her scalp into a soapy lather. Once more she groaned at the luxury of it all.

He chuckled "I take it you like my magic fingers?"

"I could stay in here forever." He continued dumping more shampoo until the suds streaked down her face. "Ah, that's good enough. It will take a long time to rinse my hair if you add any more."

"Sorry. I've never washed a woman's hair before."

How sweet. "You're doing great." To show him her appreciation, she dragged his face down to her level and kissed him lightly. Unfortunately, that one touch set off another chain reaction of desire. Finn must have been affected too, because not only did her scales flash pink, blue sparks shot off his arms more intense than any explosion she'd set at the mine.

Finn broke the kiss and wagged a finger at her. "Don't start, young lady. Your hair is still full of soap."

She laughed and let him finish rinsing her hair. When he was done, she raised her arms. "A little help here? I can't reach my underarms. Rub hard so it doesn't tickle."

"I'll scrub and scrub until your skin shines."

True to his word he cleaned her body again—every single inch of it—including between her legs. By the time he was finished, her body glowed and pulsed with more desire than she'd ever known before.

"Now I have to get clean," he said. "I think the castle mold rubbed off on me."

He didn't smell at all, but maybe he wanted her to touch him like he had her. "Hand me the soap," she commanded.

"But you're in handcuffs."

"Just you wait and see what I can do." She pushed back the teak chair out of the heavy flow of the shower, and Finn stepped under the shower. Being close to a climax already from all the touching, she lathered her hands and stroked his cock. "Have to make sure this is clean."

He laughed, but when he closed his eyes and clenched his fists, Kaleena pumped harder. Not that she wanted him to come, but to have his cock in her hand after all this time brought her so much satisfaction.

He finally grabbed her wrist. "Enough," Finn said, his voice rough. "I'm weak around you, and I want our first time to be special."

"Oh, it will be. I have no doubt.

CHAPTER ELEVEN

As Finn slipped Kaleena's fingers from his cock, she could almost believe she and Finn were in a dream, partly because this shower was reminiscent of their secret waterfall cove.

His eyelids lowered and he leaned closer. "Do you know why I stopped you?"

She could guess. "Tell me."

"I've been on edge since I realized I was going to finally meet you in the real world. I kept denying you existed because no real person could be that amazingly wonderful, but I was wrong. You are real, and I want you more than anything."

He hovered over her before he lightly ran his tongue across her lips, begging for entrance. Her body heated, and her dragon scales illuminated her skin. When they came up for air, she placed her hands on his chest the best she could. "You should be me. My dragon is bigger than your wolf, which means my needs are greater." Sure, she was teasing him, but it would be fun to see his response.

He stepped back, picked up the bar of soap from the shelf, and dragged it over the tip of her nipple. "Now that's where you're wrong."

She grinned. "Prove it."

"Give me one minute." He ducked into the shower and then ran the soap over his hard-packed muscles before scrubbing his face. "Acacia had said that this face-changing thing was an illusion, but I swear it changed my skin somehow." He rubbed harder and then rinsed. A second later, he tossed the soap back onto the ledge and turned off the water. Inhaling, his gaze raked up and down her body.

Oh, Finn. Her heart soared. Their first lovemaking should probably take place in a bed, but she couldn't wait long enough to walk there.

He nodded to her wrists. "I wish like hell you didn't have on those cuffs. I have so many plans for you."

"Tell me about it." Everything about the man excited her—always had, always would. Because her healing dragon had outdone herself, Kaleena placed her hands on one of his shoulders. "It's your turn to sit on the teak stool. I want to show you some plans of my own." She yearned to play out all of her fantasies with him, no matter how long that took.

After dragging the seat to the middle of the shower, he sat down. Finn grabbed her waist and drew her close until she was forced to straddle him, her throbbing mound pressed against his dick. While she had a strong need to take him hard, she wanted to taste him again.

"Oh, Kaleena, what you do to me."

Kaleena wrapped her arms around his neck and leaned in close, positioning her breasts inches from his mouth. His teeth elongated and hair sprouted on his face as he ran his hands from her hips to her tits.

"Finn?" she asked, not used to a man's face changing right in front of her.

He ran his tongue over his sharpened canines. "It's okay. My damn wolf is so excited right now, it's hard to keep him in check."

Finn grabbed one tit and massaged it while he sucked hard on the other nipple. Bolts of electricity shot up her spine, forcing her to grind against his cock for more friction. She wanted to run her hands through his wet hair, but that would mean leaning back too far. Damn these cuffs and damn Rathan! Kaleena decided that gripping Finn's hair on the back of his head would do just fine. When she did, it seemed to be a big turn on for Finn as well.

He growled and hummed as he switched to the other breast. He then dragged his hands to her back before running them down to her butt. When he squeezed her ass, another wave of ecstasy shot through her.

Finn looked up at her. "I want to take my time and explore every inch of you, but I have to have you now. Lift up a little."

His desperation made her even wetter. With her hands secured around his neck, she partially stood. He then guided his cock right into her needy opening.

Oh holy goddess.

Maybe it was because he was much bigger than she'd ever imagined, but the slight pain from him stretching her wide actually enhanced the high. Lifting up and then dropping down again in order to encompass all of him, the tip of his cock finally hit her back wall, and she moaned.

Blue sparks flew off his body until he glowed one solid color. "Geezus, Kaleena!"

Needing more of him, she dipped her head and devoured him, delving her tongue into his mouth. He tasted different from any man she'd known, so fresh and sweet, causing white-hot need to swamp her.

As if there was a competition for who could explore faster, they dipped their tongues in and out then darted them around, testing, teasing, and tempting one another.

She broke the kiss, wanting his mouth elsewhere. "Suck on my tits again." The combination of his mouth on her nipples and his cock inside her surpassed everything she'd ever imagined.

Kaleena leaned back to give him access while she slid her wet pussy back and forth, easing his cock in and out. With each glide, every nerve ending fired as her climax built. In her one hundred years, she'd never experienced such a high.

When he gently bit down on her nipple, the wave of ecstasy was so great that her climax rushed in and consumed her. Her inner walls squeezed and contracted around his cock until a second later, Finn buried his head against her chest and pummeled his hot seed into her.

Their climaxes came too quickly, but it couldn't be helped. Weeks of dreaming had made her too sensitive to his touch. With their breaths slowing, Kaleena clung to Finn, never wanting to let go.

They held onto each other until noises sounded in the hallway. Slightly embarrassed for having forgotten that

Nessa had probably returned a while ago, she sat up. "I think dinner is here."

Finn glanced up at her. "You go ahead. I'm not sure my legs will move."

He was teasing, but that made him all the more charming. When she lifted off of him, her legs became a bit wobbly. Needing to do some more cleanup, she turned on the shower to rinse again. "I have faith in you, cowboy. A hot meal will perk you right up. Don't forget you need to help me dress."

Finn stood. "I'll be happy to do that."

She wagged a finger at him. "No funny business though. The food is ready."

Once Finn helped her towel off, they headed back into the bedroom. She needed to figure out what she could do about not walking around naked. Shifters who weren't dragons didn't seem to have a problem with nudity, but Kaleena did.

"I have an idea," Finn said.

"What's that?"

"Find me a button-down shirt with long sleeves."

She could do that. From the wardrobe, she removed a pink cotton shirt and handed it to him. "Will this do?" she asked.

"Perfect. Now turn around."

With efficiency, he placed the front of the shirt across her chest and then tied the sleeves around her neck. He then secured the shirttails around her waist and spun her around. Finn smiled. "That works."

Kaleena looked down at her new outfit. "Are you sure you weren't an engineer?"

He grinned. "Bartenders always solve other people's problems. It's their own issues that they struggle with sometimes."

"You have issues?" she asked with a concerned look.

"All of my anxieties and concerns stem from one source —a certain sexy dragon shifting redhead." He winked, and her muscles relaxed.

"I never meant to be the source of dismay for you. I'll try to make it up to you." Kaleena flashed him a smile.

Finn stepped closer and tugged her against his chest. "You better." He kissed her hard, but stepped back a few seconds later when more voices sounded in the corridor.

He helped her put on her panties and a pair of pants before getting dressed. Once they finished, Finn wrapped an arm around her waist as they made their way to the kitchen.

As soon as they reached it, Kaleena stopped dead in her tracks. "Mom? Dad?" It didn't surprise her that Tory would be there, but she hadn't expected so many of her family to show up.

"You were able to shower," her mom said. She then glanced at Finn. "I'm glad."

Even though her mom's comment implied she approved of Kaleena's soon-to-be-mate, heat still raced up her face. She had no doubt they both had that *I just got laid* look.

As if the rest of the group had no idea what had gone on in the bedroom, the others rushed toward her and asked her questions all at once.

Kaleena held up her hands. The table was laden with food and Kaleena's stomach grumbled. "How about we all sit and I tell you what happened? If any of you haven't been introduced yet, this is Finn—my mate. He's from Earth. And he saved me."

He held up a hand. "Trust me I couldn't have done it without a lot of help from all of you and those pottery ladies."

Kaleena's mom seemed to be holding back a smile. "I heard what Acacia did. She definitely is talented." Her mom turned to Kaleena and nodded to her cuffs. "Speaking of which, one of the four sisters should be able to get those off."

"I hope so too. It can't happen soon enough."

Finn pulled out a chair and then helped her into it. "If some of you didn't know, these cuffs were poisoning me, but I haven't felt anything since we left the castle."

"I'm so happy," her mom said.

The crowd chattered again, and her father passed the plate of yams to her mom.

"This smells wonderful by the way," Kaleena said. "Thank you and everyone else who brought something."

Her father received a basket of rolls, took one, and passed it on. "As soon as you finish eating, I'll contact the sisters again to see if they've returned. Then I'll drive you there."

"That would be wonderful."

Once Kaleena drank a glass of wine and ate a few bites of the delicious Avonbelle bread, her body started to truly heal. "Where's Declan?" she asked, looking around.

Her mother looked off to the side. "He's with Thane."

"Was he injured in the skirmish?" Guilt attacked her. Her two brothers would never have engaged in a fight with the Royal Guards if it hadn't been for her.

"I'm afraid so. Two of the guards teamed up on Thane and stabbed a claw right about here." Her mom pointed to a spot above his heart.

Her own heart took a dive to her stomach at how close he'd come to being killed. "How is he?"

"Declan will do his magic, and then Thane's dragon will have to take over."

Well that put a damper on any kind of celebration.

"Kaleena, just so you know, Stone and I wanted to come and help," her younger brother Ramsey said, "but Declan thought if too many of us showed up, it would tip off the Royals."

"He was probably right. I'm glad you stayed back and remained safe. Someone had to watch over the business." Ramsey ran the lab, and Stone handled much of the SinCas business. While they were all excellent fighters, they were needed more at the office. "No doubt Rathan, who by the way is the one who had me kidnapped, will be on the warpath now that I've escaped," Kaleena said. "I need all of you to be careful and on the lookout."

"You can count on us," Ramsey said.

"Thank you. You can help the most by making sure he doesn't sabotage the mine or blow up the lab. I wouldn't put anything past him. Just so you all know, it appears he has enough power from the dark lighters to succeed." Why he needed to add her powers, she didn't know.

"You don't need to worry about him harming our property," Stone added. "Birk is there now to make sure nothing happens."

Birk, her wonderful cousin, always took his job too seriously. "I can't believe Rathan was behind this," her mother said. "I don't even think your aunt Teresa cares for him. He has no respect for anyone. The fact he took his own cousin and tried to turn you into a dark lighter is proof enough."

"That's for sure."

"While I want nothing more than to take him down a peg, he rarely gets his hands dirty," her dad said. "But his time will come."

Kaleena looked over at Finn who was listening to every word but saying nothing. It was probably better that he not rock the boat right now by asking too many questions or making some inflammatory remark about the Royals. Her brothers, cousins, and father, were easy to incite when one of their own was harmed.

"How did Rathan get the drop on you?" her father asked.

"I was at The Wing's bar where I usually go on Friday night. As the band I'd come to hear was warming up, this guy Christian asked me for a dance. I wasn't going to accept, but he insisted." Kaleena didn't want to look over at Finn, knowing he'd be scowling. While it was rather embarrassing, she outlined how someone had drugged her. "I can't be sure if it was Christian though. He said he was going to take me to the hospital, but I ended up in that cell. He could be there too, but I didn't see him. They could have him someplace else."

"Your cousin Anderson called from the police station and said your car was spotted at the bar. It's back at your condo now."

"That's a relief."

"I'll see if I can find this Christian fellow," Griffin said. "If I do, I'll ask him what happened." Nessa's brother had been quiet up to this point, but she could always count on him to be the levelheaded one.

Nessa cleared her throat. "Kaleena is clearly tired. Let's give her a break from all the questions until after she's finished eating. Be sure to take seconds and thirds everyone. We don't want the food to go to waste."

Bless Nessa. For the next few minutes, dishes were passed around, and more wine was poured and consumed. "This is divine," Kaleena said. "Nothing like practically starving for a few days to make you appreciate real food, especially a fantastic steak from...." She glanced at the white bags with the logo of a man in armor next to a slain wild boar. "Highlander's Steakhouse."

"Very true," her mother said.

"Kaleena," Dad said. "I for one agree with your assessment of Rathan wanting revenge. He's a proud man, one who will not take your escape lightly. I think you should stay at the country house for a while. I'll double the guards there."

She sagged. "I appreciate that, but I do have a job, remember?" She then listed about ten things that should have been taken care of yesterday. "If I have an escort to and from home and don't leave the SinCas building, I'll be fine."

"Dad's right," Stone said. "We can't be too careful. I deal with all the same people you do. I can help out. We all would feel better if you stayed away from the office—at least until things settle down."

As much as she didn't want to agree, they had a point. Besides, it might give her a chance to spend some quality time with Finn. "How long do you think I'll have to stay holed up there?" Rathan was the impetuous sort.

"Just until we can learn Rathan's intentions," her dad said. "Then we'll make sure he never tries anything like that again."

The only way to stop someone as evil as him would be to kill him—during a battle of course. "Just so you know there are more white lighters being held captive in the bowels of the castle."

"In the same place where you were held?" her dad asked clearly concerned.

"Yes."

Her cousin piped up. "We have the camera recording from Finn's travels. From that we should be able to pinpoint their exact location."

"Excellent. We'll put a plan together to free them, but first we need to make certain you remain safe."

She pictured their desperate faces and her heart turned heavy.

"Did Rathan say why he took you?" her mother asked.

"He did." She explained about him wanting to use her magic to help the Royals. "The scary part was how incredibly powerful their dark lighter, Sanditra, is. If I'd been there much longer, there is no telling how long I could have held out. On that last day, I was beginning to feel this evil swell inside me."

"Oh, sweetheart, I am so sorry that happened, but you are strong. I'm sure you could have fought her."

"I believed that for a while, but I doubted it more and more each day."

Her mom rubbed her arm. "I'm proud of you for

fighting so hard. Did Rathan say if any of your other cousins were involved?" her mom asked, clearly worried.

"No, but he did say Aunt Teresa had no idea what he'd done."

"I'm glad to hear it. I didn't mean to upset you by bringing it up. I'm sorry." She turned to Finn. "So Finn, what do you do?"

CHAPTER TWELVE

Once Kaleena finished her meal, her strength had almost completely returned. "We need to call the Four Sisters."

Her dad pulled out his phone. "I told you I'd take care of it. You need to rest."

"I'm so thankful for everyone's help, but I'm fine. Really—other than having these cuffs."

Her dad smiled just as he reached one of the sisters. He kept nodding, and then said they'd be there shortly. "Acacia said she and her sisters just arrived back home and to come on over. She will do what she can to help."

"Great."

Once she and Finn were settled in the back seat of her dad's car, Kaleena must have fallen asleep against him, because it seemed like only seconds before her dad came to a stop in front of the darkened pottery shop.

"Wake up, princess. We're here," her dad said.

Just as they reached the front door, a light in the back room turned on. A moment later, two women cut across the store and opened up. "Oh, Kaleena! I've been anxious to hear how the escape went," Acacia said.

Magnolia, her older sister, was with her. Kaleena hadn't been to the shop in a while. It seemed that the only time her family members came here was to ask for help from one of the four sisters. As strong as their powers were, there were many things the sisters wouldn't interfere with —like swooping in and saving someone. They did however make sure the Royals didn't get too out of hand. Kaleena would be forever grateful for that.

She held up her wrists. "I think Nessa explained about the cuffs, right?"

"Yes."

Kaleena told them once more about the poison and how it—or a dark lighter's spell—prevented her from shifting or using her magic.

Acacia's eyes widened. "I can't imagine losing my magic." She visibly shivered.

"It was horrific. Seems my cousin Rathan engaged some dark lighter to put a hex on me."

"That bitch. Which one was she?"

"I can't be certain, but it was probably Sanditra. Rathan had assigned her to help me tap into my *evil* side."

Acacia hissed. "We've tangled with her before. She's lucky I don't go there right now and kill her."

Oh dear. Finn would think this woman was crazy. Listening to her now, maybe she was. Here she thought, Poppy, was the impulsive one of the sisters, always pushing the boundaries, but she'd never go so far as to murder someone. She and her sisters vowed to help, not harm. Then again, a Guardian had been kidnapped.

"I tried to get these off, but I can't find a keyhole," Kaleena said.

"Hmm. Let's see what I can do." Acacia placed her hands on the cuffs and closed her eyes. Her fingers trembled and seemed to become transparent as she hummed. She then ran her hands over the cuffs and mumbled something that sounded close to a spell—though what language she was speaking was anyone's guess. When she finally let go, the cuffs sprang open, and her hands returned to normal. Wow.

With shaky fingers, Kaleena lifted off the cuffs and set them on the table. "Thank you so much."

Acacia smiled. "No problem. I will dispose of these. I could sense they contained much evil. Not only was there poison inside, a curse was placed on the cuffs. With them removed, your ability to shift will return, as will your magic." She smiled sweetly. "Is there anything else I can help you with?"

Use your magic to kill Rathan. "You've done so much already. I can't thank you enough."

They chatted a bit more about how Finn managed the rescue, and then the three of them left. All during the half hour ride back to the mining complex, Finn said little. Most likely he was still trying to figure out exactly who these sisters were. They would appear to be pure magic to an outsider, and that wouldn't be far from the truth. Besides being able to teleport, Acacia had been able to transform Finn's face to look like another, and then remove the cuffs without any tools. Even the Guardians were a bit stumped as to the extent of their abilities.

Finn reached over and rubbed her wrists. "How are you feeling?"

"Good. Real good."

Once back at the mining complex, her dad stopped in front of the solid wall. He slipped out of the driver's seat and swiped his dragon scale over one of the flatter areas.

Finn leaned across the front seat. "What is he doing?"

"Opening the garage door."

"What garage door?"

Kaleena almost laughed at his surprise. "There's one there. You just can't see it, which is the point. It works the same way as the entry door Nessa took us through. Remember when she used a scale to open that door?"

"Vaguely. I was still in shock from the flight to take note of everything. For someone who prefers solid ground, it's taken some time to get used to being swept off my feet and carried a thousand feet in the air."

She smiled. "Don't tell me you're afraid of heights?"

He glanced off to the side. "Only if I have no control over when or how high I fly."

She chuckled then ran her hand down his arm. "I'll make sure you feel safe when you're with me."

"I just need a bit of warning, that's all."

"You're doing amazingly well. I've met many of the people of Earth, and I dare say most would be begging to go back if they'd been through what you have."

"That's only because they don't have you here." He leaned over and kissed her cheek.

Finn was the most wonderful man she'd ever met.

Once the large rock groaned opened, her father slipped back into the car and drove into the lit parking space.

He cut the engine. "I'm going to find your mother and then we'll head home. You going to be okay here all alone, sweetheart?" he asked as he twisted in his seat.

"I won't be alone. I have Finn. Besides, not even Rathan and his powerful dark lighters or guards can break in here. Rest assured, I'll be sleeping soundly tonight." She gave him a big smile.

"I'm glad to have you back. I haven't slept a wink."

The three of them exited the car. When they reached her room, she hugged her father goodnight. "Thank you for everything."

"No thanks needed. Now get a good night's sleep."

"I will." Assuming she could sleep with her mate next to her.

Her father held up a hand. "Oh, when you go to the country house tomorrow, I'd like you to drive instead of fly. You know how easy you are to spot in the air. Those pink scales really stand out." She was mostly black with only a few pink ones, but it wouldn't do any good to argue with her father. Once when she'd shifted, a Royal had been near by. No doubt he reported her distinct coloring. If they did spot her, she didn't need to put Finn in danger.

"Fine."

"In fact, I don't want you to use your own car either."

"I couldn't if I wanted to. It's not here."

"True. I'll have a car the Royals haven't seen delivered tomorrow." Her father clasped her shoulder. "Not to scare you, but I wouldn't be surprised if Rathan sends a dozen men to find you."

"You think he'll have every road watched too?"

"It's possible. That's why I've decided to have a caravan

escort you. Some will be driving and others will be flying to stave off an attack from the air."

"Ugh." She hated all of this.

"Don't worry. It'll be over soon." He leaned over, kissed her forehead, and then strode off.

Exhaustion finally hit her, and she turned to Finn, the bright light in her life. "Let's go to bed. It's been a long day." She tried to smile, but even her lips seemed tired.

"That's an understatement." He placed a hand on her back to lead her inside the room and that one touch woke her up and had her body burning with desire in seconds.

Mate, mate, her dragon shouted.

I know, but aren't you tired? You've been working non-stop for days.

Finn rejuvenates me.

Me too.

Kaleena had thought she had it bad after she'd dream-walked with Finn, but having him in person by her side ratcheted up her desire to new heights. With Finn being a shifter too, he probably had it just as bad. Add in the whole newness of her land, and he must be overwhelmed. "Is Tarradon what you expected?" she asked, wanting to learn more about this wonderful man.

"Not really. Our people can't cloak themselves at will. That's a bit disturbing, but I guess I'll get used to it."

She stepped closer, needing to absorb his healing energy. "I hope so."

"There's something else that amazes me. I thought we had some pretty powerful witches back home, but I don't think any of them could do what those sisters can do."

Ophelia was as powerful, but her father had mentioned

that once she left the light realm to live on Earth that she swore she wouldn't interfere—much. After all, she had sent Finn to her. Kaleena cupped his face, thrilled to have the use of her hands again. "They are special ladies."

She pressed her lips to his but then pulled back when his gaze went elsewhere. His depth of concern worried her. *Please don't tell me you want to return to Earth.* "What's wrong?"

"I'm worried," Finn said.

"About?"

"That Rathan guy. You can't hide for the rest of your life. I know I couldn't enjoy life if I couldn't shift and run free. I imagine it's the same with you and flying."

"I have no intention of hiding." She was a Sinclair, and Sinclairs never cowed to anyone.

"You heard your father. Rathan will be searching for you—or rather his men will. You even said they are exceptionally well-trained soldiers."

"They are, but Guardians are bred to fight." Needing some comfort after that discussion, Kaleena reached behind her back and untied the knot from around her waist and then slipped her shirt over her head before dropping it on the floor.

From the way Finn's eyes turned amber when he zeroed in on her breasts, she sensed he'd already forgotten what they were talking about. Good.

"Kaleena, I had no idea it was going to be like this."

He better be talking about the way he responded to her and not how her life would always be in turmoil and danger. "Like what?"

Finn wrapped his arms around her waist and his heat,

combined with hers, created a deadly combination. Even though they'd made love not that long ago, it only made her want him more.

"I can't get you out of my head. My wolf is going crazy." He didn't even wait for her to tell him it was the same for her before he kissed her.

The instant their tongues touched, she reached between them and tugged open the button on his jeans, and then unzipped his pants. Slipping her hand into the opening, she grasped his erection, and when she gave it a slow stroke, an unexpected wave of desperation assaulted her. The mating pull kept increasing with each touch.

His thumbs brushed the sides of her breasts as she pumped his cock hard. Kaleena couldn't wait and had to break the kiss. "Enough! Lose the jeans, my sexy wolf. You wouldn't want me to set your ass on fire to get you moving, now would you?"

Finn laughed, gave her a sexy grin, and then winked. "Oh baby, I do love an aggressive woman."

He had no idea just how assertive she could be when she wanted something—and Kaleena wanted Finn McKinnon. Having her freedom and her magic back while being with him proved she could have it all.

As if they were in a race, they both shucked their clothing while continuing the kiss. Having the ability to touch him fully now, Kaleena slipped her mouth from his and nibbled her way down his chin and then to his throat. Needing more, she planted kisses between his pecs, down his abs, and then followed the line of light hair that led from his belly button straight to his magnificent cock. All the while she dragged her fingertips and nails across his glorious body.

His scent overwhelmed her dragon. In desperate need to taste him, she dropped to her knees. When she dragged her tongue around the head of his dick, Finn groaned.

"You can't imagine how many times I've pictured this moment," he whispered.

His sentimentality thrilled her. "Me too."

Afterward, she would tell him how she'd known for many years that they were meant to be together. Only when she couldn't stand the separation did she engage the dream link. However, now wasn't the time to talk. Her dragon was shooting flames up her spine, demanding that Kaleena take him now. Her nails began to extend, and she had to concentrate on retracting them.

Behave, she demanded.

I can't help it. Our hormones are screaming for us to mate with him, her animal spat back.

We will. Soon.

Kaleena grabbed Finn's hard length and trailed her tongue from his balls to the tip. His fingers shot to her head, and he threaded them through her hair, clutching hard. With his other hand, he stroked the side of her face, and the tension from his grip in her hair and gentle touches caused a chain reaction of lust and desire so strong that they went straight to her core. She loved a strong, sensitive man, and Finn responded to her in every way.

When she drew him deep into her mouth, he pressed his hips forward. A second later, a shot of cum tinged her tongue. This time, Kaleena was smart enough to back off.

She looked up at him and winked.

"You are in so much trouble now, baby," Finn said, his eyes glowing amber.

"You talk a good game, but can you deliver?" Teasing him in person was such a high.

In a flash, he lifted her to her feet then swept her up into his arms. Two strides later, she was on the bed with Finn on top. He kissed her hard, and as he slipped in between her legs, her anticipation skyrocketed. They might have engaged in this kind of behavior in their dreams, but having him in her arms was so much better.

He swiped his rough tongue across her slit and her body arched. Finn reached up and pulled her back down to his sexy mouth. "Easy there. I've only just begun." He blew a hot stream of air right on her clit.

Remembering their wonderful shower adventure, she shouldn't be so excitable, but she was. "Oh my goddess! I'm trying. I can't think when you do things like that. I have waited a long time for this." Like twenty years since Finn needed to grow up before she could contact him.

Finn gave her another long lick and looked up at her with the sexiest grin. "Don't think Kaleena, just feel. I've waited a long time too." With one hand massaging her breast, he dipped his tongue into her opening, bringing her closer to a climax.

Kaleena planted her feet on the mattress and pressed upward for more control. She wiggled and pumped as she clutched his forearms, loving the way his muscles bunched with each sway of his body.

Every one of his licks caused her to shoot higher and higher. When her nails dug into his skin, she tried to let up on the pressure, but her dragon wasn't having anything to do with it.

If you don't stop, Kaleena said, *my nails will go through his skin*.

Her animal relented.

"Finn, please."

Instead of letting up on the violent pleasure, the man had the nerve to flick her clit once more. The total bliss was so intense, Kaleena released her hold on him and grasped the sheet as an orgasm swept in and carried her away. Her vision blurred, and stars burst on the back of her lids.

He stopped, and the lack of stimulation forced her to open her eyes. Finn's were hooded, but the amber color still glowed, and his body was shooting off blue sparks in rapid succession as he slowly crawled up her body. Their lips met in a fiery passion-filled kiss coupled with nips and moans as their tongues came together. Needing air, they released after a minute, and it was only then that she noticed Finn's hair had grown a bit longer, and the whiskers on his chin had darkened.

He dug his now-lengthened claws into the mattress on either side of her head, and what sounded like a low rumbling growl came out of him. He bent toward her ear and gave it a small nip.

He whispered, "I need you so badly, Kaleena."

She smiled and then rubbed herself seductively against his cock. "Then take me."

CHAPTER THIRTEEN

Finn had never been so excited in his life. Sure, their love-making in the shower had been phenomenal, but her hands had been tied. To have her touching him all over and then go down on him was beyond anything he'd ever experienced. And when he tasted her intimately, his wolf had clawed for release, forcing Finn to struggle to keep him under control. And things were only getting hotter.

Images of the ways they'd make love in his dreams ran across his memory like a fuzzy movie, but when Kaleena licked her lips, Finn forgot about his choices of positions and just pounced. Bracing himself on one elbow, he engaged in more slow kisses while he cupped her face. Kaleena's lips reminded him of sunshine and blue skies, making him picture a future full of happiness with her.

At first it was a little intimidating to think of her as this giant dragon woman while he was merely a wolf, but then he looked into her eyes and pride filled him. He'd always been drawn to the strong, competent type—and no one was stronger than Kaleena Sinclair. Who else could survive a room full of knives while being poisoned? To think she succeeded in fighting off the lure of the dark lighter, further convinced him that Kaleena was the best thing to happen to him.

"Finn?" she asked after breaking the kiss. "Where did you go?

Heat raced up his face. "Just thinking how amazing you are."

"You should know by now that I'm a show-me kind of girl."

He laughed. Ducking his head, he nipped at her nipple and then sucked hard. She arched her back, grabbing his shoulder with one hand while sinking the other into his hair to hold him against her breast. Kaleena let out a gasp. "So good. Ah, yes."

Her ecstasy turned him on even more. Wanting to touch her all over, he slipped two fingers inside her to make sure she was ready for him. She was.

Kaleena sucked in a breath, whimpered, and then tightened her hold on him. Her lips quivered, and her body glowed. Seeing the pink scales appear under her skin would take some getting used to, though Finn had no room to judge. He was shooting off blue sparks faster than any Fourth of July finale. His new goal was to aim for a full-on pink explosion.

When his cock turned painfully hard, he rolled on top and plunged into her in one slick thrust, his body fitting like a key into her wet lock. He groaned in complete rapture while his wolf howled, *Mate!*

The emotional connection was so high, he almost

burst. Finn wanted this to last, so he pumped into her a few times and then slowed. "You feel so fucking good," he moaned.

When she wrapped her legs around his waist, Finn feared he'd lose his ever loving mind. The tightening contractions of her sheath around his cock caused him to pulse and throb so hard, he had to take deep breaths so he didn't shoot off like a teenager.

Not sure how much longer he could hold out with the slow motion, Finn pushed in then retreated from her warm heat. He gripped her upper shoulder with his left hand and lifted himself up a bit on the other side. As he reached between them with his right hand and pressed on her clit, Kaleena gasped and bucked.

"Fuck me harder," she called out.

Not only did Finn do as Kaleena asked, he also flicked and then pinched her clit. Just as his rhythm stuttered, she tilted her head and let out a primal scream. It was when she tightened her inner walls around his cock and started to spasm that Finn finally let go and lost it too. Together they had climbed up to that climactic ledge and soared.

If this was what life with his mate would be like, he wasn't sure he'd survive, but for sure he would be damn happy through it all.

Kaleena must have put a spell on him because Finn wasn't able to move for the next few minutes. When he finally pulled out, he lovingly gazed at her and leaned over, softly placing his lips on hers for a moment. He then stumbled to the bathroom on shaky legs to retrieve a damp washcloth to clean them both up with. By the time he returned though, Kaleena was sound asleep. She didn't even flinch or make a sound when he gently cleaned her.

After washing himself, Finn doused the lights and climbed into bed. Drawing her into his arms, he snuggled up against her back as he pulled the blankets around them. With his arm under her pillow he placed his other hand on her hip. She let out a happy little sigh and wiggled even closer, entwining her fingers through his and pulling their joined hands up toward her chest and tucking them under her chin.

Finn smiled to himself and buried his nose into her hair, inhaling her delicious scent. Being next to Kaleena soothed his soul. While he missed his family and friends, this was where he belonged. She completed him.

Rathan paced his castle office. He'd been summoned to meet with his father like a commoner. If the king planned to lecture him, the least he could do was walk over to Rathan's side of the castle.

Wishful thinking, his dragon grumbled.

Most of the previous summons had been to inform Rathan that he wasn't doing enough to bring in more dark magic. He hated the old man. His evil father wasn't even a full-blooded dragon. He'd been born a demon—and a disgraced one at that. If his powers hadn't been stripped, he wouldn't have needed to seduce him mom—weak woman that she was.

Rathan glanced into the mirror to make sure he looked like a prince before heading over to hear what the old man had to say. Most likely this chastisement was for losing Kaleena. How his father had found out about her capture and subsequent escape he didn't know. Most likely his guards told him. If Rathan heard the screeches and cries of the battle overhead, they must have too. A few well-placed inquiries would lead him to the truth.

By the time Rathan finally figured out the reason for the fight and sent someone to investigate, Kaleena had already escaped. She'd been spotted outside with a man, but it had been too dark to see his face. Rathan couldn't figure out how she had managed that feat. She had no magic. He'd seen to that. And none of his men had reported any kind of a breach.

It didn't matter. He'd find out soon enough, but damn, the whole incident galled him. Losing Kaleena was a huge blow to his plan and to his ego. He'd had such high hopes of breaking her—his own cousin.

With his head held high, Rathan marched down the large castle hallway, turning right then left. Every guard stood at attention when he walked by—as well they should. Rathan better not encounter his brothers since he didn't need their shit piled on top of his already foul mood. His two sisters, at least, he could handle.

Luck was on his side when he made it to his father's office suite without any interruptions. The guard standing watch knocked on the massive wooden door, pushed it open, and then announced him. When Rathan entered, his father, the king, was seated at his desk scribbling something in a ledger. It smelled of rich leather and tobacco smoke mixed with something sickenly sweet—like cheap cologne.

The man actually believed he ran his kingdom, when in reality without Rathan's steady help of infusing dark magic into him and the others, none of the Royals would stand a chance against their enemies. Sure, his brother Tarik trained the guards, but it was Rathan who searched far and wide for the most powerful dark lighters.

When he reached the desk, his father did not look up but rather continued to jot something down in the ledger. "Father?"

"Just a moment."

Just a moment? Did he think his time wasn't valuable? Rathan was busy organizing search parties for Kaleena and didn't need to be having this needless conversation.

Just as he was about to speak his mind, his dad finally set down his pen. "I hear you have quite a situation on your hands. Another failure, Rathan?"

He'd figured this meeting was about placing blame, but Rathan wouldn't confess to anything. What if this wasn't about his cousin? "To what are you referring?"

"Why your cousin's escape, of course."

Damn. "How the hell did you hear about that?"

"The whole fucking palace watched the air fight with her two brothers. Guards do talk, you know. What are you doing to find her?"

"I have people looking for her now."

His father shoved his chair back, got up, and strode around his desk. Rathan stood straighter, refusing to be cowed by this man. When his father had the nerve to poke him in the chest, Rathan considered hauling off and hitting him. Too bad the guards would come running and toss him in jail for hitting the king.

"What the hell were you thinking taking that girl?"

That girl? She was his niece. "Weren't you the one who suggested I grab her? And weren't you the one who said she could help us since her powers are so extensive?"

"I never told you to do any such thing." His father crossed his arms over his chest and looked off to the side.

What the fuck? That was a blatant lie. Now Rathan was even more pissed off. "Are you insane? I have spent my life trying to find enough dark lighters to satisfy your insatiable need for power. I'll tell you exactly what you said. *Rathan, I need more power. The dark lighters are depleting too fast, so go and find powerful white lighters and turn them. That kind of power should out last us all. I'm told your cousin Kaleena inherited powerful white lighter abilities.*"

His father huffed and waved his hand through the air as if he was swatting away something annoying. He then turned his back on Rathan. "You misheard me."

What?! He hadn't misheard the bleating old windbag at all. Rathan clenched his fists and started to take a step toward his father, but before he could call him out, someone rapped on the door. His father turned, raising an eyebrow in surprise when he noticed Rathan's stance.

He smirked. *That's right old man; be very wary of me. I will bury you someday.*

A second later, his younger brother Ander came in. Shit. On the surface, he was every woman's dream man— fair haired, handsome, and eloquent. Underneath, he was a snake.

"Oh, I'm sorry, I didn't mean to interrupt," Ander said.

Like hell he didn't. He wanted to watch a beheading —his.

"How can I help you, son?" their father asked in a gentle tone.

Rathan's blood boiled. His father never used a gentle tone with him or referred to him as son. Rathan always felt like he was more of an annoyance and treated like no more than a hired guard. Bloody so-called family would all feel his wrath one day!

Ander glanced at him and his barely noticeable evil smirk disappeared quickly. Then the little shit turned to their father all proud and pretentious. "It's not good, Father. Several members of the press arrived at the castle asking why white lighters were being held captive in our castle. I told them that was a total falsehood. Unfortunately, they had a lot of details. I informed them that under no circumstances would the Royals be involved in such a degrading travesty and explained that they needed to check their information properly. We take great pride in the people of Tarradon. Do you have any idea what happened to bring this all about?"

"Ask your brother. He took the girl and then let her escape."

Rathan's temper got the best of him. "You ordered me to take her, you...*Your Majesty!*" he shouted once more, hoping this time his father would cop to the truth, especially since Rathan had no fear of him anymore.

His father turned dark red and was in Rathan's face in seconds, grabbing a hold of his lapels. He shook him as he yelled, "You better watch your mouth. That's a damn lie, and I will not be disrespected like that."

It took all of Rathan's control not to kill him. He didn't because in the back of his mind he wondered if he could.

After all, the king had been infused with so much dark magic over the years—thanks to him—that if he attacked him, he might kill Rathan. On top of that, Ander would jump to their father's defense in a heartbeat—the little traitor.

When Rathan didn't fight back, his father let go and then shoved him.

His brother spun to face him. "What the hell were you thinking?"

"What difference does it make?" Rathan wanted to repeat that he was only following orders, but Ander would never believe him—his father's little scene made sure of that. And dear old dad sure as hell didn't care if one of his children took all the blame, just as long as his reputation remained squeaky clean. *Asshole.*

"What does the press know?" his father asked Ander.

"They know it was Kaleena. How shall I address their concern?"

As if Ander didn't already know the answer before he came in.

"Deny their allegations and keep denying them until they believe you. Tell them that one of Rathan's men was under the misconception that this woman hadn't paid her taxes. He brought her in for questioning, but she was released when she identified herself as a Sinclair. Unfortunately, it took a few days before we realized our mistake."

Bullshit! "My men are well trained," Rathan said. "That will make us look like fools."

"We have our overall image to be concerned with. Fire the lot of them and make it public."

That was uncalled for. "It's hard to find good men, men who have magic and who are willing to fight for us."

"We need to make an example of someone."

His father was all about image. Behind the scenes he was ruthless. It was why Mom wasn't allowed outside of the castle walls without a ton of guards. "What about my image?"

"What image? That of a fool? And a very careless one at that?" He turned to Ander. "Go soothe the press. We have those cells in the east wing—the ones that have never been used. Take them there and show them we house no prisoners or any kind of white lighters."

"Yes, Father."

Ass kisser. He didn't know which one was worse—his father or his brother.

Once Ander left, Rathan spun to face his father. "Am I to disband the Searchers then?"

His father's face turned white. Good. Without the Searchers, no suitable dark lighters would be found, which meant his father would slowly become useless without his power. "Let's not be hasty. My power is draining each day, and I need more. We can keep the Searchers on low key duty until some of this attention has died down."

So now he likes what I do for him? "Didn't you just say that you've never asked for my help in finding dark lighters?"

"I don't recall saying that."

Rathan wanted to strangle the man. He only said what suited him. The rest of the world could be damned. If only Rathan had the magic to make his father revert to being a demon, he would. "Fine."

"Just find that Sinclair girl and kill her. And make it

look like an accident. We don't need her going to the press. I fear they'd believe her."

No, we couldn't have that now, could we? For a split second, Rathan almost considered telling the press what kind of man his father was—an evil megalomaniac who didn't give a damn about the people in the province. Unfortunately, that would cause an uprising of epic proportions, and Rathan might lose any power he had.

At least with Kaleena dead, it would be a warning to the Sinclairs not to interfere with him again.

Just as he was about to leave his father called him back. "And, Rathan?"

"Yes, Your Majesty?" Rathan wouldn't call him father to his face ever again. He didn't deserve that title any more than the royal one.

"Remember, only her death will make this go away and if you fail, it will be your death that I will use to keep the family name clear."

Rathan didn't give away one bit of his shock at the open threat from his father, but rather allowed a strong nod in recognition, and then marched out of *His Majesty's* office chamber.

Fucking fatherly love and care, my Royal ass!

CHAPTER FOURTEEN

"This is a country house?" Finn asked. "It's almost as big as the Royal castle.

Kaleena chuckled. "It might have the same stone exterior and three turrets, but it's a fraction of the size." She pulled under the porte cochère and then into an area that contained several parked vehicles. "It was built around fifteen hundred. When my great-great grandfather bought it, it was rather rundown. He started the restoration process, and it's been ongoing ever since. Thankfully, it never gets really cold in Tarradon. If it did, I imagine the heating bill would be outrageous."

Finn smiled. "I'll stick to my two-bedroom wood-framed house." Kaleena rolled down the car window and waved goodbye to her father's escorts. Those in the sky were already heading back to town.

Now that she'd arrived safely, Kaleena could let down her guard a bit, though she wasn't under the delusion that

Rathan's men wouldn't continue to find out whether she was there or not. As long as she frequently checked the sky, they should be safe.

"I understand that something this large can seem impersonal and cold," she said. "I can't wait for you to see my condo in the city. It has a great view, but it's much smaller. Since you seem to like cozy, I think you might like where I live." At least she hoped so. Though compared to US standards, her condo would rival any penthouse in New York City.

She cut the engine and slipped out of the driver's seat. Finn followed and then nodded to the row of vehicles along the side of the house.

"Do those cars belong to the servants?" he asked with awe.

"Yes, but we prefer the word *employee*. The Royals have servants." A simple answer was the best. She didn't need to explain that their staff was quite large. Add in the security staff, and they employed a lot of people. Most importantly all employees were treated as family.

It was a shame the house wasn't used all that much anymore. She missed seeing everyone and their children. Growing up, her family used to vacation here for the whole summer, and she and her siblings would play with the employees' kids, running and laughing all over the countryside.

Kaleena unlocked the car trunk, and Finn grabbed her suitcase. "Is there someplace I can buy some clothes? I can't wear these much longer," Finn said, plucking his shirt off his stomach.

"There are clothes for you inside."

"For me?"

Kaleena stopped and faced him. "Some of the employees went shopping this morning and bought you the basics. I figured you'd need something to change into."

Finn straightened his shoulders. "I could have shopped myself."

"Do you have Denlars, my dear man?" When Finn just looked at her with his eyebrows raised, she decided not to tease him further. "We do take dollars and other currencies here since many of the shifters travel back and forth to Earth."

"Do they accept credit cards?"

She chuckled at his hopeful expression. "No wolf man —only cash."

"Then thank you, but how did you know what size to buy?"

She smiled and wrapped an arm through his. "You are very welcome. As to your size, I checked out the tags on your old clothes. Plus, I am a pretty good judge since I buy clothes for my brothers on occasion."

"You didn't have to go to all that trouble."

Kaleena smiled. "It's the least I can do for you saving my life." She sobered. "I really don't know how much longer I could have held off against that dark lighter. The poison was weakening my resolve, and Sanditra was doing her damnedest to get me to do horrible things. You literally saved me from a dishonorable death."

"You are strong. You survived." Finn set down her suit-case, and when he slid his hands around her waist, her dragon instantly woke up. This constant state of arousal had to stop or Kaleena feared she might become distracted and lower her guard.

"I'm glad you think so."

"Other than the obvious reason for not wanting darkness inside you, would performing these feats have really killed you? One of our Wendayans back on Earth claimed that crossing over to the dark side would alter something inside her, but that's all."

"All I know is that on Tarradon, the dark magic is like a cancer. It would eat away at my white magic and eventually destroy me."

Finn tightened his grip. His warmth and caring bolstered her spirits. "I'm so sorry you had to go through that. You must have been petrified."

"A little, but I knew I had to stay strong and keep the faith that the Guardians or you would find me."

He leaned back and studied her. "I'm glad I was successful."

"Me too, and can I say I'm glad that's over?"

He cupped her face. "Is it though? Even you said Rathan will want revenge. That's why your father sent us here. It is still dangerous, and we need to be vigilant to make sure you are always protected."

"I'll be careful, I promise. I will always be with you, and trust me, I don't plan on leaving your side anytime soon." She winked at him. "Now come on. Let's get settled and find something to eat. Then I want to show you something.

"I don't think we should chance being out in the open," Finn said. "Your father warned you about staying hidden."

"No one is around," Kaleena said as she led him behind their country home. "I'll be able to sense a dragon should one come near, even if he is cloaked."

"How?"

"Our white light magic allows us to detect them—but not the other way around if we are cloaked."

Finn glanced to the sky, but he didn't see anything circling overhead. He then checked out the surrounding area to see if Rathan's men might attack from the woods. He couldn't even hazard a guess as to how many acres this estate encompassed. No other structure appeared for miles.

She dragged her hands down his face and turned his head toward her. "Stop worrying. We're in the middle of the country. We'll be okay. Besides, it's been days since I've been in the fresh air. Now that the curse has been lifted, my dragon is begging for her freedom." She tapped his nose. "It's mostly your fault, you know, that she needs this release." Kaleena grinned.

"My fault? How?"

"Our lovemaking excited her too much. She needs to fly." She kissed him quickly. "I won't go high or far, I promise."

That didn't make him feel much better, but he understood. "I'll admit my wolf is chomping at the bit for a run too, but I'll watch you first and then shift," he said. That way he might be able to help detect, and then possibly deflect any intruders should they come by land. "Show me what you've got, fly girl."

Finn was excited to see her in her dragon form. Dragons were magnificent and so regal.

"Do you want to come with me?" she asked. "You can shift afterward. Of course, you could shift first and I could take your wolf for a ride."

Don't even think about it, his animal said.

I won't let her take you. We need to patrol down here. Finn held up his hands. "I think I'll sit this one out. Besides, I want to be able to watch you."

Finn dropped to the ground, leaned back onto his elbows, and crossed his ankles. The sweet smell of grass elevated his mood, but not enough to make him lose focus. "Don't be gone more than a minute, okay?"

"I know what you're doing, you worrywart. Trust me when I say that I have magic on my side. I will sense someone coming."

"Go." The woman was too stubborn for her own good.

Kaleena stepped back, and a moment later she was in her full dragon form. My goodness, but she was gorgeous. While she was mostly shiny black, there were enough iridescent pink scales to make her something to behold.

Holy shit, she's big, his wolf said.

Finn was willing to admit he was a little intimidated by her fifteen-foot height and forty-foot wingspan, but he might feel small even if she'd been a bear shifter. To think Kaleena possessed all that power too. Wow.

She turned to the side and shot out a little fire. "Show off," he called then laughed.

A second later she was in the air, soaring high into the sky. Finn was spellbound by her agility and speed. She tilted one wing toward the ground and the other to the sky, gliding on the wind. Sunlight struck her pink scales, creating a glorious vision. This was his woman, and he couldn't be happier.

She did two loops in succession and then nosedived toward him. When she didn't seem to be slowing down, he jumped to his feet to move out of the way. At the last second, she pulled up and shot straight to the sky once more. While he'd been to many air shows that specialized in acrobatic planes, none had been this fast or this nimble.

On her next approach, she slowed before landing. A second later she was his beautiful Kaleena once again, magically dressed in her same outfit.

He held open his arms, and she ran to him. "You were amazing," Finn said.

The hug that followed altered something inside him and once more created an intense need to be with her and to protect her. Just as he was about to kiss her, out of the corner of his eye, a dragon magically appeared in the sky, and his senses shot to high alert. "Kaleena, look!" Finn pointed to the black outline in the sky. "We have company."

"Shit. It isn't my family. I know all their colors. It has to be one of Rathan's men. Go hide."

Like hell he would. There wasn't time to tell her she should have listened to him in the first place. The only thing to do was shift and fight, which Finn did just as Kaleena turned into her dragon once more. The tall grassy field wasn't enough to hide him for a surprise attack, so he remained where he was.

Finn could race back to the castle and call for help, but by the time he arrived, her battle would be over. Besides, he didn't want to leave her alone.

Kaleena might be fast, but could she fight a dragon soldier? He'd soon find out. The two giant animals met twenty feet off the ground, where her opponent immediately went on the offensive. He reached out and clawed her face with his giant talons. In return, she growled and shot fire at him, but the sleek animal dodged the flames.

Finn had never felt so helpless in his life. He couldn't jump twenty feet in the air and attack. Damn. All he could do was to wait for the two of them to return to the ground before he engaged in any kind of battle.

When the intruder came at Kaleena again, she managed to get out of the way by swooping upward and then circling behind him. Charging at him, she tore a part of his wing.

Go, Kaleena!

The black beast opened his mouth, and a high-pitched screech echoed all around. Finn wanted to cheer out loud, but all he could manage was a howl.

Even though the pain seemed to be intense, this monster swept one wing forward, allowing him to turn around. Mouth open, he dove at Kaleena again and latched onto her throat. Finn froze.

Help her, his wolf begged.

How? They're twenty feet in the air.

We'll howl and bay in order to draw his attention away from her, his wolf offered.

Before Finn could address that plan, her attacker let go and Kaleena plummeted to the ground. She landed with a thud. One of her wings sagged, and she was holding her head at an odd angle, as if that last bite had been fatal. Desperation speared him as adrenaline rushed through his veins. He couldn't lose Kaleena. He'd rather die.

The beast landed in front of her and raised a claw, looking as if he was about to impale her in the chest. Finn had to stop him somehow. Without giving any thought to his own safely, he growled and then charged.

The attacker twisted toward him, taking his gaze away from Kaleena. She remained on the ground with her wings fluttering and thumping. Clearly, she was injured badly— unless this was some kind of ploy. Maybe she purposefully dove to the ground because it gave her the advantage.

I don't think so, his wolf said. *She's barely breathing.*

Shit. That meant every second he could give her to either recuperate or plan her next move was a good thing. Out of the corner of his eye, he noticed that Kaleena had wrapped her wings around herself, hopefully to help her heal.

This evil dragon's wing was injured too, and Finn decided to attack that vulnerable spot. He ran at him and scraped a paw at the webbing between the wing bones. Despite the injured state, his adversary swatted at Finn as if he were a pest. Finn tumbled and rolled ten feet, but he righted himself and shook off the shock of the impact. When he glanced over at Kaleena, she still hadn't risen, and adrenaline flooded his veins.

We got this, his wolf said.

I'm counting on you, Finn shot back.

Okay, he needed to think. If this beast had been a wolf,

Finn would have attacked his throat. Even if that killed a dragon, how could he reach fifteen feet off the ground?

Not the neck. Bite him slightly above his heart.

Finn stilled. That instruction had not come from his wolf. The voice was feminine. Had Kaleena communicated with him somehow? How could that be? They weren't dream-walking and they sure as hell hadn't mated.

What the fuck difference did it make? It seemed to be sound advice. Finn could leap fairly high, but he certainly couldn't jump ten or more feet to this black dragon's heart.

Try, his wolf begged.

Finn had no choice. Head down, he charged the huge animal. Claws digging into the dragon's wing, he scurried up the long spine, gaining purchase with each push. Just as he was in a position to crawl down to the dragon's chest, the beast dipped his snout and shot fire at him, searing Finn's skin. The shock from the heat paralyzed him.

A second later, the pain crippled him to the point where he was forced to let go. After tumbling to the ground, his body bounced, sending an ache so intense, Finn wasn't sure he could move again. The dragon then opened his mouth, as if in glee, and then dragged a talon down Finn's burnt body. His vision blurred, and as much as he tried to roll over to get away from this monster, he couldn't.

A roar sounded behind the beast, drawing his opponent's attention away from him. Like a Phoenix rising, Kaleena unfolded her wings and soared into the air. Finn had never seen a more beautiful sight.

Dipping her head, she nosedived toward her evil attacker. Her mouth was aimed straight for the dragon's chest, which wasn't covered with the same tough scales as the rest of his body.

The last thing Finn remembered was four flapping wings, a lot of squawking, and a stream of fire shooting above his body.

CHAPTER FIFTEEN

Kaleena paced the bedroom where Finn lay in a heap on the bed in his wolf form. She faced her brother, happy he'd responded so quickly to her distress call. "What do you think?"

Declan shook his head. "I've finished the last of the treatments for the burns. Now it's up to Finn to finish healing."

Her brother's ability to heal was legendary, but maybe Finn's Earth genetics were different from other shifters on Tarradon, and it disrupted Declan's magic. Her brother said he hadn't wanted to overtax Finn's wolf, so he'd performed his healing magic in small bits over the last twenty-four hours.

"How long before he wakes up?"

Declan cupped her shoulder. "Honestly, I can't say, but since Fate has connected you two, he should feel your concern and healing love. If he does, he'll pull through." He dragged his hand down her arm. "If I recall, he wasn't the only one injured in the battle. How's your arm doing? A broken wing needs to be tended to."

Kaleena didn't have time to worry about herself. "I'm fine. When Finn attacked that monster, it gave me time to heal myself. All that's left is a little soreness." To prove it, she lifted both arms over her head and held in the wince.

He glanced at her cheek and placed a hand over it. "If you won't let me fix the last bit of soreness, then let me repair this scar."

The bright red slash from the gouge mark had yet to mend but with time it would disappear. She concentrated all her efforts on her wing and not on the inconsequential facial scratch. "Fine."

Heat poured through her body from his touch, and she almost pulled away from the ache. Closing her eyes to concentrate on her brother's healing warmth, she inhaled and counted backward from ten to one. When he lifted his hand, all of the pain disappeared. She opened her eyes and touched her face. "It's gone!"

Her brother smiled and tapped the end of her nose. "I've still got the touch, little one. If your arm remains sore, call me, okay?" Her brother's concern lightened her heavy heart.

"Yes, I promise, and thank you." She glanced back at the bed.

Declan wagged a finger at her. "And stay inside, please!"

"Don't worry. I will." She shook her head. "Damn Rathan and his men."

"Our guards will make sure no one gets in here."

Being a good prisoner wasn't in her genetic makeup, but until both she and Finn were strong, she'd stay inside the country estate. "I have no doubt."

"Just so you know, I asked a few of the workers to dispose of the dead body," Declan said.

"I'm glad. I never want to see that creep again." She'd washed her hands ten times to get that man's blood off her talons, but she couldn't remove the image of him struggling for his last few breaths. Even though the man took orders from Rathan, he didn't deserve to die for something he might not have believed in. "I never want to kill another soul. Fighting is one thing, but killing is another."

"You had no choice. Rathan sent him to kill you."

"I know, but I wish our dear cousin would have come himself. I would have enjoyed that kill."

Declan chuckled and moved closer. He looked down at her. "Rathan would have killed you. Don't tangle with him." His voice held a deadly serious tone.

She wasn't about to say that if Finn hadn't attacked the Royal Guard when he had, she'd be dead. "I'll try not to." She lifted up on her toes and kissed his cheek.

"I'll leave you to your nursing duties." He smiled and then left, his boots smacking against the tile floor.

Once his steps faded, Kaleena rushed over to Finn. Declan had healed her lover's burns. That in and of itself had been an amazing feat.

"Finn, can you hear me?" She placed a hand on his head, hoping to somehow transmit her love to him.

For years she'd always known that he would be her mate, but having him here in person made a world of difference. Because of her special abilities, she was given a window into her mate's life. For her, it happened about twenty years ago when Fate must have decided she was ready to see the world that he lived in. Now, Finn was with her, and Kaleena would do everything in her power to make him strong again.

She sat next to him on the bed, believing what Declan said. If she talked to him, he might not respond, but he would hear the love in her voice. "Hey, baby. I was just thinking about one of the images I received of you and your family." She smiled at the memory of his youthful feistiness. "You couldn't have been more than eleven at the time." She sighed. "What a daredevil you were. You provided me with such wonderful nightly dreams." She continued to stroke his body.

"I'm not sure whether your parents owned the horses or not, but you and Devon decided to go for a ride in the hills. Being the youngest child, you wanted to prove you were a man, so you challenged your brother to a race. Do you remember that?" She didn't expect him to respond, but hopefully he could hear her, and the memory might help bring him back.

"Anyway, you were in some field. I'm not sure why your horse spooked, but it did, and you went flying. When you landed, my heart nearly stopped. I can still see the way your leg bent. It was something awful. I had no doubt it was broken." She smiled. "Brave, Finn. You worked so hard not to cry out. Devon on the other hand kind of freaked, but like a good older brother, he rushed to your side and told you to shift. And you did. I can only imagine how much that hurt. Devon stayed with you for about an hour and then must have figured that your wolf wasn't mature enough to heal you. So what did he do? He lifted you up and placed you on the back of his horse and took you home."

She remembered waiting until the next night to find out what happened. "Someone by the name of Kathryn Berta was called in to help heal you. She lit some candles, placed an herb packet under your head, and chanted. Miraculously, you roused in a few hours. Your leg was a bit sore for a day or two, but as soon as it healed, you were raring to go riding again. You really wanted to prove to Devon that you could beat him in a race."

A muscle twitched under her hand, and her heartbeat rose. "Finn?"

Her pulse soared and Kaleena sat up straighter. The bedroom door opened and Tory entered. Kaleena didn't need to turn around to know it was her. Their twin connection seemed to be working overtime of late.

Her sister placed a hand on Kaleena's shoulder. "How is he?"

Tory had been her rock since the attack while Finn tried to heal. "I felt him move."

"That's good." As if together they could reach his wolf, Tory placed a hand on Finn's body too. "Come on, Finn. Kaleena's really worried about you. You need to wake up."

A leg shot out and then retracted, boosting her spirits. Kaleena leaned over and pressed her lips to his ear. "I love you, Finn McKinnon."

A second later, his eyes opened but then closed again. "I think he's coming out of it," her sister said with excitement.

Kaleena rubbed an unscathed part of his body to stimulate him. "Come on, Finn, you can do it."

As if she'd willed him awake, Finn's wolf whined as he opened his eyes. His gaze darted around in obvious confusion. She bet the last thing he remembered was passing out after being attacked by that monster guard. Kaleena glanced at Tory then back at Finn and smiled. "You're at the country house. You're safe now."

Finn huffed at Tory and then rolled over. He slowly shook his body as if testing whether he was completely healed.

Only then did Kaleena remember that if Finn shifted, he'd be naked. "Tory, it might be better if you leave. I'll explain why later," she said.

"Sure." Tory leaned over and hugged her. "I'm just happy he's better. Bye, Finn."

As soon as she left, Finn shifted and sure enough he was buck naked—just the way she liked him. Kaleena grinned. "It's so good to have you back. How do you feel?"

He sat up. "Confused how I got here, but I think I'm okay." He looked down at his body, and his eyes widened, probably at the lack of burns.

"What do you remember?" she asked.

He winced. "That I was going to lose you, and I couldn't let that happen." Finn pulled her in and hugged her tight. "I didn't know what to do. When that dragon clawed at your face and then injured your wing, I saw red."

"What you did was fantastic, especially with the way you somehow managed to get on that guard's wing. Those few seconds gave me time to gather some strength."

"I'm not sure I remember much after he shot fire at

me. Can you fill in the gaps? And why am I not burned? I remember the intense heat and searing ache."

"You have Declan to thank for that. He healed you."

"Ah, yes. Declan is a healer. I will thank him, but how did you escape?" he asked.

"When I saw how the guard had injured you, it gave me this incredible boost to rise and attack. I only had enough energy for one shot though, so with my claws extended I charged, and sunk my talons through his chest and into his heart." She waved a hand, not wanting to relive that moment again. "He died quickly after that."

Kaleena swallowed hard to keep down the bile. It wasn't her first kill, and it wouldn't be her last, but that didn't mean she liked taking a life.

"I'm glad he's dead, but how are you? For real?" Finn reached up and gently touched her face. "I can't believe it. There's hardly a mark. When I saw that dragon had gouged your face, I thought for sure there would be a lot of damage."

She smiled. "It was pretty ugly, but Declan healed me too."

Finn glanced down and ran his hands over his body. "He's a miracle worker. I'm not sure even Missy could have healed you without a trace."

It took her a moment to remember Missy was Kathryn's daughter and that she had become the healer in the family in Silver Lake, Tennessee. "Maybe not."

He checked her out. "You look so amazing, all healthy and alive. I can't believe it."

She cupped his face. "I'm good now that I have you

back." She wouldn't mention the sore wing. Her dragon would heal her soon.

"I think I should check you out to make sure there are no other scratches or gouges," Finn said with a gleam in his eye that screamed trouble.

"Is that so? Did you suddenly get a doctor's degree?"

He slipped an errant strand of hair behind her ear. "Let's just say I have a magic touch."

She chuckled, and it felt damned good. How Finn could joke at a time like this she didn't know, but most likely it was his coping mechanism for having nearly died.

In a flash, they were stretched out on the bed, kissing and touching. As strong as Finn felt in her arms, she didn't want him to overtax himself, so she reluctantly broke off the kiss. "You know I've been worried sick about you. You might believe you've recovered enough for play time, but how about if we get you something to eat before I let you devour me?"

"Can I have you for dessert?" He winked.

She giggled but wrinkled her nose. "No offense, love, but you might want to shower first."

Finn laughed. He lifted his arm and took a whiff. "I guess I am pretty gamey. I still smell like burnt hair and flesh."

"How about you clean up while I ask the cook to prepare a meal for us?"

"Sounds good to me. Just so you know though, I still expect you to give me my sweet treat after we eat." He gave her ass a little slap on his way to the shower.

She squealed and grinned. "Oh don't you worry, I'll take care of your sweet tooth."

Finn couldn't believe they'd both survived fighting a dragon. Okay, he didn't actually do much of the fighting, but he had distracted the beast long enough for Kaleena to kick its ass.

Finn downed his drink. "By the way, this wine surpasses anything I've ever tasted on Earth."

She looked down for a moment. "Actually, the vines we use are from France."

"Really?"

She laughed. "You'd be amazed what we've learned from your world. Our philosophy is if we don't harm anyone in the copying of ideas, we're good. It's not like we'll be competing for resources or customers."

That made sense. While Finn loved talking about Tarradon, he had something that had been on his mind ever since he awoke. "Kaleena, you mentioned that you'll need to hole up here for a while because there is a possibility that Rathan will send someone else, right?"

"Yes."

"As nice as it is here, Rathan knows you are here, so what do you think of taking a little trip to Earth?" Her eyes lit up. "It would be a perfect place to lay low, and you would be protected there as well. Besides, I feel bad with the way I left my family, and I want to let them know that I'm okay. I know my twin Chelsea is worried."

When Kaleena smiled, a huge weight lifted. She then sobered. "I'm sorry I put you in such a tenuous position. As for going to Earth, I think it's a splendid idea."

His pulse jackhammered. "You do? That makes me so happy."

She polished off her wine. "For a short visit at least. I understand what it's like to miss family. Hell, when I went to school in Colorado, I would leave every almost every weekend to come back here, partly to visit, but also because my dragon became very antsy without her weekly flight. I worried that if I didn't fly on Earth, my shield of invisibility might disappear, and that would be bad."

"I can understand that. My wolf is the same way." He tried to wrap his head around his real need for the visit. "It's not just that I owe them a good explanation, I want my family to meet my mate."

Kaleena leaned back in her seat smiling, appearing relaxed and happy at the acknowledgment of them being mates. "I want to meet your family in person too. Your mother seems like such a wonderful person and your dad is so strong and in control. I would enjoy learning more about your siblings too."

Her comment surprised him. "How would you know about any of them?"

"Yeah...about that...I kind of watched you growing up." She explained how Fate had decided that she'd be one of the lucky ones who could view her mate's life.

The idea fascinated and maybe horrified him at the same time. "When I went out on dates, did you like spy on me?"

She sipped her wine as if she needed a moment to think what to say. "It's not like I could watch at will. Fate picks those moments too. So, no, I never saw you on a date. I would have been so jealous."

He relaxed until he realized his plan was not without risk since they might not be as safe as he thought. "What's to stop Rathan and his guards from following us to Earth?"

"He can't. We're called Guardians in part because we guard the portals. Normally, the Royals don't have much desire to visit Earth, as they aren't into technological advancement, but there have been times when they've tried to send one of their minions after us."

"Like Slater Coghill—the dragon shifter who came after my brother's mate."

"Yes. That was an unfortunate mishap. Trust me, I'll make certain the rest of the team is prepared to stop anyone from entering, especially since we suspect Rathan might try something sneaky."

"That's a relief. You said they aren't into technology? Why is that exactly?" Maybe it was why the castle jail cells had keys instead of an electric device to open them.

"I might have misspoken. They do have cell phones and some drive cars. They're smart enough to know they must keep up somewhat so that the rest of the realm doesn't overtake them. I think what they really want is to have the good stuff for themselves, while the rest of the realm remains in the dark ages."

"So they can control them. Geez, they sound like tyrants the more I learn about them."

Kaleena reached across the table and squeezed his hand. "They are indeed."

The idea of the two of them remaining on Earth appealed to him more and more, mostly because she would be safe there. "What do you think of moving to Earth for good but returning on weekends?"

She shook her head. "That would be the easy way out. The Royals need to understand they can't take what isn't theirs. I am a Guardian, and I have responsibilities. We are here to help protect the good of Tarradon."

Her philosophy resonated with him, but he didn't like that Kaleena was willing to put her life in danger. "So you're willing to die for your principles?"

Saying the word *die* had his gut churning. He couldn't lose Kaleena now, not after he just found her.

"It's who I am. A lot of people rely on me to keep them safe. If Fate chooses that as my path then I must accept it. I could go to Earth and die a different way. All we can do is live and love to the best of our abilities."

"I get it, I really do." She needed to live on Tarradon.

While he didn't want to rush her, the thought of seeing his family had Finn excited. "When do you think we could go back to Earth?"

She finished off her wine. "How about we finish dinner first?"

"Seriously?" She nodded. This was too good to be true. It would be like he never left if they could transport to Earth with a snap of a finger. "So what's the catch?"

"What do you mean?"

"What's to stop us from visiting whenever we want?"

Kaleena sighed. "It's complicated. You're really close to your family and love them unconditionally, which was one of the reasons why I was so attracted to you in the first place."

"I hear a *but* coming."

"Finn, it will be really hard to explain why we need to leave all the time. Your folks might understand, but others won't. Next thing you know, your family will want to visit Tarradon."

"Why would that be so bad?" For the first time ever, they were butting heads, and he didn't like it. "They are aware of dragons, and trust me they've kept their fair share of secrets and more than just about your kind. Remember, Slater Coghill showed himself, and they didn't tell anyone." At least he didn't think they had.

"That's true." She frowned. "I am sorry for what he did to your brother's mate. He was a rogue working for the Royals. It was why the four sisters had to intervene."

"They were responsible for his disappearance?"

"Yes, they basically sucked him off Earth. I believe my dad told you he's now in jail."

Something was amiss. "Yes, but if this rogue dragon shifter got through your gate, what's to stop others?"

"The Guardians will be more diligent, but there's always a chance that someone with strong dark magic can follow someone who's been given clearance to enter, especially if they can cloak themselves."

"That's scary."

"Do you see why I was hesitant to tell your parents that they could travel back and forth whenever they wanted to?"

He did understand. "Yes. Will you be able to tell if we have a dark lighter hitchhiker?"

"As a Guardian, I would, but other dragons can't."

"Then I guess their visits will need to be highly supervised." In other words, Kaleena and he could escort his family to Tarradon.

She sighed. "I know how important this is to you. How

about this? We visit when we want, but we can't go running around Silver Lake announcing we're there. Everyone in town knows you and will ask questions about your whereabouts."

"I like that compromise. Short visits it is."

CHAPTER SIXTEEN

"It'll be midnight on earth when we arrive, right?" Finn asked.

"Yes." Kaleena still had some trepidation about traveling to Earth, but her father assured her that he would contact Ophelia and have her keep watch. He also agreed to beef up security at the gate so she and Finn would be safe.

Dad also believed that given the situation with Rathan, heading to Earth right now was the smartest move. He understood that being cooped up for days, if not weeks, would drive her—and her dragon—crazy.

Not only that, Finn had grown up being very social, always around people and chatting with them. If he was only with her and their employees, staying indoors all the time could put a strain on their relationship and their animals.

Not to mention when Finn had spoken about returning to Earth, she heard the shimmer of joy in his voice. Underneath it though, she had sensed his pain from being separated from his family. If she ever had to leave Tarradon for good, her ache would be as great. Knowing that, she wondered if she would be able to ask that of him.

Tory met them at the main entrance to the country home and handed Kaleena something. "This is one of my dragon scales. I had a special spell put on it that allows us to communicate since our twin link can't travel between realms."

Once when Kaleena had been in a car accident in Colorado and had injured her shoulder pretty badly, Tory later told her she had no idea that she had been harmed.

They hugged. "You are the best sister in the world."

Her twin placed the leather thong with the attached scale around Kaleena's neck. "This way you'll always have me with you."

Kaleena fingered the gift. "Promise me you will be careful too."

"If you're thinking Rathan will mistake me for you, he won't," Tory said. "We not only have different hair, our colored scales aren't the same."

"It's not that. They might kidnap you in order to lure me out into the open, or try to use your magic for their own purposes." Doubt about leaving arose, but one glance at Finn convinced her she needed to take the chance.

Tory rubbed her arm. "I'll be careful. Now go and have fun, but hurry back. Always keep the scale with you so I can reach you."

"I will. We won't stay long as I need this witch hunt to end once and for all."

"Amen."

After a final hug, Kaleena led Finn outside. With their bags slung over their shoulders, she walked with him about fifty feet from the main entry door before stopping. Sticking her hand in her pocket, she withdrew one of her dragon scales.

"What's that for?" Finn asked. "I don't see any doors that need to be opened."

"A portal is a door. Watch..."

Kaleena set down her bag and then drew her arm in a large circle three times to the right and twice to the left. When the air wavered, she swiped the scale across the opening until one spot glowed, and a portal appeared. She then replaced her precious scale back into her pocket and picked up her bag. "Ready?"

"Yes, but when I came here, Ophelia didn't do that. Hell, she left right before the portal appeared."

"That's because my father created the portal from this side. Come on. It only stays open until we are on the other side and then it closes so no one can find it and use it."

She held out her hand, and Finn clasped it. From his strong grip, he was worried something might go wrong, and she couldn't blame him. Kaleena had been a bit afraid the first few times she traveled too.

"I want you to picture your house since we need a precise destination," she told him.

He closed his eyes. "My house is now clearly in my mind."

Special portals, like this one, needed extra care. Finn had drawn a map for her, but that didn't guarantee pinpoint accuracy.

"Here goes," she said. A second after they stepped into

the portal, they landed in the middle of a street. "Damn. Something went wrong." Maybe she hadn't pictured the location clearly enough. Kaleena glanced around. "I hope no one saw us."

"I doubt it. The lights are off in the nearby homes." He pointed to a cute white house. "That's my place, and my car is thankfully still parked in the driveway."

His house was small but befitted the understated Finn. He lifted her up and spun her around. While she was thrilled he was so happy, she'd feel better if they didn't continue to stand in the street. "We need to get out of here. A car might come, and that could be disastrous."

"Fine. Come on."

As Kaleena followed, she rubbed her arms, forgetting what winter was like on Earth. "Brrr, it's cold."

"You'll be warm once we're inside." Finn said it with so much cheer that nothing seemed to dampen his spirits. He wrapped an arm around her shoulders and pulled her close. Once he reached the front stoop, he set down his duffel bag, fished out his key, and opened the door. Finn then guided her inside and flipped on the lights. "Ugh. It seems musty in here." He flipped a switch and something clicked on. "The heat will take the chill out of the air in a moment."

She set down her bag and wrapped her arms around his neck. "You know what? I don't mind what it smells like because now I'm safe, and I'm with you. What more could a girl ask for?"

He grinned. "Okay, safe girl, let me show you to my bedroom." He shucked off his jacket, tossed it onto the back of the sofa, and she followed suit.

"I can't wait, and that's the dragon's truth."

All through dinner, she'd wanted to jump his bones, but when he brought up the idea of coming to Earth, she hadn't wanted to disappoint him and delay their departure another day. Now that they'd arrived, she couldn't wait to indulge in the fantasy of loving him. It had been too long since they'd make love.

He clicked on the bedroom light. The bed wasn't made and several pairs of clothes were strewn on top. "Sorry. I changed my mind about ten times about what to take with me."

"That doesn't sound like you."

"Truth is, a few minutes before midnight, I'd given up that Ophelia would even show, so I started to unpack."

Kaleena moved closer and ran a finger over his lips. Just touching him set her body on fire. "Remind me to thank Ophelia for sending you to me."

Being with Finn brought her so much joy she could almost forget what had caused him to come to Tarradon in the first place. So much love was pouring through her that she reached out and tickled him.

His eyes went wide, and he grabbed her wrists. "Oh, no you don't."

"You're ticklish." She hadn't known.

"Am not."

Men. Possibly to prove that he was at full strength, he lifted her over his shoulder, stepped two feet to the bed, and tossed her down. Never had anyone done something like that in her life. Surprise shook her first and then laughter. Finn's fun side was finally emerging, and she couldn't wait to learn more about him. Coming to Earth had been the best decision she'd made in a long time.

He stood at the edge of the queen-sized bed and looked down at her before slowly crawling on top of the bed. He raked his gaze up her body, looking like a man on a mission. Never taking his eyes off her, he straddled her, and then shoved his excess clothes on the floor. Not saying a word, he reached behind him and unlaced his boots before kicking them off. As if he wanted to torment her, he lifted his heavy pullover sweater over his head and tossed it aside too.

Kaleena pushed up on her elbows. "Let me unbutton your shirt."

His eyes were already glowing amber, and sparks were flying everywhere. "How fast can you do it?"

"Very fast," she said though she had no intention of moving quickly. Tonight was all about seduction—and mating. "You do believe we are really mates, right?" she asked, wanting to make sure Finn truly was on board. This was a no-going-back event.

Finn dropped onto his hands and dipped his head, bringing his lips close to her ear. "With my whole heart," he whispered.

Her body glowed and pulsed at his romantic words. "Me too." There was one sticking point left to discuss. "I know on Earth that when a bear and wolf mate, they retain their own form, but dragons are full of magic. When I mate with you, you will become a dragon too."

He sat back on his heels. "For real?" The excitement in his voice thrilled her.

"Yes, for real, and I will become a wolf."

He narrowed his eyes. "Does that mean you won't be a dragon anymore?"

She loved his innocence. "No, silly. We each will become both animals. We can use that to our advantage." Especially in battle.

"Wow, I can't even wrap my head around becoming a dragon let alone being able to fly."

She smiled and kissed him. "We will talk about it later. Now where was I, huh?"

He grinned then nipped her bottom lip. "I believe you were supposed to be removing my clothes."

Kaleena tugged the bottom part of his shirt out of his pants and eased the first button through the hole. After she finished undoing a few more, his abs peeked through, and she licked her lips. "Oh yes, I remember now." Kaleena winked, scooted out from under him, and then knelt to make the chore easier.

After she undid another button, she snatched a kiss. Finn reached under her arms and swiftly undid her jeans. With a little juggling, he managed to get her out of her pants and panties, and then placed her back on the bed. The clothes soon joined his on the floor.

With no warning, he slipped a finger inside her, and the intensity with which the burgeoning lust grew inside her was huge. His touch had ignited a passion so deep, that she glowed from the inside out, and she was forced to suck in a breath.

His eyes widened. "I love when you change color."

"You have no room to talk." He was pulsing blue himself.

"Very true." He cupped her face. "You know what I

love about you?"

"What?"

"How your eyes change from really dark blue to purple when you get excited."

She'd hoped for something else. "I hate to break it to you, but every female dragon's eyes turn purple when excited, and the men's eyes turn teal. Your amber eyes are so much better."

"They're only amber when I'm with you."

"Then you must be ready now."

Finn dragged his hands down her shoulders, and then slid them inward to cup her waist. "Oh, Kaleena, I want you more than you can imagine."

Her need was just as great. "Maybe we should get down to business then, huh?"

As if a shotgun went off signaling the start of a race, they ripped off the rest of their clothes and shoved them aside. Once naked, Finn dropped down on top of her, and the kisses that followed were strong, eager, and so very desperate. Their tongues darted in and out then swirled around each other, tasting, loving, and tempting. When Kaleena dragged her hands down his back, she was thrilled that Finn was whole again. Once they mated, he would never be vulnerable to the dragons in Tarradon again.

Needing more of him, she lifted her hips and rubbed against his hard cock. Finn moaned then broke the kiss. "I can't get enough of you, Kaleena. You are the air I need to breathe. You are my heart and my soul."

Thank you Fate for giving me a romantic! "You say the sweetest things. And you, Finn McKinnon, are my life."

He grinned then dipped his head and nabbed a nipple.

Sparks crawled up her spine, and as her pink scales showed through her skin, heat suffused her. She arched her back and called out, "Harder."

Finn encircled her other breast and gently pinched the distended tip. Her nails began to grow, and she dug them into his skin, careful not to press too hard. Everything about this man turned her on. When he drew her tits together, scraping his teeth across one nipple and then the other, she thought she'd explode.

Kaleena grabbed his ass and squeezed, enjoying the play of his muscles under her fingertips. Needing him to hurry, she wrapped her legs around his waist and once more ground hard against his erection, her pussy rejoicing at the delicious contact.

Finn lifted his head and smirked at her. "Impatient, baby?"

"Yes. How about popping your clutch so we can head on into high speed?" Kaleena giggled.

"Funny girl." Finn lifted his head. "You're asking for it."

"Yes, I am."

One side of his sensual mouth ticked up into a devilish grin, and he slowly licked his lips. Finn crawled lower, forcing her to drop her feet to the bed. Once he moved between her legs, she planted her heels on his back. Palming her tits, he swiped his tongue across her opening, and shards of pure bliss slid up her spine. His blue sparks shot everywhere, proving she and Finn were meant to be together—forever.

Kaleena pressed her head against the pillow and closed her eyes. After only a few strokes, he was able to take her breath away and transport her to a world of wonder. She dragged her hands over his head, bucked, and lifted her hips as her climax built. It was when he let go of her breast and slipped three fingers inside her, touching on one particularly sensitive spot that the biggest climax of her life rained down on her.

Her yell sounded primal even to her, and for the next few seconds, she floated on a cloud of pure ecstasy.

Finn's breathing, along with the amount of his blue sparks, increased. He then elbowed his way upward until their lips were an inch apart. "You taste exquisite. My wolf is going crazy. I have to have you now. Are you ready?"

"Oh my goddess, yes! I need you so badly Finn, take me now," she panted.

He placed his hard cock against her opening, rubbing her moisture around to lubricate his way. Then without asking again, he drove in hard, and in one thrust, he was thoroughly embedded in her tight sheath. Her pussy enveloped him and clung to his hard cock, forbidding it to leave her body. Stars burst forth in her field of vision, and sound ceased to exist. Kaleena needed him, wanted him, and just plain had to have all of him.

They both moaned as he started to pull back but then he thrust in again. Finn set up a pounding rhythm, and Kaleena pumped her hips to meet each of his thrusts. They kissed, tongues lashing against each other, and their passion unfolded.

Finn then lifted her arms until they were extended above her head. With his body against hers, he hammered in hard, clasping her hands tightly. "Ugh, I just can't get close enough," Finn said. He groaned again as he continued his relentless and delicious torture.

"Please, don't stop." Her body heated with each plunge, and flames licked up her torso, edging her closer to the time when she and Finn would finally become one.

His teeth sharpened, and his facial scruff thickened. His eyes darkened with lust, as he dragged his mouth down to her neck. The anticipation of mating with him made her soar higher than any dragon could fly. This was it—a once in a lifetime commitment.

Her body was slick against his, and she could feel the sweat from his face drip onto her neck with each powerful thrust of his cock. As their passion built, her whole body became as taut as any tightrope that was about to snap.

"Oh, Finn. Need. You. So much. Oh! Do something. I can't. Please!" Her voice came out breathless and strained.

"I got you, love. Just hang on, beautiful." His voice was gravelly and deliciously sexy.

Finn swiped his tongue along her shoulder blade then returned to that soft sensitive spot right above her collarbone. She dragged her lips to his neck where her teeth sharpened against his sweat slickened skin. She couldn't help but lap up his salty essence. When he grabbed hold of her hips and plowed into her again, his teeth sunk into her neck.

Bite him, her dragon demanded. Jeez, the divine sensation made her forget to complete their mating cycle.

And bite him she did. As soon as her teeth drove in, his blue glow encompassed them both, and her pink scales turned pure white.

As much as Kaleena had dreamed about this moment, her imagination had failed to do it justice. Transferring her magic and power to him and then receiving his gifts in return went beyond all of her comprehension.

Their fangs withdrew at the same time, and they gently licked each other's mating mark. Kaleena's body went as limp as a noodle—make that a very satisfied and happy limp noodle. Finn seemed to possess a bit more strength than she did for he managed to roll onto his back and take her with him.

How she found the strength to talk, she didn't know. "Holy smokes, that was beyond amazing. Was it everything you thought it would be?" she asked.

"Much more than everything, my beautiful mate," he said as he slid a hand down her back and stroked her butt cheek. "I just want to stay here in our own little bubble forever."

Kaleena snuggled against his chest. "Sounds like a plan."

They lay wrapped in each other's arms, bursting with love. She needed to tell him before he fell asleep. "Finn?"

Kaleena smiled, knowing what she was about to say would wake him up. She lifted her head and stroked her hand through his hair.

"Mmm?" He gave her a little squeeze.

"I love you, my mate."

Finn's eyes came open, and the light amber in them glowed again. "I love you too, beautiful." He smiled and kissed her lightly as he rolled her onto her back. Gently, he slid into her and began a slow rhythm as he made love to her once more.

Just as they reached their peak, Finn nuzzled her neck, and she heard him whisper, "Forever and always, baby."

CHAPTER SEVENTEEN

The sun was out in full, but there was a decided chill to the air. Kaleena pulled the borrowed jacket Finn had lent her around her shoulders. "I bet your folks will be so excited to see you," she said as she slipped into the front seat of his car, happy for the warmth. "I can't wait to meet them."

He rushed around to his side and jumped in. "I'm sure they will be surprised to see me, and they'll probably be a little bit shocked too. They only kind of believed me when I told them my dream was real. Hell, I wasn't sure that I truly believed you existed until after I walked through that portal in Tarradon and met your dad." She reached out and rubbed his leg, igniting his wolf.

"I'm glad you took my plea seriously. Not being able to mate with you would have been worse that spending the rest of my days in that stinking jail."

He looked over at Kaleena and smiled. "You exaggerate, but I'm flattered. It's why I can't wait for my parents to meet you in person and see how amazing you are. I definitely didn't want their last memory of me to be that of a rather eccentric son."

"You're anything but that. You're brave, honorable, and fearless."

Her words had him puffing out his chest a bit. "Trust me, I wasn't any of those when your father picked me up and flew me to the city." He'd been scared shitless and probably less than honorable in some of his thoughts.

She laughed. "The first time flying is always the worst."

"I'll admit having huge claws wrapped around my body was a bit unsettling. I had no idea if he'd drop me or not."

Kaleena grinned. "Poor Finn. I am sorry I wasn't the one to initiate you. A bit of warning for you could have gone a long way."

"True."

The drive to his parents' place took about three minutes.

"You live close to each other," she said.

"We do. Everyone in the complex is a shifter, whether they are bear, wolf, or a lone tiger. It's not required that they stay here, but most do. "

"Interesting. We don't segregate like that on Tarradon." She dropped her head against the seat. "I have to tell you that I'm a bit anxious. What if they don't like me?" She sat back up and twisted toward him.

Finn glanced over at her. "Are you kidding? They'll love you." *Just like I do.*

She drew down the visor mirror. "I should have brought the pink lipstick. This red is kind of garish."

"You are beautiful with or without makeup."

He pulled into his parents' driveway. He then jumped

out of his side and braced against the cold wind. What a change from her realm. Kaleena must feel the cold more than he did since she was used to being warm. He rushed to her side to open her door, but she beat him to it.

She stepped out and rubbed her arms. "Sorry. I didn't know you were going to do that."

This was the first time he'd driven her. "I was raised to be a gentleman."

"And I like you being one." She slipped her arm through his, and with their heads down they scurried to the front. Finn was a little nervous knocking on his parents' door without calling first, but he wanted to explain things to them before they had a chance to contact the others.

When he depressed the handle and pushed, the door opened. They stepped inside, and he welcomed the heat. "Hello? Anyone home?" he called.

A shriek sounded from the kitchen, and a second later his mom rushed out. "Oh, my! It's really you!" Tears streaked down her face as she hugged him. She leaned back and clasped his shoulders. "I can't believe you survived! Your dad will be so happy. When we didn't hear from you right away, we thought the worst."

"I'm sorry. I had no way of calling home. Is he here?"

"Yes." Before she called his name, she looked over at Kaleena. "I'm Celia, by the way. You must be Kaleena." She nodded. "It's no wonder my son was willing to leave his life behind to go after you."

His mate actually blushed. "Thank you. I owe him my life."

Familiar footsteps sounded, and his father shot down the hallway. "Finn? Is that really you?"

"In the flesh." Seeing his parents again made him swell with joy, but it was tinged with sadness knowing their reunion would be short-lived.

His dad hugged him hard. "Missed you, son." He leaned back and studied him. "Let me take a look at you. You don't look any worse for wear."

"I'm good—really good."

He wouldn't tell them that a dragon had almost killed him nor that Kaleena—also a dragon—had slain the beast. They both decided it would be best for now to keep that part a secret. Telling them their own son was now a dragon would be too much to share right now.

Kaleena said that those from Earth couldn't sense a dragon shifter, only other dragon shifters could, so their secret was safe.

"This is Kaleena," Finn said proudly. "My mate."

His dad smiled. "Well, well. So nice to meet you. So what kind of shifter are you exactly? Or are you one?"

Well, shit. Way to go, Dad.

Kaleena looked over at Finn. What the hell. They'd find out sooner or later. "Kaleena is a dragon shifter."

Their eyes widened. "Really? Like the one that nearly killed your brother?"

"Yes, but he was a bad one." Finn stabbed a hand through his hair. "Can we have this conversation later?"

"Oh, sweetie, I'm so sorry. Of course." His mom placed a hand on Finn's shoulder. "Have you two had lunch?"

He was hoping she'd ask. "No, and we'd love some."

Mom looped an arm through his and leaned her head against his shoulder. "I can't tell you how worried I've been about you. I can't believe you really traveled to another realm."

"Let's sit and I'll tell you everything."

They entered the kitchen and sat at the counter while his dad pulled out a carton of milk from the fridge and poured them each a glass.

"If I'd known you were coming," his mom said, "I would have prepared a meal."

"That's why I didn't tell you. I didn't want you to go to any trouble. You know what I would really like though?"

"Name it," she said.

"A PB&J sandwich."

"Really? You come home after being gone four days and that's all you want?" His mom loved to cook.

"I've had a hankering for it ever since I left."

Kaleena ran a hand down his arm. "If I'd known, I would have made you one."

Finn smiled at his mate. "When we return you can fix one for me."

"Deal."

"One peanut butter and jelly sandwich coming up then."

As she busied making them lunch, his dad faced them. "So, Kaleena, tell us about yourself."

Finn had warned her she'd get the third degree, and she said she'd be ready.

"I work for the family's mining business, which is called SinCas. It is owned by both my family, the Sinclairs, and my uncle's family, the Caspians. One digs for gems and the other for metals. I run the Public Relations Department for both."

"Mining? Sounds a lot like the United States."

"It might surprise you to know that much of Tarradon looks like it does here. We have cars, cell phones, and even high-definition televisions."

Actually, what he'd seen of Tarradon didn't look all that much like the States—at least landscape-wise. If he had to pick a country, he'd say it resembled Scotland, with its acres of lush grass and rolling hills. Not to mention the castles.

"That's remarkable," his dad said.

Finn wanted to take the pressure off her. "Kaleena went to school in Colorado to study business."

I thought we weren't going to say that many Tarradons had visited Earth, she telepathed.

Oh fuck, I forgot. Finn jerked at the mental intrusion. Even though he knew that once a shifter mated, the two of them could communicate telepathically, it still surprised him.

She rubbed his arm then squeezed it before letting go.

"I had no idea. So do many Tarradons come here?" he asked.

"Not many," she said.

Good save, he telepathed.

She glanced over at him and smiled.

His mom placed the plates with sandwiches in front of them. "Finn tells me that you were in danger on Tarradon."

This time he'd let her tell them what happened. "Yes, but it's a long story."

"We'd love to hear it."

For the next ten minutes, Kaleena gave a rather sanitized version of how she'd been held captive, and how Finn managed to free her.

His mother's eyes were wide the entire time. She looked over at him. "So a white lighter, as they call their witches, changed your face?" she asked him.

"Yes, but it only lasted a few hours."

"That's remarkable."

"Her family then helped us reach a safe house." He decided not to go into detail about how Nessa swooped in and snatched them off the field behind the castle in the nick of time. "We believe the man who took her is furious that she escaped and will try to retaliate. Instead of holing up until he can figure out what to do, we thought we'd come here."

His father patted him on the back. "Good call. I'm glad you did."

"Me too."

His mom sighed. "Chelsea will be so excited to see you. She's been so out of sorts with you gone."

Finn's heart cracked. He'd worried his twin would be having issues dealing with their broken twin link. He knew he was having a hard time with the separation, but seeing Chelsea would make it even harder to return to Tarradon. "I miss her too."

Mom grabbed her phone. "I'm going to call her now. Maybe she can get off work and stop over. How long are you staying?"

Kaleena grabbed his arm. *"We have to leave tonight,"* she telepathed. *"There's been a development on Tarradon. I just got word."* She rubbed her finger over the necklace her sister had given her.

He'd wondered why she'd suddenly turned quiet. *"What happened?"*

"I don't have any details. Tory just said we need return."

"When? Right now?"

"No, at midnight."

Damn. "I had planned to stay a while, Mom, but it turns out something just happened back in Tarradon, and we have to leave tonight."

"Oh, no," his mom wailed. "Can you stay for dinner at least? You know your brothers will want to see you."

"I'd love to see them too."

When the rest of Finn's family arrived, Kaleena hit it off with all of them, especially Chelsea who was a lot like Finn —warm and friendly. They spent almost two hours chatting and sharing stories, but eventually it was time to leave. His parents and siblings were even better in person than what she'd seen through Finn's eyes growing up.

"It's almost eleven thirty," she telepathed Finn. *"We have to go now."*

"I know."

Finn stood. "I hate to break up this family gathering, but Kaleena and I have to be getting back."

Chelsea clasped his hand. "Kaleena's still in danger there, right?"

"Yes, but there's just been a new development. As much as we had planned on staying a lot longer, we have to straighten this out." He hugged his twin.

"When will you be back?"

Finn dragged a knuckle down her cheek. "As soon as I can, I promise."

"You'd better."

His mother hugged him next. "Is there any way you can communicate with us to let us know you're okay? Tarradon sounds so much like here that I thought maybe there was some kind of device you could use."

He smiled then quickly sobered. "If anything bad happens, I'm sure Ophelia will let you know."

"How can Ophelia find out?" his mother asked, glancing between the two of them. "Does she use some kind of magic?"

Finn smiled. "Yes." He kissed her cheek. "We really need to go. The portal won't stay open for very long."

That wasn't true, but Kaleena didn't want to tell them that she could create the portal at any time. Not only didn't she want to delay any longer, it was safest at midnight and noon when the Guardians would be watching on their end.

After one more round of handshakes and hugs, they finally left. Once they stepped out of the house, the cold air made her shiver. Without speaking, they rushed to his car. They'd spent the entire day and evening with his family and hadn't had the chance to discuss what Tory's message might mean.

Finn started the car and peeled out of there. "Do you know anything else?" he asked.

"Tory didn't say, or maybe she wouldn't say. Nessa caught the man who drugged me. That's all. They think he has information we can use."

He drove too fast down the dark street, but he never

once went off the road. Those who lived on Earth were definitely better drivers than on Tarradon. With the population mostly made up of dragons, the top choice of transportation was flying. Hell, even those who owned cars didn't use them all that much. When they did chance traveling by car, they were often a danger to others.

"I still don't understand the need to rush home," Finn said. "The man who drugged you will be punished, and Rathan will still be at large."

"I know this is hard to believe, but Christian—that's his name—says he wants to make amends."

He glanced over at her. "And you believe him? Most criminals say they are remorseful so you'll go lighter on them."

She dropped back her head. "I know, but he seemed different, almost caring when he carried me out of the bar."

"What happened when you got outside?" Finn asked.

"I passed out. When I awoke, I was in that horrible cell." The image made her groan.

"It's still not going to be safe when you return. It doesn't matter if this guy cops to being the one to have drugged you or not."

"True, and I know I won't be safe until Rathan is put to rest, but I had the sense he was willing to give us information about what my cousin is planning to do next."

"I see."

From his tone, he didn't. Kaleena rubbed his leg. "As wonderful as it was to be with your family, this wave of guilt keeps hitting me. I wasn't born to run away. I need to fight for what is right."

Finn didn't answer. He pulled into his driveway and cut

the engine. "You need to do what you have to, and I won't stand in your way."

She leaned over and kissed his cheek. "I'll make it up to you, I promise."

Finn flashed a sexy grin, and then wagged a finger at her. "You better!" He pushed open the car door. "Come on, we need to gather our things."

They had come to Silver Lake with the understanding that he'd show her his town, and they could have a fun time together, but Tory's urgent call had changed all that. If she ever confronted Rathan again, Kaleena would do her damnedest to make him pay—with his life.

Once they gathered their gear and stepped into his front yard, she removed her magical dragon scale and created the portal.

"Can anyone with one of those scales do that?" he asked, his voice tinged with amazement.

"No. Only the Guardians have the power. Ready?" She held out her hand, and let out a breath when he placed his hand in hers.

They stepped through the swirling circle of air, right into the bedroom of the underground mine.

Kaleena set down her case. "Finn, I really am sorry our trip was cut short. I know how much you wanted to spend time with your family."

He pressed a finger to her lips. "It's okay. I understand it's something you have to do. I've spent my life surrounded by men who possess the same kind of drive."

"You are the best. I love you, my mate. Have I told you that before?"

He chuckled. "Yes, and I love you too, beautiful, but I have no problem hearing it again."

"We can return to Earth just as soon as this mess is cleared up."

He dropped his bag and stepped closer. When he leaned in and kissed her, it was as if the Royals didn't exist and life was blissful.

A second later a knock sounded on the door. "It's Tory —time to find out what's really going on."

CHAPTER EIGHTEEN

"We need to head over to the SinCas building," Tory said.

"Why?"

"Because the rest of the family is gathering there."

Tory offered to drive Finn and Kaleena back into town. Even though Kaleena lived in Edendale, more people seemed to be around than usual. Dragons might need less sleep than humans and other shifters, but from the noise pouring out of the nightclub bars, she questioned if these dragons slept at all.

Once her sister parked at the SinCas facility, they took the elevator to the top floor of the mostly empty building. What sounded like loud drilling vibrated inside the elevator.

Finn grabbed Kaleena by the waist and pulled her close. "What is that?"

She smiled at his protectiveness. "It's just the lab techs at it again. They're experimenting with new ways to separate the rocks. They only do the loud stuff after hours. If you really want to experience demolition techniques, I can take you to our processing facilities near the mine, but you'll be advised to wear ear protection."

Finn's grip lightened. "I'll pass for now."

"Smart."

The elevator reached the top floor, and Tory led them to the end of the hall to one of the large conference rooms. Inside, Nessa was pacing along the back wall, glaring at Christian who was cuffed and seated at the end of the table across from her father.

"What's he doing here?" Kaleena whispered to Tory. Kaleena thought this would be a brainstorming time to discuss what to do with him.

"He wants to help you. Give him a chance."

Her sister had gone soft. "Help? You told me he admitted to drugging me. Help like that I don't need."

"Kaleena, come sit down," her father said, acting as if Christian was the victim.

She and Finn took the seats to the right of her dad, while Tory settled in on the left. Nessa remained standing or rather pacing, looking like a caged animal. Knowing her, she was probably upset that she'd caught Christian prowling around outside.

Kaleena didn't even want to look at the guy, but she did so out of curiosity. Guilt was written all over his face. "Why did you drug me?" she blurted before giving anyone a chance to talk.

"It's like I told her." Christian nodded toward Nessa. "I work for the Royals as one of their lawyers and when—"

"So Rathan put you up to this?" she nearly shouted. Why would Christian admit that? His confession alone was enough to imprison him for life. Nessa moved closer to Christian as if she expected him to bolt, but there was something about the way he held his head high that made Kaleena want to hear him out. "Go on."

"I swear to every goddess in the light realm that I had no idea our government would kidnap you."

"What rock have you been living under? I don't buy that you're that naïve. You're a fucking lawyer." Kaleena's sympathy suddenly shattered.

"I've only worked there for six months. All I do is draft legal documents to people who are in arrears of their taxes. Nothing more. The first time I even stepped foot in the castle was the day I was summoned and told to drug you."

"By Rathan?"

"Yes."

His sincerity was believable, but she wouldn't be tricked a second time. "Why did you agree to the kidnapping?"

He looked her right in the eye. "I agreed to drug you because they threatened to kill my sister, Clarisa, if I didn't."

A woman by the name of Clarisa worked in the accounting department at SinCas. Only now did Kaleena realize she'd never asked him for one piece of vital information. "What is your last name?"

"Milan." He cocked his head as if he was waiting for her to connect the dots.

Well damn. If someone ever threatened Tory, she'd do whatever it took to keep her from being harmed. "Clarisa works here. Didn't you think of that before you carried out their orders?"

"At the time, I had no idea you were a Sinclair."

Kaleena tried to keep a low profile so he might be telling the truth. "Did you ask Rathan why he wanted me drugged?"

"Prince Rathan said you had stolen money from him. Had I known who you were I would have questioned him further. He showed me your picture then told me to slip this drug into your drink. I didn't know it would incapacitate you so quickly. I swear."

Kaleena visited The Wing's Bar on a regular basis, so finding her wouldn't have been hard.

Nessa crossed her arms, a disgusted look on her face.

"Do you believe him?" Kaleena telepathed Finn.

"I don't know what to think. I can't get past the fact that he hurt you."

Nessa moved close and loomed over Christian. "Tell me, why were you really skulking around outside of the SinCas building today?" she asked.

"I wanted to speak with Kaleena. Before I did, you found me and dragged me in here."

"Did you ask for her inside?" Nessa demanded.

"Yes. I went into the jewelry store and pretended to be looking for an engagement ring. I chatted with a woman who told me Kaleena wasn't in the office—that it was her day off. I didn't believe her and feared Rathan might have done more than just talk to her about taxes." He turned to Kaleena. "I know I was the one who set you up, but I can't live with myself knowing what I've done." He lifted his bound hands and then lowered them, probably forgetting he was now the captive. "I'm just relieved you are free."

"So am I, but just so you know the kind of man you've

been working for, Rathan kept me drugged and held me prisoner in a stinking, filthy cell for days. Had it not been for Finn here and my family, I might still be there." She hadn't meant for her words to come out so bitter, but the memory slammed into her hard.

Finn placed a comforting hand on her arm, reminding her she was safe now.

"I'm so sorry," Christian said. "I want to make it up to you. You have to believe me." He glanced between Nessa and her. "If you want, I can go back and leak false information to Prince Rathan if that's what it will take to keep you safe."

The idea intrigued her. The word *safe* bounced in her head, giving her hope. "We'll keep your offer in mind, but let me ask you this—didn't you think we'd prosecute you?" Kaleena asked.

"I don't care what happens to me. I just want my sister protected. I figured if they tried to get me to do their dirty work once, what's to prevent them from trying again? I told Prince Rathan I wanted to quit, but he said I couldn't because I knew too much. My only options were to keep working for him, imprisonment, or death. Jail seemed like the best place to me."

That did suck. Much of what Christian said could be checked out. Kaleena needed time to think about her options. "Nessa, why don't you take him someplace safe?"

Like to their underground holding cell. Thieves were caught periodically trying to sabotage the mines or attempting to rob their jewelry store. They needed someplace to keep them while they decided how to prosecute.

"My pleasure." Nessa grabbed Christian by the arm and

dragged him out of his chair. He was cuffed, so she doubted he'd try to escape. To his credit, he didn't resist.

"What will happen to my sister?" Christian called out as Nessa hauled him to the door. "If Prince Rathan finds out I told you, he might kill Clarisa."

Kaleena glanced at her dad. He nodded. "We'll provide her with protection."

Christian's body sagged. "Thank you."

Once they left, she faced her father and Tory. "What do you both think?"

Her father stroked his chin. "He could be telling the truth."

"He's still guilty of drugging me. You can't forget that."

"That's in the past. We need to worry about the future. What if we can use him to set a trap for Rathan?" her father said.

Her mind spun trying to come up with a scenario that would work. "What are you thinking?"

He looked over at Finn then back at her. "From the way you keep looking over at your young man, together with the slight red mark on his neck, I assume the two of you have mated?"

Heat raced up her face. She was over one hundred years old and shouldn't be embarrassed to admit she'd had wild, passionate sex with Finn, but this was her father. He'd know if she lied however. "Yes. We have mated."

He smiled. "That is wonderful news. Since you just arrived back here from Earth, I'm guessing Finn has not yet taken his maiden voyage as a dragon?"

"No," she said before glancing over at her mate who was focused on her dad.

"Are you aware that new dragon shifters are highly powerful?"

She'd heard that was true, but since none of her dragon friends had mated recently to a non-dragon shifter, she had no data to back that up. Her father most likely did. "I've heard that, but while Finn might have the strength and endurance to fight, I dare say he is untrained," she said.

Finn sat up straighter. "I am a quick study if someone is able to teach me what I need to know."

She rubbed his arm. He was her white knight. "Thank you. Thane can train you. He makes us do drills and take classes on fighting all the time, but the Royals are highly skilled too. While we have more magic on our side, their abilities are considerable."

"What if we fight Rathan together?" Finn asked, sounding excited. "Can the two of us take him down?"

Everyone glanced around. "You would have surprise on your side," Dad said. "Have you tried to shift into your wolf form yet?" he asked her.

"No."

Her father leaned back in his seat. "I'm sure Finn can help you avoid a dragon attack by darting into the woods. It might give you time to regroup."

Finn squeezed her hand. "I'll do whatever I can to help. I can see the advantage of being able to shift from one form to another. If we're near a forest, hiding as a wolf is easy. We'll blend into the background very well. The possibilities are wide open if we can emerge from the dense foliage and shift into our dragon form then take to the air."

She smiled at his level of excitement. Kaleena could almost picture it in her mind. Rathan would come in cloaked, but she'd be able to sense his presence when he drew near. If she and Finn shifted into their wolf form, and cloaked themselves, they could hide. Staying invisible when their signature was small would take less energy than when in their dragon form. Once Rathan showed himself, they would have a moment to form a plan.

Relief poured through her. "I like it. I think it can work. I hate the fact that Rathan assumes he can do what he likes without consequences."

Tory leaned forward on her elbows. "What makes you think Rathan will show up? He sent his minion the last time," her sister said.

That was a problem. "Maybe that's where Christian can come in. We just need to figure out what he should tell Rathan to make him take on the challenge personally."

Her father smiled. "I like the way you think, Kaleena, but you need to be prepared in case he arrives with an army of men."

Well shit. "We'll take our chances. The biggest problem, as I see it, is not being found out before Finn is ready to fight. While it was safe to remain underground at the mine, Finn couldn't train there since he needed to be outside. Rathan's man found me at the country house, so that location is out of the question."

"I agree. You'll need a safe place to hide and not be spotted while flying," her father said, as if reading her mind.

"Have any idea where we can go?" Kaleena asked.

"Yes, but you'll need to leave Avonbelle."

The realm was vast. Rathan and his men wouldn't be

able to canvas everywhere. "Do you have a place in mind?" Her father had extensive contacts.

"I'll give Gregor Kearn a call. He lives in Drifsdown in Grindale province. You'll be safe with him and his Guardians.

That was the next province over, but it was still far away. While each of the four provinces of Tarradon had their own set of Royals, she'd never heard of them interacting or working together.

Kaleena looked over at Finn, worried about the long trip there if they flew. "I like the idea of being safe, but I'm not sure I can train Finn myself. Can you spare Thane for a few days?"

"Have Declan set it up. He runs the show."

Declan might be technically in charge of things, but their father still controlled the roost. Everyone listened to him and to Uncle Laird. Her brother, Thane, was a master strategist and fighting was his specialty. She hoped he would be free to help.

Finn yawned, and only then did Kaleena realize it was past two in the morning.

She pushed back her chair. "I think we're going to hit the hay. Let me know if Gregor Kearn can help out."

Her father reached over and squeezed her hand. "Will do. Sleep tight and we'll be in touch tomorrow."

CHAPTER NINETEEN

When Finn had been almost torn apart by the guard Rathan had sent to take out Kaleena, Declan claimed that Finn's physiology was different from the shifters in their realm. Because her dad claimed Finn would be a strong and powerful dragon, he couldn't wait to test it out.

"Tell me again why we have to drive," he said, failing to tamp down his frustration. He finally had the chance to sprout his wings, so to speak, and now he was stuck in a car for ten hours.

"I couldn't chance that something might happen on the way to Grindale."

"Were you afraid that if I flew alongside you that I might fall out of the sky or something?"

She looked over at him. "No, silly. We could have been spotted. Learning to hold a cloak takes time and training. If any of Rathan's men had seen us, we would have been attacked, and both of us might have been killed."

He reached out and rubbed her leg, trying not to let

that one touch excite him too much. "I never want to put you in danger. I'm sorry."

Keeping her eyes on the road, she reached out and squeezed his hand still on her leg. "Don't be. I'm sure I won't be the best or smartest wolf the first time either. Look, it's a long way to fly, and you're not used to maneuvering in and around the air currents."

That was a nice way of saying he wasn't ready. Finn had let his excitement get the best of him. He pressed on her leg once more and then removed his hand, not needing her to be distracted either. "Do you think Rathan has scouts out looking for you now?"

"I have no doubt of that. Failure is not an option for him. When we last spoke, I could see the greed in his eyes. He'll stop at nothing until I'm captured again or dead."

Finn's gut clenched and his protectiveness flared. "I thought you said that when a Guardian is cloaked, others can't detect him." Whether he would inherit any of her magic was yet to be seen.

"That's true, but it takes energy to stay invisible. And who's to say I'll be in my dragon form when he finds us?" She sighed. "How about we not talk about Rathan for now and enjoy the trip? Just so you know, I don't like being confined anymore than you do."

Damn. He'd been a jerk. Kaleena had mentioned that driving was not her choice of travel. "Again, I'm sorry. I'm a bit uptight about this whole dragon shifting thing."

She flashed him a reassuring smile. "You'll do great."

Easy for her to say. "What if I can't get off the ground?"

She grinned. "You getting up won't be a problem."

Did she have to bring up sex? "Getting it up isn't, but flying might be."

She glanced over at him. "Don't worry. I'll make sure you succeed."

"I appreciate that." He leaned close to her. "You know what my issue is right now?"

Her hands stiffened on the wheel. "What?"

"Sitting next to you, while my wolf—or is it my dragon —wants you so badly." That damn leg rub did him in.

Kaleena grinned. "That so? You should be me. My dragon is going crazy too. I'm surprised she's lasted this long without demanding some kind of release."

He had an idea. "Have we crossed into that other province yet?"

"Yes, why?"

"Because I'd love to find a cozy spot for us to stop and have a little backseat fun without worrying about Rathan's men spotting us."

She laughed. "Oh, Finn McKinnon, you are so good for my soul. I wanted to suggest the same thing, but I worried your mind wouldn't be on making love."

"Are you kidding me? I can barely contain myself." He slowly eased her right hand off the wheel and placed it on his crotch.

"Oh, my. Any dragon shifter would be pleased to call that his own."

He laughed, but quickly sobered when Kaleena made a sharp right turn down a dirt road. She slowed only because four sheep crossed their path. "I wonder where their owner is?" she asked.

"You can always fly overhead and check out the area."

"I could, but see that copse of trees?" She nodded to a spot less than thirty feet off the road.

The large trunk would block anyone's view. "I do. It has many possibilities."

"That's what I was thinking." Kaleena drove onto the grassy area and stopped the car. "Race you."

Feeling as if he were a randy teenager again, he jumped out and sprinted to the shaded area, but Kaleena beat him. "Damn, you're fast," he said.

A little out of breath, she planted her palms on his chest. Without a word, she kissed him, and his wolf lost his inhibitions. Waves of lust slammed into him hard, and it was all he could do not to tear off her clothes and impale her.

Her fingers made fast work of his jeans. She tugged them down halfway before they bunched around his knees, but that didn't stop her from dropping to the ground, grabbing his cock, and then drawing it deep into her mouth.

Finn reached behind him and nearly clawed the tree bark. They might have had sex only this morning, but it felt as if it had been ages. The moment they'd mated, his need for her had grown.

"Easy, there," he panted.

Kaleena totally ignored him, cupping his balls and then tightening her hold. Each lick sent him closer to his climax. When she took him to the back of her throat and swallowed, Finn's eyes rolled upward, and it was all he could do to grip her hair and gently pull her back. Embarrassed that he had just about gone off like it was his first time, he leaned over and lifted her chin. "My turn."

She smiled and stood. Needing to undress, he toed off

his shoes, and then stepped out of his pants and briefs. The ground was riddled with roots, but he didn't care. All he could focus on was Kaleena Sinclair, his mate. "I want you so badly right now. I have to taste you, kiss you, and then drive my cock so deep into you that you can't breathe or think."

"Talk is cheap," she said as she slipped her top over her head and had her bra unhooked in seconds.

The moment he spotted her tits, he forgot everything. Finn lifted her pendulant breasts and marveled at her delicate nipples. His mouth watered as he bent over to taste each one. Kaleena grabbed his shoulders and leaned her head back.

"Yes, Finn. Suck harder."

Wanting to please her, he did just that. Each lick and pull was meant to give her pleasure, but he swore it heightened every one of his senses tenfold. He reached between her legs and cupped her, but her jeans prevented him from doing what he wanted.

Finn stood and fumbled with her pants. She laughed as she swatted his hands away. "Let me."

With a speed that was not to be believed, she removed her shoes, jeans, and panties. Had they been in bed, he would have enjoyed divesting her of them.

The moment she was naked, her scent swirled in the air, and he swore his senses were more intense than ever before. As much as he wanted to lick her and give her multiple climaxes, he couldn't wait. His weakness around her would have to be addressed at some point but not now.

As if she too were overly anxious, she rubbed up

against him, grabbed a handful of his hair, and tugged to lower his mouth to hers.

They opened up at the same time and couldn't taste each other fast enough. When he grabbed her ass and lifted her up, Kaleena obliged by wrapping her legs around his waist. At that moment, the whole world, except for the two of them, ceased to exist. Nothing was going to keep them apart for as long as he lived.

She clutched his shoulders as he leaned back against the tree. Freeing one hand from her hip, he reached between them and slipped his cock straight into her wet opening. He wanted to roar at the glorious bliss pummeling him. Instead of shouting his joy to the world, his blue sparks shot everywhere and slowly merged into one big blue glow. His scales were lit from below, but he couldn't tell their color as her body blocked his view.

"Finn, yes," she yelled as Kaleena pressed her feet against his thighs and rode him hard.

The wind blew her hair over her mouth, and she had to shake her head to move it out of the way. The speed of their pounding increased, and their breaths became harder to come by. With each stroke his climax brimmed.

Help me hang on, he begged his wolf, or maybe it was his dragon he was talking to. He didn't know or care. One of them needed to do something or he would explode too soon.

Kaleena lowered her mouth to his neck, and her sharp teeth pressed against his skin. Her pink scales pulsed inside her body, and heat radiated in every direction to the point where he could no longer control himself.

"Kaleena, come for me." He lowered his mouth to her neck and bit her.

Her teeth sank into him, and as Finn's cock exploded, her inner walls clamped down tight on him. Waves of ecstasy filled him, and he held her close. It was as if they'd mated for the first time over again. The joy was that immense.

When she released her grip, her eyes rolled back in her head. A second later, her body went limp, and her legs slid to the ground, but he held on tight.

She dropped her head on his chest. "That was intense."

"I'd say Earth shattering. Do you think our need will always be like this?" He lifted her chin to look into her beautiful purple eyes.

"Good goddess, if it does, it might kill us, but we will definitely be happy, satisfied, and well loved."

He kissed her and the stirrings began anew. It was only when a tractor rumbled down the dirt road that they broke apart and quickly dressed, smiling and laughing. Finn had never been this giddy in his life, but clearly Kaleena had altered his world.

"I've never done anything like that before," she said as she zipped up her jeans and slipped her feet into her sandals.

Finn had, but he decided to keep that tidbit to himself. For sure it hadn't been nearly as fantastic or life altering. "It was truly something I'll never forget." He nodded to the oncoming vehicle. "We better go before I need a repeat performance."

She grinned. "Let me know if you want to stop again. Maybe we can find some place a little more private."

Kaleena wasn't sure what to expect when she arrived at Gregor Kearn's estate, but it wasn't something this lush and vast.

"It's a castle," Finn said with awe. "I hope he isn't as crooked as the Royals in your province."

She smiled as she headed down the long drive that was bordered by tall shade trees. "Hardly. Gregor and my dad have been friends for years. They met because each of the four provinces has a family of Guardians. According to Dad, Gregor Kearn's family earned their wealth over the centuries. They were farmers first and then bankers."

He shifted in his seat and twisted toward her. "How does one become a Guardian?"

"Fate decides it. The Guardians are given magical powers that enable them to defend against evil."

"The evil being the Royals?"

"I wish the Royals were the only bad ones. We have dark lighters, shifters, and humans who do unspeakable things. It's what makes our job hard. As for the Royals being less than honorable, I know the ones in Avonbelle are. They've been too rich for too long, and they refuse to relinquish any of their power to the common folk. It doesn't seem to matter to them that they had to enslave people to get what they want."

"There are corrupt governments all around our globe, so there is no reason to believe it wouldn't happen here."

As soon as she pulled to a stop, the front door of the massive stone castle opened, and two uniformed men rushed out. Before she could undo her seatbelt, the men opened their car doors.

"Welcome to Kearnwood, Ms. Sinclair. Mr. Kearn is expecting you. Leave your luggage here. We'll take it in."

"Thank you," she said as she held out her hand to allow him to help her out.

Kaleena was used to wealth, but this place surpassed anything her parents owned. Not that they couldn't have afforded something grander than their country home, but her father liked understated estates.

"This is incredible," Finn telepathed.

"I know, and to think we'll be safe here." It was a double win.

"We might not want to leave." He grinned.

Kaleena would never inconvenience Mr. Kearn that much, and even if he wanted them to remain, she needed to get on with her life and enjoy Finn. That wouldn't be possible until the issue with Rathan was resolved.

Once inside, one of his attendants led them down a long corridor that was twenty feet wide and almost thirty feet high. "I've never seen anything like this before," she said checking out some of the gold-framed paintings on the walls. The Palace of Versailles in France and this castle had a lot in common.

"If you think you've never seen anything like this, what about me? I've never seen a castle in America, though we do have a few historic ones. As you've seen, I'm more of a small house type of guy."

That was what she loved about Finn. He seemed happy with his life. "I hope you can enjoy this place then."

"No problem."

At the end of the long corridor, the manservant opened large double doors. "Mr. Kearn is awaiting you."

They stepped inside, and the gentleman behind the desk stood and came around to greet them. He was probably several hundred years old, but he didn't look more than the average fifty-year old human. Given his shoulders were broad and skin taut, he appeared to be in excellent health. Dressed in blue jeans, a white button down shirt, and a black jacket, he looked elegant yet approachable. The dab of gray at his temples gave him an air of sophistication. He looked exactly as her father had described him.

Kaleena held out her hand as she stepped toward him. "Mr. Kearn, thank you for welcoming us."

"Call me Gregor, please." He faced Finn. "And you are the realm's newcomer who saved Kaleena."

"I had a lot of help."

"Come sit and let's discuss your plan for taking down that dastardly villain, Rathan Abercrombie."

CHAPTER TWENTY

Finn was nervous. And well he should be. He'd never flown or transformed into a huge beast before. Hell, he wasn't even sure he had the ability. Shifting into a wolf was easy, but a fifteen-foot tall dragon was something else altogether.

"I take it dragons don't need a white moon in order for their first shift to work?" he asked Kaleena.

They were in the field behind Gregor's castle that was surrounded by dense forest. His wolf would be able to conceal himself quite easily. His dragon? Not so much.

"No," Kaleena said. "I had heard that when a human mates on Earth, he or she can only transform on the white moon. I always wondered why."

He shrugged. "I never asked. I was maybe three the first time I shifted, but I have no idea what the moon was doing at the time."

Kaleena stood in front of him and smiled. She then

placed her hands on his shoulders. "Do you remember what I told you?"

He hoped he did. "Close my eyes and picture a large dark beast with wings. For my first time, I should wave my arms." It seemed corny to him, but what did he know? Many concepts on Tarradon were the same as they were on Earth, but a lot weren't.

"Yes. As soon as you shift, I will too. Once you've transformed, take a few steps and flap your wings hard. You should lift off the ground and be able to fly. Don't go too high at first, until I teach you how to ride the air currents. If you show off, you could lose altitude."

"And crash. I get it." Finn started to unbutton his shirt.

Kaleena held out her hand. "What are you doing?"

"I don't want to ruin my clothes. I don't have many. I dare say changing into something the size of a large tractor would shred these."

She smiled then shook her head. "You're a dragon now, remember? You have magic on your side. The moment you start to shift, the clothes will disappear. When you return to human form, they will be like they were before you shifted."

"I've seen you do it, but I wasn't sure it would work for me."

For the first time today, she appeared uncertain. "I kind of assumed my magic would transfer to you."

"But you can't be sure, can you?"

"No. Okay, get naked. I'll sit back and enjoy the show." She gave him a saucy wink.

Finn whipped off his shirt and shoes, and then unzipped his jeans. From the glow in her glorious purple eyes, she was debating whether to jump his bones now or wait. If they hadn't nearly consumed each other an hour ago, he'd take her right there in the field. "No touching. I have to learn how to fly first."

She grinned then turned her back. "I'll be good."

Most likely her dragon was trying to convince her to enjoy the moment once more, but Kaleena was working hard to stay focused. Finn undressed then stepped away from his pile of clothes. "I'm closing my eyes now."

Blanking his mind to her delicious scent, he concentrated on the sweet smell of grass and the pleasant scent of frenlan, which smelled suspiciously like pine to him. He recalled what Jamison Sinclair looked like the first time he appeared in his dragon form, and Finn urged his body to take that shape.

Just like shifting into his wolf, his bones began to crack. For a moment, Finn thought his wolf would appear. Oh, shit. He'd forgotten to flap his arms. Simulating the movement of wings, he raised then lowered them. His shoulders pulled outward, signaling the change, causing adrenaline to charge through every vein. His head filled with visions of flight, and then his toes elongated, his ears drew downward rather painfully, and his arms stretched outward. When his backbone expanded, it was as if he was bursting apart at the seams. The pain was mixed with wonder at his success.

"Open your eyes," Kaleena called, sounding far away.

Inhaling, he did. Kaleena appeared quite small in front of him. Finn lifted his arms, or rather his wings, stunned by their large size and how light they felt.

"I did it," he telepathed. He wondered if she could feel the awe and excitement coursing through him.

She grinned. "You did. And what a glorious dragon you are." She stepped closer and ran her hand down his chest. "You have dark maroon scales interspersed with the black ones. For a moment, I was worried they'd be pink."

"I guess I have to thank Fate for that," he telepathed.

"You do."

A moment later, Kaleena was facing him, snout to snout. There were no words to describe the sense of power overwhelming him. Shifting into a wolf gave him a feeling of fearlessness, but his dragon form was different. Dare he say better?

His wolf snarled. *You can't run in the forest as a dragon. Remember that.*

His animal was right, though how he'd be able to talk to both his wolf and dragon at the same time, he had no idea. His wolf already tried to control him, the horny bastard. Heaven help him if there were two beasts demanding action. Finn might never have a say in anything again.

"How do you like it?"

She probably could tell what he was feeling, but in case she couldn't, he wasn't about to say that sex was on his mind. As much as he wanted to devour her again, he had to learn to fly first. *"Just trying to take this all in. It's quite marvelous."*

A wave of hope radiated off her, giving him the boost he needed to do this.

"Ready?" she telepathed.

"Maybe."

"Come on. It's easy."

"Easy for you."

Kaleena flapped her wings once and rose thirty feet in

the air. Wow. Even though he didn't like heights unless he was in an airplane or firmly holding onto a rail, he followed her lead. The powerful push surprised and delighted him as Finn rose to her height. Her eyes glistened, and his dragon seemed to think of nothing but making love to her. That momentary lack of concentration caused him to plummet back to the ground and land on his butt.

He could hear Kaleena laughing in his head. *"It wasn't funny,"* he telepathed looking up at her.

"Oh, Finn, you are my hero."

"Don't mock me." He rose to his feet—or rather to his claws that were at least four feet long. They were thick and strong enough to carry a big load.

It seemed that Kaleena didn't need to flap her wings very often in order to stay aloft. He wanted to try again. Stretching out his impressively long wings, he looked upward and flapped. This time, he seemed to rise much faster. He passed Kaleena and kept going.

Only when he looked down did he realize that if he fell, he might not survive the impact. Flying parallel to the ground seemed his best option. As soon as he leveled out, he beat his wings faster and faster. Wind rushed past his face and the exhilaration of actually flying was like nothing he'd ever experienced. The air was much colder up there, but oh so pure.

It was only when he glanced down again that he forced himself to slow. Holy crap. The castle was miles behind him, and he was now over water. The landing might be softer, but then he might drown. He needed to ask Kaleena about a dragon's affinity for swimming.

A blur swooped in front of him. Startled, he brought

his wings into protective mode. Big mistake. Down he went, until he remembered he could fly. Waving his wings once more, he changed his trajectory from down to up. Once he regained some loft, he spotted streaks of black and pink once more. Never in his wildest dreams did he believe an animal could move that fast.

She did a loop in the air, impressing the hell out of him.

"Show off," he telepathed.

"I just wanted to show you what you're capable of. Try it."

It was scary enough to be in the air like this, but to fly upside down would petrify him. Even though Kaleena didn't transmit any words, her aura of encouragement reached him.

"Okay, here goes." Just in case swimming wasn't one of his new talents, he charged over the land once more and flapped furiously to gain momentum. Lifting one wing, he tilted into a hard bank. That wasn't so difficult. Drawing the other wing back while he swung his top wing forward, he flipped over.

"Whoa."

"You got this. Now repeat those same moves and right yourself."

With Kaleena's continued encouragement, he flipped over. It might not have been a graceful loop, but at least he hadn't crashed and burned. The next time he needed it to be smoother. Kaleena appeared next to him.

"I want to try that again," he telepathed.

"Then do what I do."

She moved in front of him. When she drove upward, he followed. *"The air current changed,"* he telepathed. That might have been obvious to her, but not to him.

"Yes. You need that to make the loop even."

She dipped her wing, and Finn did the same. She remained sideways for a lot longer than he had, but that was probably what made her look as if she were gliding instead of flying. After a few seconds, she flipped upside down, headed east for another few beats, and then righted herself. While Finn wobbled a little, the move was much more comfortable.

"This dragon thing isn't so hard after all," he announced.

A second after that arrogant announcement, Kaleena bashed into his wing and sent him spiraling downward once more. Holy hell. He'd watched enough biplanes do their acrobatic maneuvers to know how they managed to get out of a spin. He lifted his head and forced his wings outward to catch a draft. His near death dive slowed.

Kaleena appeared beneath him as if to catch him should he fall, but Finn couldn't let that happen. Fighting against the wind and gravity, he fought to level out. Too close to the ground, he succeeded.

"Nicely done," she telepathed. *"Ready to go back?"*

As much as he wanted to play for a few more hours, it might help if he listened to some pointers first. *"Lead the way."*

The trip back to the field behind the castle only took a few minutes. In that time, Finn studied the terrain, noting where he could land and hide if need be. Kaleena landed with grace, and he tried to do the same. Finn reached the ground shortly after her, but with more force than he would have liked.

She shifted and he followed suit. Kaleena ran up to him and jumped into his arms. "You were right to undress first.

Now you're naked—just the way I like you." She wrapped her arms around his neck and her legs around his hips. Divine pleasure filled him.

"You're dressed, which is wrong on so many levels," Finn said.

Before she could answer, a squawk sounded overhead, and he glanced upward. Holding Kaleena tight, he started to drag her toward the woods for safety.

"It's one of Gregor's men," she said.

Finn relaxed his grip. "How can you tell?"

"His men are mostly green interspersed with different colors. Why we are black with colors, I don't know. It's just the way it is."

"Are all dragons in this province green?"

"Not all. I know it's confusing. We've intermingled for years, so we have many combinations. There is one constant. If you see an all black dragon, watch out. Those are most likely evil. It means they believed they were too good to mate with a white lighter, human, or other shifter." She dragged a hand down his naked chest. "Gregor knows that Rathan might come after us, so he's having his men make periodic sweeps of the area."

Finn was impressed with her knowledge. "Is that what you and your family would have done if someone from here had sought refuge in Avonbelle? Do sweeps to look out for the evil ones?"

"Yes."

"Nice." Not that he cared if anyone saw him naked, but it might make Kaleena uneasy the next time she ran into one of Gregor's men. "Do you want to try shifting into a wolf?"

She grinned and his inner animal went wild. "I'd love that."

"I'm going to test your theory about whether I can keep my clothes intact. I'll put on my briefs and then shift. I'll just go commando if they gets ruined." Finn winked at her. If he were ever back home and his clothes remained intact after a shift, there would be no end to the questions about how he'd managed that feat.

"So do I just think of a wolf, and poof, I'll be one?" she asked.

"That's hard to say. I learned at such a young age I've never had to teach anyone." He recalled what his oldest brother had told his mate the first time she attempted to shift. "How about this. Think of yourself as being one with a wolf. Once that image runs through your mind, start running and hopefully the rest will follow."

To give her visual, he shifted and then faced her.

Her eyes brightened. "You're beautiful," Kaleena said as she moved closer.

"I am not beautiful. I am a strong beast that can rip out a person's throat," he telepathed.

"You're still beautiful, and just so you know you can rip out someone's throat as a dragon too, but if you want to do real harm, take out their heart."

He loved her sense of humor. *"Got it. Now stop stalling."*

Finn turned around and trotted toward the forest, hoping she'd follow. Not wanting to make her feel self-conscious, he didn't look back, but the sudden intake of breath implied she'd started to shift.

A moment later a gorgeous black animal with streaks of dark mahogany came up alongside him. She nudged him

then took off. Finn smiled. His woman would always challenge him. Putting on his afterburners, he raced after her.
As if she were born to be a wolf, she charged into the
forest and hid behind a tree.

Because they were mates, along with the fact he could
hear her breathing, he was able to find her right away. The
energy between them was growing to the point where Finn
could no longer keep from ravishing her.

One second he was a wolf and the next a human. It
took Kaleena a moment to figure out how to change back,
but when she did, the sight was worth it. Her hair was a bit
tangled, and her clothes askew, but she took his breath
away.

She tugged at the waistband of his underwear. "See?
They stayed on."

"Well, I'll be damned."

With a quick yank he tossed them off. "Now it's your
turn. No one can see us in the dense foliage."

"Oh, Finn McKinnon. How have I lived this long
without you?"

CHAPTER TWENTY-ONE

"I know it's not the same as being outside in the field, but watch as Kaleena and I demonstrate a simple attack move," Thane said.

The three of them were in a large room in the basement of Gregor's castle, and Finn was anxious to learn how to fight. He was very thankful Kaleena's brother had been able to fly out and help him.

"I'll use this whip to simulate my tail," Thane said. "It can be one of your most powerful tools. Shooting fire at a dragon might make you look like a bad ass, but our scales are fairly heat resistant, so don't waste your breath."

Finn smiled. "No pun intended."

Thane laughed. "Naturally, your end goal is to stab a claw into the dragon's chest right about here." He tapped a spot near the center of his chest, slightly above the heart. "Dig the claw in and the end will puncture the organ. That is the only way to kill one."

"How do I get that close?" Finn asked. "And if I do, what's to prevent him from doing the same to me?"

Kaleena slipped the whip from her brother's hands. "Like this." In a second, she had the ends wrapped around her brother's wrists. "No claws? No killing."

"I see. Easier said than done I'd imagine."

Thane unwrapped the leather from his bound wrists. "Surprise is the key. I dare say if the two of you attacked Rathan, one can distract him from above while the other can fly in from below to deliver the fatal blow."

"Given my inexperience, I might have to opt for the top spot."

Kaleena smiled. "I'd be happy to dig out Rathan's heart, but you need to be prepared for fights in the future, and Thane here is the best trainer in the realm."

"She exaggerates." Her brother turned to Kaleena. "You might consider taking him ocean diving too. It's one more skill that could come in handy." Thane turned back to Finn again. "It could even save your life someday."

That sounded intriguing. "Dragons can swim?" They were such bulky creatures.

"They love to swim. While we keep our wings tucked into our sides, our tail is a powerful propeller. Kind of like how whales swim."

That made sense. "How long can you hold your breath underwater?" He loved to swim, but only on top of the surface.

"Three to four minutes maybe, but like human skin divers, with practice you can stay down longer. I believe your Earth record is about twenty minutes."

Finn whistled. "I'm impressed." Not only with the record but with the fact Thane knew that tidbit.

"Diving for us is mostly used as an evasive maneuver. We're near the coast here, so it might come in handy."

"I'm up for it," Finn said.

Thane pointed to his shoulder cap. "If I didn't mention it, a dragon's wing is a very vulnerable spot. Rip it or break it and a dragon will lose the ability to fly well."

He'd seen one of Rathan's men harm Kaleena's wing, and she'd been incapacitated for some time. It was why she'd needed to finish the job on the ground. "Got it."

"Ready for some real life fighting outside?" Thane asked.

"Absolutely."

Kaleena remained in her human form and watched Thane put Finn through some dragon drills. On the way over to Grindale province, Thane said he'd not seen any other Royals. For the time being, they'd be safe.

She leaned back on her elbows in the open field, admiring her mate's grace. Sure, he'd stumbled through a few exercises, but he was an incredibly quick learner. And strong! Oh, my. Her father had been right when he claimed that newly formed dragons were highly powerful.

Twice, Thane had come after Finn with what she thought was a bit too much intensity, yet Finn had been able to dodge his attacks by performing a loop with pinpoint perfection. As much as she wanted to join him in the air and have her and Finn tag-team her brother, this was Finn's time.

The blue sky was dotted with white puffy clouds and the air was pure and balmy. She closed her eyes for a moment and tilted her face to the sun. Kaleena hadn't been this relaxed in a while. A loud roar, together with a deep pain stabbing her chest, jarred her out of her reverie. She jumped to her feet. Finn was hurt.

He fluttered his wings and nosedived toward the ground. *"Keep your head up and whip your tail back and forth to give you some loft,"* she telepathed. Her brother would pay for this.

Thane flew underneath Finn as if to stop his free fall, but instead he flipped onto his back, reached out with his claws, and grabbed Finn by the chest. Fire flew everywhere, nearly encapsulating her brother.

"Stop it, Finn."

He was scared and in pain, but her brother must have been trying to teach him a lesson. If Thane wanted Finn dead, he'd be dead. Thane flipped them over and pushed upward, carrying Finn with him. A minute later he let go and motioned for them to land.

Once safely on the ground, they shifted into their human form. Kaleena ran over to them. She didn't know who to go after first. As much as she wanted to comfort Finn, she wanted to give a tongue lashing to Thane.

Her brother held up his hands. "It was for his own good."

Was he kidding? "It's his first day!"

"That's true, but Finn is more advanced than some dragons I've been training for a while. He has such raw talent that it scares even me. But Finn's careless. He doesn't know how to use his power."

Finn rose to his feet, and rubbed his shoulder and chest, both of which were probably sore. He came over to Thane and stuck out his hand. "Thanks for the lesson. I kind of thought I was invincible for a few minutes."

Thane smiled. "You have a lot of potential, but you need to learn when to conserve your energy and when to attack."

Okay, she must have had her eyes closed when something happened. If those two were fine with the outcome, she wouldn't complain. "So are you guys done for the day?" she asked her brother.

"I think Finn could use a nice refreshing swim. If Rathan finds you here, the water might be a good place of safety." He turned to Finn. "Remember that while dragons enjoy the water, it's not a place to fight. Our wings enable us to float on the surface, but underneath they can weigh us down. I'd feel better if you had some experience there."

"I appreciate it. It's the same for my wolf. While we can swim, I'd rather be in my human form."

Thane patted him on the back. "Good luck, and listen to Kaleena. She's been trained by the best."

She laughed. "Are you heading back to Edendale now?"

"Yes, but I can return if you need me. Finn has the skills. He just needs to practice."

Kaleena hoped time was on their side. As soon as her brother took off, she hugged Finn. "I was so worried about you." She ran a hand down his chest. "Did Thane stab you with his claw?"

He cupped her hand in his. "Just a little poke and I

deserved it. I was goofing around, and he wanted to show me that losing concentration for even a minute can be deadly."

"I felt your pain, so don't do that to me again."

Finn leaned over, and when he kissed her, his air battle was nearly forgotten. As much as she wanted a repeat performance of their amazing adventure in the woods, Thane was right. Finn needed to learn to maneuver in water.

She stepped back. "How about a quick swim? Afterwards, maybe I can show you a very private spot I learned about."

"Oh yeah?"

"One of the guards told me of a waterfall hidden in the forest near a certain cove."

He grinned. "Now you're speaking my language."

They both shifted into their dragon form and took off side by side. His speed and agility looked as if Finn had been flying for years instead of only three days. As they headed west, Finn would occasionally dip toward a line of trees or check out a rock cropping, but he never lingered.

"The landscape is beautiful and unique. I love the deep purple rock formations," he telepathed.

"They are different from anything I've seen on Earth, though they kind of remind me of your Grand Canyon."

"I can see the resemblance."

Wanting to give Finn time to figure things out, Kaleena remained quiet though vigilant throughout the flight. While Gregor had his men patrolling, she wouldn't put it past Rathan to send some scouts into each of the other three provinces. Even though the chances of the Royal

Guards spotting them were slim, she wouldn't let down her guard.

Thankfully, Rathan had no idea that Finn was a dragon. Even if he saw him, Finn's markings would be unidentifiable. If he spotted the two of them together, Rathan might assume the pair was someone else.

After a wonderful but too short flight the ocean came into view. The ports were busy with fishing as well as recreational boats, and she wouldn't be surprised to learn that one or more belonged to their host. Kaleena veered to the right and Finn followed. When she came to a more secluded and rugged coastline she slowed.

"The key to diving into the water is to know how high you can be and not break your neck," she mentally told me. *"Watch me first. Just before you enter the water, you must bring in your wings."*

"Can you go in claws first?"

"You can, but it's harder to keep your wings from spreading out. You won't go as deep either. Ready?"

"Yes."

Finn circled while she dove. Close to the surface, she spread her wings wide to slow down, and then folded them into her body as tightly as possible. Taking a deep breath, she entered the water and swept her tail back and forth to push deeper. The fish scattered as she neared the bottom.

Waves from a splash above disturbed the sand below, and Kaleena soared upward to meet Finn.

"Slow down your tail movement or you'll tire too fast," she telepathed.

Finn followed her instructions. As soon as he decreased his speed, his body seemed to relax. Thirty seconds later, he rose to the surface. Because he didn't open his wings to float, he descended once more.

Instead of telling him what to do, she surfaced and showed him. Finn shot up out of the water fifteen seconds later and landed next to her, creating a big wave.

"You're a goof," she mentally said, laughing in her head.

"Just testing to see what my limits are." With that he lifted one wing and then the other as if he thought he could swim. He soon figured out that wasn't going to work. *"How do you manage to get around in the water?"*

"Only by swimming underwater. Come on, let's head to the shore."

Kaleena dove down ten feet and whipped her tail to propel her forward. She hoped Finn didn't decide to fly to the shore. Wet wings were heavy which would make the journey a difficult one.

When they reached the gravelly ground, she spread her wings to dry them, much like the cormorant birds did on Earth. Finn did the same. The clear sky and warm air had them dry in a matter of minutes.

"Ready to head over to the waterfall?"

"Would it be easier in our wolf forms?" he telepathed.

"First we'll fly, and then we'll run." Kaleena had forgotten about her increased powers until now and it almost made her giddy.

The two of them left on their journey. Having this uninterrupted time together where the evil of the world seemed far away was a precious gift, and Kaleena planned to enjoy it to the fullest.

They flew over the steep cliffs, and when they reached the forested area, she motioned for them to land and shift.

It was Finn who went straight from dragon to wolf without going through the human state. Never in her wildest dreams did she think that was possible. Concentrating on her wolf form, she shifted and landed on all fours.

"I love it," she telepathed. *"It will shorten our trek by a half hour at least. Follow me."*

Kaleena took off, enjoying the view from being this low to the ground. The occasional vast field of ferns took on a new meaning, and she spotted several squirrels and birds foraging for food, but the slithering snake had her moving a little faster. While he was no challenge to a dragon, shifting with all of these close packed trees would not be wise. It was one reason why she wanted to come here. They'd be safe from the enemy.

While Kaleena was fast, Finn might have been faster, and he kept up without breathing hard. Kearn's guard told her that if she kept to the path, she'd hear the noise of the falls and be able to locate them.

It was Finn who howled first. *"I hear the water and can smell it."*

Without another word, he moved in front of her and charged down the path, cutting through the forest, lithely jumping over a log and dashing in between trees. Seeing him in his wolf form thrilled her. He had mostly dark brown fur with a sprinkling of gray around his face. His shoulders were wider than hers and his legs longer.

After a fun chase, they made it to the falls where Finn immediately transformed into his glorious human form and Kaleena followed. He spun to face her. "It's almost like in the dream!"

She thought so too. "But I've never been here before. The water is as crystal clear as the one I'd conjured up."

Finn grinned. "I can't wait." He kicked off his shoes and unbuttoned his shirt. "I can see there are some advantages to being naked after a shift."

She laughed. "Do you always have sex on your mind?" *As if I don't? I wouldn't mind him naked all the time.*

"I heard that," he said as he finished undressing. "Need help?"

"I'm good." Kaleena stripped in record time. "Race you to the water."

There was something about Finn that made her want to challenge him.

He took off and dove into the pool of water, looking like a professional diver. She jumped in. Strong hands grabbed her waist and dragged her to the surface.

"I love you, Kaleena Sinclair."

Her heart soared at hearing the words. "I love you more."

He moved closer. "Is that how we'll always be? One wonderful challenge after another?"

She couldn't quite tell whether that bothered him or not. "Only if you're okay with it."

He tapped her nose. "It's one of the many things I adore about you. You're fearless, kind, passionate, and sexy as hell."

"How about showing me then?"

Finn glanced over to the waterfall. "You're on."

CHAPTER TWENTY-TWO

Finn still couldn't believe how his life had turned around in such a short period of time. Not only did he have a kick ass woman that he loved, he could now fly.

Because Finn swam in high school, he had no problem beating her to the falls. A quick duck and he was on the other side with the cave wall to his back. He hopped up onto a ledge that was maybe four feet deep and ten feet long. The water level only came partway up the front of the ledge so where he sat was dry. Kaleena surfaced two seconds later, coming up directly between his legs. She smiled.

"This is better than anything I could dream up."

"Now when we dream-walk, we can come back here together." Finn bent over and kissed Kaleena so passionately he almost toppled off the ledge. Their tongues entwined as if they were each trying to draw in as much solace and love as possible from their mate. They'd experienced something amazing in shifting into each other's animals, and now they could revel in the comfort of each other's arms.

As they pulled apart, Kaleena panted. She leaned forward and wrapped her arms around his waist. Holding onto the spot right above his ass, her mouth landed directly in front of his cock.

Cocooned in their own world, Finn wanted to forget about Prince Rathan and make sweet love to his mate. He didn't know whether it was his wolf clawing for release or his dragon, but if he didn't have Kaleena soon, no telling what his body might do.

Finn watched as she ran her tongue from the base of his cock to the tip and around the crown.

"It's no wonder I'm so desperate to have you when you do that," he said, looking down at her as she continued to lave his dick in a show of love. Finn knew why; Kaleena Sinclair was his mate and the woman he loved.

She tilted her head. "It's because I'm sexy, precocious, tempting, smart, and talented."

Then Kaleena showed him just how talented she was when she engulfed his cock into her hot mouth. When the tip hit the back of her throat, she swallowed.

He gripped his hands on either side of her head and groaned. "That description nails it, baby."

Needing to taste her, Finn grabbed Kaleena under her arms and lifted her up next to him. He slid off the ledge into the water and then spread her legs wide. After easing open her folds, he leaned close and inhaled. Between the fresh aroma of the river and her unique womanly scent, Finn's body went crazy. His animals seemed to be arguing with each other, trying to decide whether to shift into a wolf or a dragon. *Dear god, help me!*

Hoping to calm his libido, Finn swiped his tongue across her slit and drank in her essence. Too bad that only made it worse. When Kaleena wiggled, he was hard pressed not to take her right away, but he wanted to bring her some relief first.

He cupped her ass and squeezed her muscled rear before delving his tongue into her welcoming pussy. She moaned and tightened her hold on his hair. Believing she was close to a climax, he released one cheek and delved two fingers into her.

"Oh, Finn." Kaleena arched her back, and then placed her feet on his shoulders as she called out his name over and over again.

As her body finally sagged from her climax, Finn hopped back up onto the ledge. He maneuvered Kaleena to her hands and knees and then moved behind her. Placing a palm lightly on her back, she rested on her elbows, leaving her luscious ass high in the air. Oh, sweet hell. He begged his animals to slow down.

Finn reached underneath and cupped her breasts, rubbing and tweaking her hard nipples, but their slickness incited a fever inside of him. His cock hardened painfully in desperate need of release.

Kaleena reached between her legs to give his dick a tug, and her strong grasp nearly made him come.

"I need you, Kaleena. Now."

If he could feel the need rolling off of her, surely she could sense he was close to exploding too. She mercifully let go, allowing him to place his hard shaft against her greedy opening.

Before he could ease into her, Kaleena drove her hips back, burying him right to the hilt, setting off a series of explosions that rippled up his spine. It was almost as if he were flying once more. Finn rolled her nipples between his fingers, and then lowered his hand to between her legs to press on her clit to give her the needed pressure.

"More," she panted.

"More what?" he telepathed.

"More of everything. I need you to consume me."

He was happy to oblige. Finn leaned over and nibbled on her neck as he plowed into her over and over again. The triple pleasure nearly undid him, but he wanted this experience to last—wanted to satisfy Kaleena and wanted to give her everything she needed and desired.

She lifted her head and twisted it to the side to give him better access to her neck. Finn ran his tongue right below her chin, but as much as he wanted to sink his sharpened teeth into her, he needed the pleasure to last. His blue aura grew, and when his gaze moved over to his arms, some of the scales pulsed a dark maroon through his skin, implying he was close to exploding.

Kaleena dropped her head down and pumped her hips back to meet each of his thrusts. Her body not only glowed with her inner pink scales, but she too shot off a ton of blue sparks. Now that they'd mated, making love gave their magic so much power it sparked an intense light show.

No longer able to contain himself, he moved his hands to her waist and sunk his teeth into her neck. When her inner walls gripped his cock, he could feel each ripple and pulse run up and down his shaft. She screamed out his name just as Finn shot his hot cum deep into her, wanting to brand her for life. If he thought flying was a high, nothing compared to this experience.

Their breaths came out rapid and Kaleena's back heaved. After wrapping his arms around her waist and placing his head against her back, he finally regained enough energy to lick the slight puncture wound. "I never want to leave here."

Excitement and pure pleasure poured off her. Eventually, her body sagged, and he had to hold her so she didn't go face first onto the ledge. Finn then gently rolled her onto her back to let her catch her breath.

After he jumped into the clear turquoise water below, Kaleena finally sat up. He reached up and lifted her down into the water, holding her against his body.

Kaleena wrapped her arms around his neck. "I love you, Finn McKinnon, with my whole heart."

"I love you more."

She laughed. Life with Kaleena was going to be fun and always exciting. "As much as I would like to stay here for a few more hours, we should head back. I don't imagine this lull will last for much longer, and I want both of us to be ready," she said.

He kissed her. "Spoilsport."

They leisurely swam side by side until they reached the shore. Once they emerged from the water, they ran around to dry off and then dressed.

"Do you want to walk out," she asked, "or be in your wolf form?"

Since he could spend more time with her walking, he

decided on the slower method of travel. "How about staying in our two-legged form?"

"Perfect."

Since the path was fairly wide, they walked hand in hand. Once they arrived at the clearing, Kaleena checked out the area before emerging.

"It's clear," she said. "Race you back to the castle?"

"Don't you ever just enjoy the day and go slow?"

"I'm a full speed ahead girl, unless I'm sucking on your cock and trying to tease you."

"What have you done about Kaleena? It's been a week since her escape." Rathan's father asked as he leaned back in his chair and puffed on a cigar behind his desk. The wrinkles on his forehead were more pronounced than usual, implying his calm delivery was covering his anger.

The smoke nearly choked him, but Rathan wouldn't give his dad the satisfaction of waving away the white puffs. "I have scouts searching for her," Rathan said, making his voice strong and bold to show he wouldn't be cowed by the man—or rather this demon turned dragon.

His father shook his head. "That's not good enough. The rumors are growing. The press is saying we are responsible for taking white lighters and turning them to the dark side."

While it was true, they didn't need their image tarnished. "Are you saying you think my dear cousin is responsible for the rumors?"

"It's possible, but you know as well as I that you are guilty of this crime."

These repeated accusations were driving Rathan crazy. His father was the one who demanded more dark magic. Where did he think all of it would come from, if not from turning these white lighters? It wasn't as if they were willing to donate their magic to the Royals voluntarily, and the dark lighters weren't as abundant as they used to be. Rathan had no choice but to force white lighters into the dark ways.

Inhaling to keep from defending himself, he nodded.

The king pointed his cigar at Rathan. "Now find your sneaky cousin and make sure she doesn't talk ever again." He shook his head. "To think I contemplated naming you as my successor."

Rathan nearly dropped to his knees. He was third in line to be king. "I thought you wanted Omar," he blurted. Tarik, while a damn fine strategist, was better suited training the guards than running the province.

"Omar only thinks about money and milking the people dry. While I appreciate his talent for now, he lacks leadership qualities. I don't think he's ready to be king." His father stubbed out the cigar. "I want you to personally see to it that Kaleena is neutralized. The last buffoon you sent never returned. Take care of it yourself."

Rathan stood up taller. "I won't let you down."

"See that you don't. Now go and find her."

As Rathan made his way back to his office, his mind raced. Getting his hands dirty was always his last option, but he'd make an exception this time. Killing his cheeky cousin would bring him great delight.

By the time he'd entered his area of the castle, he'd come up with a plan. Thorn, one of the palace guards approached, and Rathan stopped him. "Find Christian Milan for me and bring him to my office."

"Yes, sir. I recently saw him with Prince Omar."

"Well, get on with it then," Rathan bellowed.

Once seated at his desk, Rathan leaned back in his chair, pleased that he had one more chance to earn his father's praise. Never would he have thought that someday he might be king, and the idea thrilled him to no end.

Fifteen minutes after the summons, a knock sounded on his large double door. Rathan smoothed back his thick hair and straightened his tie. "Come in."

The door opened, and Christian was shown in. "You needed my services, sir?"

From the way he was avoiding eye contact, he would be easy to manipulate. Rathan pointed to a chair facing his desk. "Have a seat." He glanced up at the guard. "That will be all." The door closed. "Did you do as I asked?"

"Yes, sir. I found Kaleena and told her I was the one who drugged her."

"Good. And how did she take the news?"

"As you would expect. She was angry until I told her that you'd threatened to kill my sister if I hadn't obeyed. It's why they didn't incarcerate me."

"Excellent." Rathan hadn't expected this young lawyer to have such success. He had a promising future. "I'd like you to find out where she is now. If you do, I'll call off my guard dogs, and your sister won't be bothered again."

Christian let out a huge sigh. "Thank you, sir. Tory,

Kaleena's twin, seems to be taken with me. I'll find her and see what I can learn."

"I'll give you two days. Don't disappoint me. Not only is your job on the line, so is your sister's life."

"I understand."

"You're dismissed."

Once Christian left, Rathan decided to find Tarik. It would do him some good to get in a few sparring rounds before he solidified his next-in-line role as the future king.

CHAPTER TWENTY-THREE

For the past two days, Kaleena and Finn had explored Grindale province as regular sightseers, sticking to the main towns to avoid being attacked. While dragons were always flying overhead, they rarely had room to land on the busy city streets.

She and Finn were at a café enjoying the sights and sounds of Veridon, the largest city in Grindale, when a familiar feeling swept over her a second before a feminine voice entered her head. Kaleena immediately clasped the dragon scale necklace her sister had given her, even though she didn't need it in this realm.

"Kaleena?" It was Tory.

Finn set down his drink, reached out, and touched her hand. "You look like you've seen a ghost."

"It's my sister," she whispered.

"What's wrong?" Her twin would never contact her unless it was important.

"I just spoke with Christian," Tory telepathed. *"He passed on*

the information to Rathan about your location. He swears he said nothing about Finn. If Rathan is to be believed, he will personally be coming after you. Soon."

Her heart beat hard. She might die from this encounter with the mighty warrior, or Finn could become a casualty, but she had to fight him. *"Did he say when the attack would occur?"*

"Christian didn't know, but from the way Rathan became animated at the news, he suspects it will be soon."

"Thanks for letting me know. We'll be ready for him."

"Love you, sis."

"Love you back. We'll be home soon."

"Take care," Tory telepathed.

Kaleena lowered her hand from her neck and then relayed what her twin had told her.

"Do you believe Christian?" he asked.

She didn't want to be gullible, but somehow she did. "Yes. The whole thing could be a set up, but according to Tory, Christian acted sincere in wanting to help. In all honesty, it doesn't matter. Even if Christian betrayed us, he did what we wanted, which was to tell Rathan where we are. We're ready. Remember, we want Rathan to come after me. He'll think it's a slam dunk because we are isolated."

Finn leaned forward. "Why do you think it's better to fight him here instead of back in Edendale? Your family could be there to protect you."

"I know, but if I'm surrounded by family, Rathan would never show up himself, and I need him dead. The only way to accomplish that is for me to fight him here. If I fail to take him down, you can finish him off."

"I know that's what you've said, but I wish you'd let us both take him."

"That might be more effective, but I need to do this for closure."

Finn scanned the customers seated around them, clearly needing a moment to think. He returned his gaze back to her. "My family has had targets on their heads at various times, so I know how you feel. I've wanted many of them dead too." He reached out and clasped her hand again. "I know that until this is resolved, you won't really be free, so I'll do as you ask."

She squeezed his hand and grinned. "Did I tell you that I love you?"

He released his grip and winked at her. "Not in the last hour."

Kaleena leaned over and kissed him lightly. "I'll try to remember to tell you more often." She picked up her purse. "We should return and tell Gregor that the time is drawing near."

The next day turned out to be a bust. Finn hadn't minded wandering around the woods while Kaleena soared into the air searching for Rathan, but Finn's frustration level had definitely mounted. Even though Kaleena had a plan, he wasn't totally comfortable with it. He was supposed to stay hidden in the forest in his wolf form and let Kaleena have first dibs at her evil cousin. She claimed that if Rathan spotted Finn, he'd probably lie in wait until she was alone.

If Christian's intel could be believed, Rathan would be

there soon. But when? She saw no reason for him not to act right away.

Kaleena had instructed Gregor's men to stand down too, so their usual grid search had been cancelled. While the field and woods were close to the castle, all evidence of anyone living there had been hidden. Not that the building looked abandoned, but it didn't appear as if anyone had resided there for quite some time.

"I'm sensing something," Kaleena suddenly telepathed as she soared above the field. A hint of fear was blended with excitement.

"Do you see him?"

"No. Rathan would cloak himself, but my magic allows me to sense his vibrations. He can't truly hide from me. He's coming."

"Does he know you can tell he's close?"

"I don't think so." She sounded unsure.

Finn debated ignoring her request to let her take on Rathan first, but if her cousin spotted Finn's dragon, he could turn tail and return to Edendale until he could get Kaleena alone. Finn wanted this threat to end here and now for her.

"Did Rathan come alone?" he asked.

"As far as I can tell."

That helped alleviate some of his anxiety. Her cousin's arrogance would hopefully be his downfall. Finn edged closer to where the forest met the field. Even though the dragon shifter probably wouldn't give a second look at a wolf, he remained hidden behind a tree nonetheless. At least from there he had a good vantage point of the area above the field.

His heart pounded hard at the idea his mate would do

battle against an experienced fighter. Yes, she had magic on her side since she could cloak herself, but even Kaleena said it took a lot of her energy to remain invisible for long.

Even though he'd watched Kaleena fight, he had no idea if female dragons were equally as strong as male dragons. Somehow he thought not, and that idea petrified him.

Kaleena suddenly let out a screech, jerking him out of his complacency. He looked up to find a huge black-scaled beast a mere ten feet from her. Rathan was attacking—or some beast he assumed was Rathan. Oh, shit!

Her tail whipped around her enemy's head, but that wasn't enough to stop him from scratching her snout with his massive claws.

Help her, his wolf begged.

No, stay put, his dragon demanded. *She can handle him.*

His dragon was right. *We'll let her tire him out first. It's what Kaleena wants. What she needs.*

Finn believed that was a good compromise. He could only wait so long before he helped—promise or no promise.

Kaleena flapped her wings with a great deal of force, and the two warriors became entangled. Rathan let out a roar as he struggled to disengage. When he failed to free himself, they began to descend, accelerating toward the ground. Just as Finn thought they'd crash, she opened her wings and let go of him before soaring upward.

Pride raced through him at that smart move. Kaleena was now above her foe. Wings tucked against her body, she dove toward him. Just when he thought she could grab a hold of his spiny back with her claws, Rathan did a loop around her and took back the upper hand.

"Come on, Kaleena. You can take this ass. Remember how he caged you and tried to steal your magic." Finn wanted to spur her on.

She rolled onto her back and let out a stream of powerful fire. He wasn't sure what that would do, but maybe it was to stall for time. Rathan moved closer and grabbed a hold of one of her wings and ripped a wide hole right down the middle.

Crap. A strong ache attacked Finn's shoulder, making him want to lick his arm to soothe it. Helplessness swamped him seeing Kaleena flail. One wing flapped furiously while she tried to gain her freedom. Her tail whipped around Rathan's back, but he was too large for her to get a good grip.

"Christ, Kaleena, I'm coming to help! Hold on." Finn telepathed her, his paws quickly changing into dragon talons.

"No! He's mine!"

Finn's dragon claws scratched at the ground, but the rest of his body stopped the shift. Damn woman. Kaleena was too stubborn for her own good.

She reached up with her claws and gouged Rathan's chest, but the dragon seemed unaffected. Had he been infused with magic too? Is that why he'd taken so long to come after her?

Finn's dragon claws pawed the ground once more, anxious to take down the bastard. *Just a few more seconds...then I don't give a shit what she wants, I won't lose her.*

She's got this, his dragon roared.

No, she doesn't, his wolf chimed in.

Damn animals. The panicked determination rolling off

of Kaleena gave him mixed signals. She had a plan; he could sense it.

Somehow Kaleena managed to get free of her foe this time, but her wing had been badly mangled. While Finn couldn't see if the skin on her face or chest had been damaged, there was no way she could hang on for much longer. Without warning, Rathan shot away from her and soared upward. What was he doing?

Kaleena tried to take chase, but her left wing was so badly torn, she was having difficulty moving fast or in a straight line. She was halfway to Rathan when he turned around and came at her again.

Before she could respond to his change in flight, Rathan stretched out his talons and whipped his tail around her clawed hands. Oh, no!

Finn had seen enough. He was going after Rathan. As Finn charged into the field, he transformed into his dragon. Finn had never cloaked himself before, but Kaleena said it was a matter of concentrating and picturing invisibility. He did so now, and when he looked over at his wings, he saw nothing. Yes!

Just as he took off, Kaleena fell from the sky. The air left his lungs, and he nearly plummeted from the excruciating pain shooting off her.

As much as he wanted to tend to her, he had to deal with Rathan first.

"Kill him for—" Those were Kaleena's last thoughts to him before she crashed in a lump on the ground.

Fury and hatred coursed through him. Rathan would pay. Finn tried to remember everything Kaleena and Thane had taught him about how to attack, but he was so blinded by grief that he couldn't remember anything. All he wanted to do was claw the bastard's heart out.

While Finn might not be able to hold this invisibility shield for long, he would take advantage of the time he did have. Both Kaleena and Thane mentioned that as a new dragon, he would possess superior strength and stamina. He could only hope they were right.

Incapacitating Rathan was not his goal. Killing him was, and the only way to achieve that was to gouge out his heart.

As Rathan dove for the ground, probably to finish off Kaleena, Finn whipped his tail back and forth, ready to wrap it around Rathan's arms. With his own claws extended, Finn charged. Rathan let out a roar when Finn deftly tied up Rathan's wrists with his tail.

Surprised you bastard, didn't I?

Rathan shot fire blindly all around and got lucky, the blaze hitting Finn's face, temporarily blinding him. Finn returned the favor, and his opponent screeched. No one had said anything about biting a dragon, but his wolf's instinct demanded that he attack the man's throat while his claws aimed for the chest.

As Finn leaned in close to bite him, his cloaking began to fail, and Rathan managed to slip his claws from Finn's grasp. With only a few seconds before his prey escaped, Finn bit down on Rathan's neck and dug his claws blindly into the man's chest.

Most of his talons failed to puncture the hard scales, but one succeeded. Rathan struggled and tore at Finn's wing, forcing him to let go. That was a mistake on Finn's part. Rathan swung his tail around Finn's wing and pulled hard. Despite his severe injury, his opponent seemed to possess some kind of super strength.

Rathan's hold tightened, and an intense searing stabbed Finn's shoulder as the tendons stretched and tore. It was almost as if his wing had caught fire.

Without warning, Finn began to lose altitude, and the ground raced up to meet him.

"Lift your head." He wasn't sure if he remembered Kaleena's words from before or if she telepathed them now.

Finn did as she suggested and also stretched out his one wing to slow his free fall. Legs ready to take the full brunt of the impact, he landed and rolled onto his good side. His head pounded, and his heart did a rapid tattoo.

Rest was a luxury right now, so he rose to his clawed feet. Finn looked up to locate Rathan, but all he could see was a huge black body plummeting straight toward him from out of the sky.

CHAPTER TWENTY-FOUR

At the last second, Finn managed to move out of the way as Rathan landed unceremoniously next to him. His foe's eyes were glassy, and the body lay in a crumpled mess. A few seconds later, the animal returned to its human form. Kaleena had shown him her cousin's picture, confirming this was Rathan.

Paralyzed by having fought his first battle, it took a moment for Finn to realize that Rathan was dead, and the woman he loved might soon be too.

Because Finn's wing was almost useless, he shifted into his wolf form. His right shoulder hurt like a bitch, but three of his legs worked well. He limped toward Kaleena and dropped down next to her.

When her chest rose and fell slightly, joy soared through him. He licked her face. *"Kaleena?"* he telepathed.

She didn't answer nor did she move. Her face was badly gouged with multiple claw marks, and the hole in the top half of her wing looked extensive. But it was the huge opening in her chest that worried him the most. The scales near her heart had been clawed away and blood was oozing out of her.

"Try to shift into your wolf form," he begged. *"Please, Kaleena. You have to be okay."*

Finn debated shifting into his human form, but he wasn't sure what good that would do. He glanced toward the castle. Why weren't Gregor's men coming to help? Hadn't they witnessed the fight?

Just as Finn was about to run to the castle for help, a swarm of dragons flew in from the east—from the direction of Avonbelle—making enough noise to raise the dead.

Oh, shit, oh shit. None of them had any colors in their scales, implying these might be Rathan's men. But if they were, why had they waited so long to arrive? Had Rathan told them that he wanted to take down Kaleena himself?

Think!

Kaleena moaned, and Finn's pulse soared. *"We have to get out of here, Kaleena."*

How he'd accomplish that he didn't know. They had mere seconds before the large army attacked them. Even if Finn shifted into his dragon, he couldn't take on six of them by himself.

Wanting to spend his last moments with the woman he loved, Finn curled up next to Kaleena and placed his snout on hers. He memorized her scent and then licked her battered face.

"I love you, Kaleena. Forever."

Just as he prepared for the attack and his last moment with his mate, what sounded like a different army of screeching banshees came from the north—from the direction of Kearn's castle.

Adrenaline shot through Finn's wolf as he jumped up onto all fours. At least ten green dragons soared upward and charged after the six dragons in the air. Finn's wolf howled, and his inner dragon roared.

Two of Rathan's men peeled off and charged toward Finn and Kaleena. Determined to protect his mate at all costs, Finn shifted into his dragon and blocked any access to her. Claws extended and wings spread, he waited for the onslaught of the beasts.

Instead of attacking either of them, they swooped down, picked up Rathan's dead body and headed back the way they came, while the rest of the Royals fought Gregor's men.

What followed was a quick and decisive victory. Bodies fell from the sky, and when it was over, it looked like what he imagined a one-sided Civil War battle would look like. Death was everywhere.

Two of the castle dragons landed and shifted into humans. Finn returned to human form too, but that was a mistake. The pain nearly crippled him.

"Kaleena's in bad shape," Finn managed to say.

"We'll take care of her." The man knelt by Kaleena's side. "Can you shift?" he asked her.

Kaleena groaned, and his own ache was compounded by waves of agony radiating off her. Finn dropped next to the man. "Try to shift into your wolf form, Kaleena," Finn begged again.

He placed a hand on her head and willed her his remaining strength. As if his love and magic was enough, she shifted into a wolf. Then the guard swept her up into his arms and turned back to Finn. "Shift into your wolf form. You're too weak from the battle."

Finn did as they suggested, hoping between his wolf and his dragon that he would heal quickly. He assumed he could return under his own power, but after taking two steps, he dropped to the ground. Damn. He was weaker than he'd thought. He must have given Kaleena what little strength he had left.

"It's okay. We'll carry you," one of the men said.

Before Finn could protest, the guards lifted him up. Together, the two carried him and Kaleena back to the castle.

Since Finn had had enough time for both his wolf and his dragon to heal him quite well, he rose from the sofa in the living room that was part of the suite just as Declan emerged from their bedroom. "How is Kaleena?" Finn asked.

Her brother had raced to the castle as soon as he'd learned she'd been injured. "I honestly don't know how she lived. Rathan's claw punctured the spot right above her heart, missing it by a whisper. All I can think of is that between her wolf and dragon, they kept her alive long enough to get help. It was a vicious wound, and she was damned lucky her heart wasn't hit."

That didn't really answer Finn's question. "But she'll live, right?"

Declan clamped a hand on Finn's shoulder. "I did my

magic, so time will tell. Kaleena is strong. I think it's her love for you that is helping her heal. Go in and keep her company." He smiled.

"She's awake?" His mate had been in and out of consciousness for almost a day.

"More or less. I've infused her with extra healing powers, but she needs you more."

He clasped Declan's shoulder. "Thank you."

"No, thank *you*."

Finn charged into the bedroom. Kaleena's face was pale and her hair was matted, but he'd never seen anyone more beautiful. Her eyes opened, and her lips almost reached a smile.

He sat next to her. "Hey, beautiful."

She reached up to clasp his hand. While her grip was weak, he believed she'd recover. "Thank you."

"For killing Rathan? You did most of the work. I merely finished him off."

"No, for holding me when I was on the ground and I thought I was dying. Your energy and love kept me going."

Finn lifted her hand and kissed it. "When I thought you might die, I wanted to die too."

"Don't be silly. You have to stay alive. You're going to be a great fighter."

He didn't care about that. Finn just wanted to be with Kaleena forever. "So now what?"

"As soon as we heal, we'll go back to Edendale and resume a normal life. Well, as normal as possible."

She gave a weak smile, but he spotted a slight twinkle in her eyes.

"What about Rathan's family? I doubt they were over-joyed when they learned he is dead. Don't you think they will want retribution?"

She turned her head and blew out a breath. "Most likely."

"Will our life always be a series of attacks then?" Finn's gut churned.

She shrugged. "I'm a Guardian. It's our way of life. The world might not know who we are or what we do, but we've been put here to rid Tarradon of evil. Will we ever succeed? Maybe not in my lifetime, but someday, we'll make things better. Even if every Royal and every dark lighter is driven from our realm, there will be evil people to take their place. All we can do is our best."

Kaleena's sense of hope made Finn feel a little bit better. His family lived under the same kind of evil shadow. If it wasn't the Changelings on Earth who were always searching for more power, it was stalkers or some common thief. "We have a lot in common—your family and mine."

She smiled even though her eyes were starting to close. Then he heard her quietly ask, "Does that mean you'll join us in our quest for battling evil?"

"I'll always be right beside you, my love."

Finn felt her squeeze his hand, and when he leaned over to kiss her, she'd already fallen asleep.

Two days later, after Kaleena completely healed, they headed back to Avonbelle and settled into her condo in Edendale. Even though Finn was physically fit, he seemed to be unsettled, and that troubled her.

Kaleena ran a hand down his chest. "What's bothering you?" she asked. She'd been around him long enough to take a guess, but she wanted Finn to tell her.

He stepped away from her and stabbed a hand through his hair. His slight rejection hurt. "I'm waiting for the next shoe to drop."

"Meaning you think the Royals will attack again."

"Yes."

She'd thought about this too. "I'm sure my aunt and uncle can guess that I killed Rathan, but I doubt they'll want to broadcast the reason why he came after me. It would give them bad press. I'm betting they will probably say he was on a goodwill mission and was viciously attacked. The torn out heart would give credence to that claim."

"I hope that's true, but where does that leave me?"

His frustration was rolling off him and paining her. "What do you mean?"

"I can't hang out at your apartment while you go to work. I can't work for your family since I know nothing about mining. I have to feel useful or I'll go crazy."

She could totally understand that. "What do you want to do?"

Finn returned to her and drew her near. "If returning to Earth is out of the question, at least on a permanent basis, do you think I could manage a bar here?"

She laughed. "You could have any job in the realm. Why would you want to do that?"

"I like people. Besides, they tell me things that might be useful to you and your family."

That had a lot of potential. Before she could respond,

the doorbell rang, and Kaleena held up a finger. "Hold that thought." She jogged to the front and looked through the peephole. Pulling open the door, she smiled. "Declan!"

He dragged his gaze down her body and then speared a look at Finn. "You both are looking good."

She threaded an arm around his. "Thanks to you."

"Thank Finn. If it weren't for him, you might not be here."

She'd been thanking him profusely for days. "What's up?" Declan rarely came unannounced.

"I have something I want to pass by Finn." He motioned for the two of them to sit on the sofa while he took the chair across from them. "I'm not sure where to begin, so I'll just spit it out. I've spoken with the others, and we'd like to have you join us, Finn, as one of the Guardians."

A blast of excitement radiated off him, but it was mixed with some confusion. She looked over at him and smiled. "That sounds wonderful," she said. "What do you think, Finn?"

"Join you? As in fight the Royals?" he asked.

"In part, yes," Declan said. "We haven't come across someone as strong as you in a long time. We could really use your help."

"I thought Fate needed to make someone a Guardian."

"Fate has," Declan said. "He, or she, paired you with my sister."

"So I'd be fighting all day long?"

"Hardly. We all hold down full time jobs. No one knows who we are or what we do, so in that sense it's a rather thankless profession—except for the person we've just saved."

"Can I think about it?" he asked.

Declan smiled. "Of course. Take all the time you want. We may not need your services for a while, but when we do, we'd like to know we can count on you."

Finn looked over at her. "Do you also battle on a regular basis?"

"I might fight," she said, "or I might gather information."

"So I could still try to get a job managing a bar and help in that way too?"

"Absolutely." Kaleena so appreciated that Finn was willing to be in her life so completely. "It will be dangerous, but Thane will continue training you, just as he trains us all."

He glanced between the two of them. "Then count me in!"

She hugged him, and her love for him continued to expand.

Declan stood. "If you're interested in a little entertainment, check out what's on every channel on the set. The Royals are sparing no expense for Rathan's funeral. I have to hand it to the family. Their acting skills are unparalleled."

"Aunt Teresa might be upset, since all of her kids managed to convince her they were saints. The others might be rejoicing Rathan is gone."

Finn leaned forward. "What did they say caused his death?"

Declan chuckled. "The protector of the realm was

viciously attacked while on a surveillance expedition. They never said he wasn't in the province."

"I guess it's a good thing that they didn't come out and say a member of the Sinclair family killed him."

"Cousin Ander, who's the most reasonable of the bunch, knows what kind of publicity nightmare that would unearth," Declan said.

She couldn't agree more. "So what's next?"

"While you were recovering, we had a meeting. I think the next order of business is to find a way to free the prisoners from the castle prison cells. The last thing we need is for the Royals to have more dark magic."

That thrilled her to no end. "I hope it's not too late for those people. The woman next to my cell had already been there a week before I escaped. If the dark lighter was able to turn her, it could be a problem."

"That's why we'd like the two of you to join us tonight in the conference room for a little brainstorming session—assuming you're up for it."

Kaleena looked over at Finn. He nodded. "Tell us what time and we'll be there."

The idea of getting back into the swing of things thrilled her. It was what she was born to do.

Finn wasn't sure Kaleena should put herself in danger so soon after her near fatal injury, but she swore she was good.

"I need to be active," she said. "It's woven into the fabric of my being."

He chuckled. "I can tell. Perhaps Declan should have

asked the four sisters to join us. With their help, I feel like the Guardians could accomplish anything."

They climbed to the top of her condo building and opened the door to the rooftop. "They don't like to interfere. They help only when needed."

"They sound like Ophelia. She basically said the same thing."

"It's a balancing act for them. They fear that if they run around and save everyone that people won't take any responsibility to help themselves."

"They might have a point."

"Ready to shift and hop on over to the SinCas building?" she asked.

"You bet."

It wouldn't be a long flight—maybe ten seconds in duration—but it beats getting in a car and hassling the traffic. One minute they were on her building, and the next they had landed on the SinCas roof where they immediately shifted back into their human form. This time he was pleased that he didn't have to search for a spare set of clothes. Life on Tarradon certainly had its advantages.

They headed down the stairwell and exited one flight down. Kaleena strode over to the first door on the right and opened it. Shouts sounded, balloons filled the air, and everyone jumped up from their seats.

He was speechless at the party atmosphere.

"What's going on?" Kaleena asked.

Her parents moved toward them. "We wanted to surprise you two."

"I hope this doesn't embarrass you; my family tends to go overboard," she telepathed.

"No, it's something my parents would have done. It looks like a welcome home party. I think it's sweet."

Kaleena looked up at him and smiled. *"You're right."*

Both of her parents hugged each of them. "I can't tell you how thrilled I am that you and Kaleena have finally mated," her mom said. "She's the first of my children to do so. It's why I wanted to throw a party."

"Thank you." He wasn't sure what else to say.

Several more members of her family came up and congratulated them. Jamison patted him on the back. "Let's everyone sit down and enjoy some cake. I could use a strong drink after having to sit on the sideline while my girl went against one of the most powerful fighters in the realm. She is something else."

Finn's gaze caught Kaleena's, and she beamed back at him as she mouthed the words, *I love you.*

"She sure as hell is, and she is all mine." He winked and told her he loved her too, without anyone hearing him.

It made him smile as he remembered how a lot of guys over the years had come into the bar and had said they wished they could find the woman of their dreams.

Damn, he was a lucky man. The woman of his dreams was a reality, and he was never letting her go. Kaleena turned toward him and slipped her arms around his waist. Bending down, he kissed her, letting his love for her flow.

"I love you, dream girl. Forever and always."

"Right back at you!"

EXCERPT FOR SEDUCED BY FLAMES

I hoped you enjoyed, Awakened by Flames. If you want to be sure to find out about my specials and new releases, sign up for my newsletter or follow me on BookBub.

Up next is Seduced By Flames, Nessa's story.

In order to stay alive, a dragon shifter and a human must join forces.

If it weren't for bad luck, safety expert, Nessa Caspian, wouldn't have any luck at all. Just when she thinks things can't get worse, an explosion traps her in the mine. Really? If she hadn't been a dragon shifter, capable of clawing her way out, she'd be dead!

When she learns the mining inspector, Kyle Harper, has to shut down her family's legacy because of all the safety issues, she's livid--that is until she realizes the super hot man is her future mate. Well crap. Now what is she supposed to do? Bite him?

Kyle hates dragon shifters. After all, one nearly killed his sister. When he meets the highly tantalizing and intelligent Nessa though, all his preconceived notions fly out the window. Part of him wants to keep her at arm's length and the rest of him wants to ravish her...

Excerpt

This damn mine would be the death of her yet.

"Come on, come on. Where are you?" Dragon shifter Nessa Caspian tapped her nails across the rock face, determined to find the gold vein. Her ability to locate metals by touch had yet to fail her, so why couldn't she sense any now? She was sure the gold was there.

Nessa closed her eyes, throwing out more energy to sense the vibrations. Her father's words of worry came back to her, cutting short her concentration. "You have a gift Nessa, but opening a new vein is dangerous, especially at two hundred feet below the surface."

Dangerous? Hah. Even if the electricity failed—shutting down the elevator between here and the surface—she could still fly up the shaft to escape.

You better be right, her dragon said. *If you aren't careful, and there's another accident, the Mining Consortium will close us down.*

Her hands shook at that terrible thought.

Sure, the wealth that this gold could bring her family and their miners would be great, but more than anything, she wanted to prove to her dad that she had the ability to find the perfect mother lode. She'd inherited this talent to read vibrations from rock from her father's great-great grandfather. No one else in the family could find gems and metals the way her ancient relative had —until now.

Once more, Nessa ran her nails across the cold rough rock, sensing small tremors. Before she could identify the source, the wall suddenly shook, and her pulse soared. This was it! Nessa could almost taste success.

Her dad hadn't wanted to dig this deep, but she'd promised him that she'd take every precaution. It was why she'd refused to allow any other workers down here with her.

An even larger vibration tingled in her fingers, returning her attention to the elusive vein. When a high tinny sound accompanied the trembling, her heart slammed against her rib cage. The frequency coupled with a distinct pitch signaled a metal was present. She wouldn't celebrate yet though. There was a fine line between gold and copper and between silver and platinum, and Nessa needed to be right this time.

After absorbing the sensations for a full minute, she was convinced the frequency and intensity of the trembling matched gold's signature. But the only way to be sure was to dig into the rock face and see the metal in its pure form.

Leaning back, she extended her arms and pointed to the area she believed contained the thick gold vein—not merely gold flecks embedded in the rock—and partially shifted her hands into her dragon talons.

She smiled at what she was about to do. If anyone on Earth had a mother lode like this, they'd celebrate for years. Hell, it might even make the history books in her realm of Tarradon.

Unlike other dragons, the fire coming out of her talons had laser precision and was coupled with an extremely hot flame, better than any store bought blowtorch. Mouth breathing fire just went everywhere, which made it useless in this situation. Plus, she'd have to be in her dragon form to do that.

With total concentration, Nessa bored through the rock, sending bits and pieces of sediment in every direction. A shard of rock flew at her, cutting through her shirt and slicing open her skin.

Oh crap. In her excitement at the discovery, she'd been careless and had forgotten to initiate more of her shift. Stopping for a moment, she concentrated on turning her human skin into protective dragon scales.

Phew. That was close. She then continued drilling. Even though the heat blew back in her face, forcing her to squint, it didn't stop her from making progress. After a minute though, her hands shook from the intense power needed to keep the flame going.

Don't fail me now, she demanded of her body. Two minutes turned into four. Then, on the next push, the shine of pure gold bounced back at her. "Yes!!"

Heart pounding, she cut off the fire and extended her claws on one hand to dig out a sample. The gold had somewhat melted, making it easy to scoop out. Extracting a small container from her pocket, she lifted the exquisite metal to her nose and sniffed, hoping it had the scent of a rose or some exotic flower. It didn't, but a girl could dream. As much as she wanted to paint her body with the stuff in celebration, she placed the scraped metal inside the box. Impossible to remove all of it from her hands, her talons glowed yellow.

She wiggled them before letting her hands return to normal. With the exploration complete for now, Nessa fully returned to her human form.

Excited about her find, she collected her light and headed back to the elevator. *See, Dad? This is the mother lode. Told you I could do it.*

Ten steps from the metal cage that would take her swiftly to the top and let her bask in her glory, the entire wall exploded, jettisoning her backward. Her mind failed to comprehend what was happening other than to tell her she was in deep shit.

Without any conscious thought on her part, her dragon took over and did the shift for her, taking the brunt of the blast. The force slammed Nessa's animal into the stone wall so hard that she crumpled to the ground. She tried to bring in her wings to avoid more harm, but something stopped her. As much as she wanted to check out the damage, between all the dust and the flying rocks, she had to keep her eyes closed until the dust settled. A sharp object pierced her skull, and she moaned at the intense ache. Where had the detonation come from? She was the only one down there.

Rocks continued to fall on top of her, and dirt lodged under her scales. Seeking as much safety as possible, she lowered her head and waited for the onslaught of rubble to stop, hoping against hope she wouldn't be buried alive.

Seconds passed and then minutes, as more aftershocks shook the area. When silence finally surrounded her, she took a deep breath to assess the situation and was immediately sent into a coughing fit. Her dragon had never coughed before, and she didn't like it one bit.

When Nessa opened her eyes to check for injuries, she had to shut them immediately. Rocks were pressed against her snout and silt fell into her eyes. While she didn't usually jump to conclusions, it was pretty obvious she was trapped hundreds of feet below the surface—all alone and with no means of communicating with anyone. Damn.

While both of those facts made her situation dire, she was a dragon after all—one with some magic at her fingertips—no pun intended. Nessa should be able to get out of there. The big question was how long would it take her, and would she live long enough to reach the surface?

The one glimmer of hope was that everyone on the surface would have heard the explosion. Sadly, there was little they could do about it. She was too far down for them to drill a new tunnel. Hell, it had taken them a month to build the shaft in the first place.

When she blew out a breath, her chest screamed in pain. Really? She chanced opening her eyes a smidge and found a mammoth rock sitting on her chest. Not only that, one wing sat under a ton of rubble. Well, double damn. It was worse than she'd feared.

Sure, she was scared, but she was more pissed than anything. This was the third accident in as many months at her family's mine. It might be better to die down here than have to go through the humiliation of having the Mining Consortium shut them down. Her father had already received two warning letters. After this, it would be lights out for them for a long while. Since she was in charge of the safety of the mines, she'd be the fall guy.

It would be one thing if Caspian Mining had been guilty of neglect, but they hadn't been. Nessa had been meticulous at keeping everyone out of harm's way.

She grunted. She wouldn't reach the surface by feeling sorry for herself. No one was going to save her, which meant it was up to her to figure something out.

The first thing Nessa had to do was move that huge boulder off her body. To do that though, she needed her claws—claws that were trapped under a mountain of debris. Ugh. This wasn't going to be easy or painless. Using much of her energy, she worked her claws upward inch by inch. Because one of her wings was not accessible, it wouldn't be of much use until she could free it.

Slowly but surely, Nessa edged her talons to the surface, tossing small rocks aside along the way. When one talon broke into view, she took a big breath.

"Ouch. Damn it." Why couldn't she remember that inhaling deeply was painful?

Move the damn rock, her dragon complained.

"I was planning on it." Sheesh. The only reason she vocalized her comment was to help feel less alone. "I'm sure help is on the way."

In a month maybe, her dragon shot back.

She refused to listen to such negativity. Grabbing one side of the boulder, Nessa pushed while she lifted her right wing a few inches. While not totally free, it was enough to help her move the rock to the side. In the process of shoving it out of the way though, several ribs cracked.

Don't move, her dragon said. *Let me heal you.*

"I have no place to go. Have at me."

As much as she wanted to pick the debris off her half-buried wing, she waited. And waited some more. *Hurry,* she pleaded.

I'm working as fast as I can.

To save energy, Nessa tried to slow her breathing and relax, but that was no easy task.

Okay, I've done what I can to repair the ribs, her dragon said, *but you will be sore for a while.*

I'm okay with sore. Thank you.

She didn't need her animal wasting any more energy healing her—energy she needed to help her get the hell out of there.

Moving more rocks, she finally managed to free her right wing completely and part of her left wing.

Exhausted from the exercise, Nessa leaned back and tried to figure out what had happened. Where had the explosives come from? She hadn't brought any into the shaft, so what had gone off? This mine was far from all of the others, so there was no reason for anyone to be excavating near there. She didn't want to consider that someone wanted her dead. She'd always believed the employees were grateful to her and her family for keeping them safe, but clearly she'd been wrong.

Nessa pounded a stone in frustration and instantly regretted her burst of anger. More pain sliced across her chest. After waiting a minute to catch her breath, she opened her mouth and shot a hot stream of fire straight at the rock in front of her. The scorching force blew right through the middle. Having a bit more room to maneuver, she began to claw away the rest of the rocks and dirt from the bottom half of her body. Because she was fifteen feet tall, it would be a huge chore to create enough room for her to stand and then spread her wings—but she had to try.

After several hours of labor, she finally had that space and stood up—or as close to standing as she could manage. Her left wing hung at an odd angle, and both of her legs were severely cut, but that wasn't going to stop her from carving her way out of there, no matter how long it took.

Knowing what she had to do, Nessa began shoving the larger rocks to the side. By heating them to a high degree, they fused, providing stability to the walls. She just hoped like hell she didn't have to repeat this process for two hundred feet straight up. She'd never make it.

Kyle Harper's cell phone rang. When he saw it was his sister, Lily, calling, he smiled and pushed back his office chair to get more comfortable. "Hey, there."

"Kyle, there's been another accident at the Caspian mine," Lily spit out.

He bolted upright. She worked for Avonbelle Insurance Agency—the agency that insured miners. "When? Was anyone hurt?"

As the head of the Mining Consortium, he would be in charge of investigating the disaster—the third one in three months at this particular mine. He straightened his shoulders and inhaled. As much as he didn't like shutting anyone down, he'd do it if the miners' safety was at stake.

Closing this particular one wouldn't upset him too

much either. After all, it was run by dragon shifters, and he knew quite well that most of the fiery creatures were evil.

"I don't know any details," she said.

"I appreciate the heads up. I'll head on over there now to find out as much as I can."

Lily huffed. "I bet it was the owner's fault."

He understood why she was a bit prejudice against dragon shifters. Her last boyfriend, a dragon shifter, had burned her back so badly she'd been hospitalized for two months. Her hatred of the species seemed well deserved.

"It's my job to keep an open mind, or at least pretend to."

She grunted. "I'll have to stop by at some point too. Whoever is injured will want to be compensated."

After he hung up, Kyle grabbed the folders from the last two incidents and headed out, ready to get to the bottom of what happened.

THE END

ABOUT VELLA DAY

Love it HOT and STEAMY? Sign up for my newsletter and receive MONTANA DESIRE for FREE. Click here

OR Are you a fan of quirky PARANORMAL COZY MYSTERIES? Sign up for this newsletter. Click Here

Not only do I love to read, write, and dream, I'm an extrovert. I enjoy being around people and am always trying to understand what makes them tick. Not only must my romance books have a happily ever after, I need characters I can relate to. My men are wonderful, dynamic, smart, strong, and the best lovers in the world (of course).

My Paranormal Cozy Mysteries are where I let my imagination run wild with witches and a talking pink iguana who believes he's a real sleuth.

I believe I am the luckiest woman. I do what I love and I have a wonderful, supportive husband, who happens to be hot!

Fun facts about me

(1) I'm a math nerd who loves spreadsheets. Give me numbers and I'll find a pattern.

(2) I live on a Costa Rica beach!

(3) I also like to exercise. Yes, I know I'm odd.

I love hearing from readers either on FB or via email (hint, hint).

Social Media Sites

Website: www.velladay.com
   FB: www.facebook.com/vella.day.90
   Twitter: velladay4
   Gmail: velladayauthor@gmail.com

www.ingramcontent.com/pod-product-compliance
Lightning Source LLC
Chambersburg PA
CBHW050712180626
46814CB00002B/407